D0957251

KEEPING MUM

Alyse Carlson

BERKLEY PRIME CRIME, NEW YORK

THE BERKLEY PUBLISHING GROUP
Published by the Penguin Group
Penguin Group (USA) LLC
375 Hudson Street, New York, New York 10014

USA • Canada • UK • Ireland • Australia • New Zealand • India • South Africa • China

penguin.com

A Penguin Random House Company

KEEPING MUM

A Berkley Prime Crime Book / published by arrangement with the author

Berkley Prime Crime Books are published by The Berkley Publishing Group.
BERKLEY® PRIME CRIME and the PRIME CRIME logo are trademarks
of Penguin Group (USA) LLC.

For information, address: The Berkley Publishing Group,
a division of Penguin Group (USA) LLC,
375 Hudson Street, New York, New York 10014.

ISBN: 978-0-425-25206-2

PUBLISHING HISTORY
Berkley Prime Crime mass-market edition / March 2014

PRINTED IN THE UNITED STATES OF AMERICA

10 9 8 7 6 5 4 3 2 1

Cover illustration by Catherine Deeter.
Cover design by Lesley Worrell.
Interior text design by Tiffany Estreicher.

For Stacy Gail.
There's no shame in a U-turn.

TO: *Roanoke Tribune*

FROM: Committee to Elect Jared Koontz

RE: Fund-raiser/Mystery Supper

This Sunday, a veritable who's who in Virginia will gather at Hunting Hills Country Club for a Murder Mystery Supper and Fund-raiser, where Jared Koontz is expected to announce his candidacy for the Virginia State Senate. Seats for the supper are one thousand dollars each, and guests will receive the opportunity to bid on the murder victim—all in good fun, of course. The event is being hosted jointly by former Virginia State Senator Holden Hobbes and Ms. Samantha Hollister, and the Roanoke Garden Society will beautify the grounds with traditional heirloom flowers suitable for 1920s Roanoke.

The event promises to be entertaining as well as politically important. Those interested in contributing or attending can find more information at Jared Koontz's website: Koontz4senate.org.

CONTACT: Cam Harris

camharris@rgs.org

CHAPTER 1

"But Samantha, he's not a Roanoke Garden Society member," Cam said.

"Oh, pish! He made a large donation once. Everybody knows him."

"But it's really better if the Roanoke Garden Society stays out of politics. We want to be a group everyone can feel good about."

Samantha turned to stare at Cam, and Cam thought she was about to be fired. She was on thin ice with Samantha Hollister anyway over that little accusation of murder the previous spring. But Samantha was back with a vengeance, and even though she was no longer an RGS officer, she was wielding her power like a machete.

"This will garner a lot of publicity. We will emphasize the gardening angle, and a lot of important people will see what we can do. Think of the goodwill it will generate!"

Cam knew the truth of it. This was the party with money in Roanoke, so it was possible they had more to gain than lose . . . other than that whole "their soul" thing. She hated her beloved organization getting political. It seemed to cheapen it.

Cam sulked and didn't manage to accomplish a thing all afternoon, so when her best friend, Annie, called at four, she was ready for a change. Unusually, though, Annie sounded as down as Cam felt.

"Meet me at Martin's at five? Happy hour—girls for an hour, then Jake and Rob can join?"

"That sounds like the prescription I need," Cam said. "Are you okay?"

"I can't even get the words out until I have my swim in a pitcher of beer," Annie said.

"Man, I hate it when we have the same day—at least if it's a bad one."

Cam and Annie had been best friends for more than twenty years. Cam thought of Annie as the yin to her yang. They were opposites in almost every way, but they fit well together.

She hung up and tried to brainstorm a little about how this fund-raiser should go, but it wasn't getting any easier. Finally, at four thirty, she fed her meter, admiring her brand-new Mustang, and went into a market, bought a Heath bar, and put quarters into a machine for two toy-surprise eggs. One of their college friends had moved to Europe and occasionally sent them Kinder Eggs, but some silly U.S. law said Americans weren't capable of telling the edible chocolate from the inedible toy inside, so she and Annie had come up with this inadequate substitute for their very worst moods. She knew her own met the criteria, and it sounded like Annie's did, too.

Annie was munching chips and salsa, half of her first beer gone. Cam set the faux Kinder Egg supplies on the table and Annie grinned.

"And just when I was asking myself what you ever do for me . . ." Annie said.

"I know. You do me a lot more favors. But at least I appreciate them."

"Well, I'm about to collect."

"You are?"

"I am. My dad played the 'Daddy Card' and I'm stuck."

Annie's father was a former state senator, and while his relationship with Annie wasn't bad as far as relationships with rebellious daughters go, Annie and her dad didn't see eye to eye on anything.

"Uh-oh. What does he want you to do?"

"He's been personally grooming Jared Koontz for his old senate seat . . ."

"Uh-oh," Cam repeated.

"I know, right?"

"No. I mean I think your bad day and mine have the same source."

"No!"

"Samantha wants the Roanoke Garden Society to host this big event," Cam said.

"The event to announce his candidacy and raise beaucoup bucks at the same time," Annie finished.

Cam reached over and gulped down Annie's beer in spite of it being about three shades darker than she normally chose.

Annie opened the Heath bar and put her half on a napkin, then took her egg and set it in front of her. Had they been real Kinder Eggs, the chocolate would have had to be broken to retrieve the toy, so Annie used her teeth to chip part of the chocolate from the toffee, and then slammed her egg on the table in mock action. One end of it went flying and their waitress rushed over in a panic.

"Erm . . . yeah. Sorry about that," Annie said. "But while you're here, could we get an IPA and an Embarrassing Light?"

"Pardon?"

"Bud Light," Cam said. "She's embarrassed. I drink Bud Light."

"It's unnatural," Annie said as the waitress walked away.

"I can't handle the alcohol," Cam said.

"Maybe you could if you ever remembered to eat. Look at you. Skin and bones," Annie said.

It was true, Cam was very thin. And it was also true she forgot to eat when she was busy or preoccupied. But she didn't think that was the only reason she couldn't handle the alcohol.

"What I meant, though," Annie continued, "was *us* stuck working for Mr. Scary-Jari Koontz."

Cam snorted. "So did you come up with anything?"

Annie grinned and leaned in. "I did, actually—a little inside joke."

"I meant for the event!"

"See, that's the beauty of it. It *is* for the event. I say we throw one of those murder mystery dinners. We let everyone coming to the event bid on who dies—all money kept for the fund-raiser—and the highest bid names the murder victim. And see, here's the fun stuff. We get the satisfaction of killing their favorite guy!"

Cam had to laugh. "By favorite you mean top bid? Okay. Brilliant! Though don't you think that's tempting fate a little, with the murder record at the events we do?"

"Yeah, but these are politicians—sad as it is, you can quit winding them up, but they seem to keep on ticking."

Cam debated addressing the mixed metaphor, but honestly, that was Rob's domain and he wasn't here yet. Her boyfriend, Rob, was a journalist, most often a sports reporter, though he had covered a few murders of late. And he was usually more laid-back than Cam, except where language was concerned. He wasn't keen on sarcasm, slang, or mixed metaphors.

"We'll definitely have to run it by everyone," Cam said.

"RGS may be skittish, but if we promise a setting with a lot of gardening features, they'll be appeased. I really like it. Have you ever been to a murder mystery dinner?"

"Yeah, but it was a college party, and the supposed murderer got drunk and was in the bathroom all night, so it was impossible to solve. Have you?"

"Yeah, actually. I met Rob at one," Cam said.

"I thought that was a young media professionals meeting."

"It was. It was the October meeting that year—five years ago. And it was set up as a murder mystery dinner. It encouraged all of us to talk."

"Oh, that's wicked! How do I not know this story?" Annie asked.

"Because every time I try to tell it, you keep jumping to the sex part—and that night, there wasn't any."

"What, all that tension of a dead body and you didn't need to . . ."

"Right. You're proving my point," Cam said. "I'm not the one who jumps into that lightly."

"Yeah. Sad, that."

The next meeting for the Roanoke Garden Society was the following Tuesday. Board member elections would also be held that day, but the acting president, Holden Hobbes, was beloved and would be listened to, so Cam felt she should start with pitching the idea to him. She arranged to meet him an hour before the meeting started at the Patrick's. Neil and Evangeline owned a beautiful garden that their gardener, Henry Larsson, managed, and each season he created a gorgeous floral mural, identifiable from the sunroom and balcony above. Cam knew Holden Hobbes would enjoy a stroll before the meeting began, and Cam liked to guess from the colors of the flowers on the ground what the mural would look like from above. Unlike the displays Cam had seen, which normally had one dominant color with strands of one or two secondary colors shooting through, the garden now seemed to have different colors clustered in different areas, each color with a circle of yellow mums and goldenrod at the center. The mums were slightly taller than the asters and sedum surrounding them, but the goldenrod reached high, almost as tall as Cam in places. Cam thought instead of appearing as one flower from above, as was usual, it would look like a giant bouquet.

"Camellia, you look lovely, as always."

Holden Hobbes was eighty-four as of his late-September birthday, but seemed spry and healthy.

"Senator Hobbes. Thank you so much for meeting me."

"Senator! Ho! I haven't been a senator since 1998. I'm in for a plea, aren't I?"

"You are. The Roanoke Garden Society has had a request from two directions . . . hosting the announcement dinner and fund-raiser for Jared Koontz. It's for your old seat."

"I know who Jared is." He didn't look particularly pleased, which cheered Cam for a reason that was in opposition to her task. She liked Holden Hobbes, and was glad he didn't particularly care for where his party was headed.

"The requests came from Samantha Hollister and Alden Schulz."

"Alden?" Holden frowned. "There was a time I hand-picked him to replace me."

"Really?"

"He was disappointing."

This wasn't the direction Cam wanted this conversation to go either, but on that front, there was at least something she could say.

"He's my best friend's father," she said.

"Annie?"

"Yes."

He smiled then. "Well then. I suppose I can forgive him his unwillingness to compromise. She's a delightful girl."

Cam noticed he never mentioned Samantha, but Cam wasn't about to bring it up. The two had coexisted in the Roanoke Garden Society since it was founded, and there was no evidence that getting between them ever solved anything.

"Annie and I thought maybe a murder mystery dinner would be a good fund-raiser. Patrons could bid on who would be killed—not really killed, of course—for the mystery."

"Oh! Now that's clever! I like that a lot. Yes. You definitely have my support."

They walked up the stairs to the balcony. Just inside was the sunroom where the meeting would be held, but Cam wanted to linger a minute to look out over the garden. The mural from above was a bouquet of asters. There were five flowers in the bouquet: a bright pink, light pink, violet, periwinkle, and white. Then there were the green stems, formed largely of the black-eyed Susan greens that had been allowed to remain and a variety of hostas. Cam thought she should have guessed it; then again, Henry Larsson didn't always opt for a flower in season to be featured. She and Holden enjoyed the view for a moment before heading into the Roanoke Garden Society monthly meeting.

The board bought in easily. Holden's endorsement and Samantha's plea swayed the few who didn't already support Jared's candidacy.

Elections were the afternoon's only disappointment. Ramona Pemberly had run for secretary and won, and Cam couldn't think of anybody she would less care to coordinate with. Mrs. Pemberly was a nagging, nitpicky shrew, as far as Cam could see. Thankfully, her husband seemed to know about his wife's less-than-flattering attributes and poked her back into line fairly frequently.

All that was left to do in the short term was plan a murder.

CHAPTER 2

"So we don't want to just buy a boxed murder game," Annie explained. She'd dropped into Cam's office in the late afternoon. "It has to be a little personalized, right? Something interesting and local?"

"I guess," Cam said.

"So I thought we'd use those Patrick Henry ghosts."

"What?"

"You never pay attention to me," Annie complained. "The Patrick Henry is haunted—you know that. Smoking man. Piano lady. The trio in the restaurant."

"I guess." Cam didn't like to admit it, but she'd had more than one sensory run-in with the ghosts of what was once the Patrick Henry hotel. It was still called that, of course, but it now held businesses in the lower levels. Neil Patrick, founder of the Roanoke Garden Society, had a suite of offices from which he and his wife ran their various foundations, including the Roanoke Garden Society, which was why Cam spent so much time there. The building also held apartments above, though Cam had only been to one of them once. In Cam's time working in the building, though, the subtle evidence of ghosts was continually present, if not particularly ominous.

"But if we do it there, there isn't a way for the Garden Society to play a central role."

"I don't mean *do it* there, necessarily. Just use the stories to personalize the game to Roanoke. Isn't it likely one of those murders was political? Or at least criminal, which is pretty much the same thing."

Cam didn't quite buy into Annie's assessment of politics, but "close enough for a game" was probably true.

"Look, my people are . . ."

"Your people?" Annie snorted.

"RGS," Cam said. "They'll want some gardening connection. We basically promised them that at the meeting where they approved this."

"So maybe that's how we choose a venue."

"Maybe. I just wanted to make sure that doesn't fall off the radar."

"Fine. Pretty flowers. Whatever," Annie said.

"Okay, and . . ." Cam wanted to redirect the conversation. She knew Annie would yield to her when the specifics came up. And at least she'd planted the seed.

"We buy a couple of games to get a feel, then substitute one of the Roanoke stories for our dinner."

That was appealing, actually. They could ask guests to come in period costume. Her face must have shown she thought so.

"Yes!" Annie fist-pumped her triumph. "I'll pull the game together. You pull together the players."

"Oh, sure. Give me the dirty job," Cam joked. She knew that was reasonable. She didn't have the contacts for all the important people, but she did have enough contacts to hit them in two or fewer degrees of separation. "When will this be?"

"Second week in November. I need recovery from Halloween and time to build for Thanksgiving."

Annie ran a cupcake shop, so holidays like Halloween were very busy, but there was also an unusual number of businesses that thought pumpkin cupcakes with turkey decorations were a perfect send-off for the Thanksgiving holiday. Cam wasn't surprised at Annie's choice of timing from that perspective.

"Isn't that early, politically?" Cam asked, thinking of the candidate.

"No. Dad says a year is good. Especially as it's only three months from the primary. And right after an election, people are either pumped from the outcome or eager to try to change things."

"All righty, then. I guess we have a murder to plan," Cam said. "But not today. My regular work calls. Plus, I need to make sure I can get our gardening details lined up, which means soliciting time from our master gardener."

Annie stuck her tongue out and left so Cam could get back to her latest deadline.

Cam got to work drafting an email to Henry Larsson. Even if the venue wasn't secured yet, she knew what they wanted. Since the party was to be set in the 1920s, the flowers should be of the heirloom variety that would have graced gardens at the time.

When she was done drafting the letter, she called and left a message for Henry to check his email. Gardening professionals weren't known for being online all the time and without a nudge, he might not see her email until the end of the month.

Cam was startled out of a dead sleep.

"So I've got it!"

Annie had jumped on Cam's bed. She lived upstairs, but

the two had an open-door policy on visits. Cam, not the baker of the pair, was used to sleeping at least another two hours. It was five thirty in the morning.

"Geez, Annie, now?"

"Well, yeah, now. I have to go to work, then you go to work. And when you go to work, you risk all sorts of bad influence from those troublemakers you work for."

Cam rolled her eyes. For the most part, the Roanoke Garden Society was made up of Roanoke's elite—money as old as the state of Virginia, people connected to . . . well . . . everybody. This event was a good example of that. The guest list Cam had finally worked up looked like a who's who of local power and influence. Sadly, it was also true that trouble found them.

"Okay, what?"

"I made you coffee," Annie said.

"Sheesh. You want me to get out of bed? I don't need to be to work until nine."

"Neil will understand."

Neil Patrick was never there that early, so Cam thought understanding wasn't the issue. And her boss, Madeline Leclerc, had never even moved into the office, as she had a home office she preferred. Cam didn't think she needed to explain all that to Annie, though, or Annie would just take it as confirmation that Cam could be flexible. When Annie was in this frame of mind, it was hardly worth resisting her whims.

"I thought we'd decided what we were doing," Cam said.

"I know, silly. We decided generally, but I found specifically!"

Annie plunked a copy of an old newspaper article next to Cam, who'd finally managed to pull herself upright.

"What is this? Microfiche?" She hadn't seen a printout like it since college. The copy looked like a newspaper article from 1925 on slick paper with very black print.

"I know, right?" Annie gave her geekiest grin.

"Which excites you, why?" Cam asked.

"Because there's nothing, and I do mean *nothing*, on the internet about this. To cheat, people would have to know the game focus—which murder is behind our game—far enough in advance to actually make an appointment with the librarian."

"You had to make an appointment?"

"Yeah. The reels are stacked behind a counter, and you have to know what date to ask for, which is already hard enough."

"How'd you figure it out?"

"Holden Hobbes! He's MC, so it's okay if he has some idea of our plan. I asked for his memory on murders in the hotel. He remembered that triple murder—it was during prohibition. But the smoking man was the fishy one. I think that's the one we should reenact."

"Fishy how?"

"It was blamed on a romantic entanglement, but he was also a lackey for a guy who ran for mayor. The candidate lost. I think we should claim the victim sold secrets to the other side about tactics or something."

"Oh! That works!"

"And *you* are the organized one who can take this and turn out who the players are without offending people, so on the twelfth, we can assign roles."

Cam had known about the role assignment. Each dinner guest would get an envelope with his or her role. Some fifteen players would be specific characters, asked to keep up some front, and the rest would be "citizens" trying to solve the crime.

A website on the technique had suggested they could also text new clues to people to prolong the game and make it more interesting. Some roles would have a call-in number, and would then get prompts. Cam figured the person assigned as a cop and the person assigned as a reporter would get the majority of these. Cam had participated in a few real-life murder investigations, and these were, indeed, the people who had sources.

By the time Cam was dressed, she was excited. Annie promised to meet her in the Patrick Henry bar at three, and they could work out any kinks. Cam just had to spend the day looking at roles and figuring out who among the guests was too important to play the role of an ordinary citizen and who might be offended in certain positions—best not to offend big donors. She would need to strategize, too, to maximize press and avoid any arguments between people who had a known history of not getting along.

"Cam! I'm glad you're here!"

Samantha Hollister wasn't exactly high on Cam's list of who she expected to greet her when she reached the Patrick Henry in the morning, especially when she was early, but she was still trying to make nice with the former RGS president.

"Samantha! How nice to see you."

"I've brought you a present of sorts."

"You have? What kind of present?"

"Joel Jaimeson!"

The name meant nothing to Cam. She tried to look pleased, but Cam knew she'd failed when she saw Samantha's frown.

"Do I know that name? I'm sorry. It's not coming to me," Cam admitted.

"Joel is only the best party planner in Virginia! And he's agreed to help with our fund-raiser!"

"Oh! Well that's wonderful, but Annie and I have most of it worked out."

"Nonsense. Joel is just what you need. I'm having lunch with him at one, and then I'll send him right up."

"Oh, well . . . thank you, then." Cam tried very hard to

sound gracious, but now that she'd placed him, she remembered that Joel Jaimeson was annoying, even from the other side of a television screen. He was so bubbly and perky that he irritated even the friendliest of hosts, though he'd managed a five-minute slot at the end of the morning show that had replaced Telly Stevens's *Roanoke Living*. He presented entertainment tips, and Cam had seen a promotion for a half-hour Thanksgiving Day special that was coming up.

This was definitely a man who would take over if he was given the room. She just wished Annie was there. She was a force all her own, and Cam felt she would need the backup.

Through Cam's distracted morning, she figured out a way to ask for help without giving anything away. It was only a stall tactic, but surely Joel knew more gossip about local celebrities than Cam did.

Cam split the guest list in two: people she knew and people she needed to learn more about so as not to offend them through the game. She wrote a list of questions, too, so she could ask things about each person and whom they did and did not get along with. By the time Joel arrived, Cam was glad he was there.

"Thank goodness, Joel. It's great to meet you. Boy, am I eager to pick your brain on this guest list!" A voice in Cam's head that sounded like Rob criticized her choice of words. Brain picking was a peeve of his. Only delicate zombies were permitted that activity.

"Guest list details? Shouldn't we get the main body of the party in order first?" he said.

"It's planned. Where we are is the guest list."

Joel tossed his head and tittered. "Show me the plans. I'm sure there may be room for improvement."

"Mr. Jaimeson, with all due respect, I need help on just a certain aspect of it. Aren't you here to help?"

"Yes, but it's critical I know what will happen, or we can't plan properly!"

"What will happen depends on what I find out about a few of the guests. The names are settled and I need to know more about these people before we can move forward. I'd love your help. And at three, I have a meeting with my co-planner. But at the moment, what I need is an informant who is better connected than I am." She hoped the flattery worked better than her earlier approach.

Joel stared back at Cam like he'd never met such impudence. His chin was pulled in in a pout and he looked ready to have a fit, but Cam didn't care at the moment. She hadn't asked for him. She hadn't planned for him. And a small part of her suspected Samantha had thrown Joel into the mix to intentionally make her life more difficult, or perhaps as a spy so Samantha could keep more control over things herself. She was sure that if Joel was more effort than he was worth, the Patricks, Neil and Evangeline, would help her get rid of him without having to confront Samantha.

"Three, then?" he asked. "Okay. We can discuss the guest list before we meet with your planner."

He sat across from her and looked at her expectantly. Cam considered correcting him about Annie's title, but instead made a mental note to text Annie. If it was just accepted that Annie was in charge, things would go more smoothly. She got several personality traits about key people and hints about relationships out of him, then Joel said he'd return to pick her up when it was time to meet Annie.

A nnie was already at the bar when Cam and Joel arrived. Annie's text about Joel's help had been very specific.

"Probably unavoidable, but if you could work with types instead of actual roles, it might help. Who knows who he's really working for?" she'd responded.

"He's working for Samantha."

"Okay, so we do know."

"Unfortunately, we've already been over guest names."

"Couldn't be helped. You needed their personalities. But if he wants to know the game characters, stick to types there."

"Got it."

Annie put on a convincing show of gratitude when she met Joel, even though Cam knew for both of them this was just an added layer of hassle.

"So Cam, you have some personality profiles worked up?" Annie asked.

"Not all of them, but several," Cam said.

"Well let's have them," Annie said.

Cam was careful to point out all the ways Joel had been helpful in sorting guest personalities, though with Joel interrupting her every other minute, he was undoing her sales pitch of him. Nobody liked an interrupter. Finally she handed Annie a profile of game personalities she'd done that afternoon so they could match.

He was excited about the twenties-era costumes and décor, and surprisingly, had some connections to look into for both decoration and costume rental. Cam was glad he wasn't a complete waste of time.

"I emailed you the fuller list," Cam said to Annie, "but I thought maybe we should talk about the victim. That player will change, depending on donations, so I thought it might be important to have our three most likely money draws in a separate batch with similar profiles, so we can shuffle them if the top-dollar guy changes."

"Or gal," Annie clarified.

"Right," Cam said. "So Joel, do you have a feel for who the top-dollar people will be?"

"Well, Jared Koontz, obviously. This is his fund-raiser."

"Should we disqualify him to keep it interesting?" Annie asked. "I mean, how fun is a fund-raiser when the main person has to play dead all night?"

Cam knew Annie had a point, and by the look on Joel's face, he knew, too.

"People will be disappointed if they donate for him, and it's not him," Cam said.

"What about this?" Annie said. "He's the sheriff, or whatever it is, so he's the main character to solve it. We will specify that up front so they know not to nominate him."

"Oh, that works. I can write that up pretty easily," Cam said. "So who are the other players someone might vote for? People someone would pay big bucks to kill—for the game, I mean?"

"My dad," Annie said.

"Who's . . . Oh!" Joel had just put together that Annie Schulz was Senator Schulz's daughter. "Right. He gets the sentimental vote!"

"I'd think Holden Hobbes would, too," Annie said.

"But he's the MC," Cam finished. "So we need to make that clear."

"Derrick Windermere might get the half-joking votes," Joel said.

Annie snorted. "You think there would be any joking at all involved?"

"That's true; he's milked fortunes from half the people invited." Joel laughed awkwardly.

Cam knew Annie's opinion of the robber-baron tycoon. He'd made a killing in finance, some of it with accusations about ethics.

"Vivian Macy?" Joel went on.

"Is she invited? I'm surprised she's not running," Annie said.

"She might run, but what better way to assess the competition?" Joel said.

"And since she hasn't announced and is a community VIP, it would be rude not to invite her," Cam added.

"I might almost look forward to this!" Annie said.

"What about a reporter?" Cam asked. "Would that make a good number two for solving the crime?"

"You're trying to get Rob front and center of this thing, aren't you?" Annie teased.

"Actually, Rob can't afford a plate, so I doubt it, but I suppose that's why I thought of it. I'm used to advocating for the reporters. It also makes for better PR."

"We'll see who of the media guests has the broadest reach—that way we can ensure the best publicity," Joel said.

Cam was annoyed she hadn't been the person to say it. It was a good idea.

They talked through several more names, then Cam claimed she had to get to the more mundane details— invitations, catering, and the like.

Joel was willing to stay, but Cam insisted it wasn't necessary. She'd had an epiphany, and really preferred he'd just go so she could talk to Annie.

"What?" Annie said as soon as he'd left.

"Isn't it wine o-clock?" Cam asked.

"Holy cow! It has to be good if you're stealing my lines."

Annie flagged over the waiter and sent their sweet tea off, requesting a bottle of pinot noir—a compromise. Red, like Annie preferred, but lighter bodied, like Cam liked.

"Okay, so what?"

"Well first, Petunia and Nick are already on for catering," Cam said. "I didn't want to argue with Joel about that."

"I figured."

"Yeah, well, I had to fight for them a little. Samantha keeps sticking her hands in this and thought they weren't fancy enough."

Cam's sister and brother-in-law owned a restaurant called Spoons that frequently catered events in the Roanoke area.

Cam thought they were very nice, but "fancy" was another tier up, and they weren't a violin-music-and-candlelight restaurant, as Samantha had pointed out. Then again, for catering, a lot of that was up to the location anyway.

"Speaking of," Cam said. "Have you figured out where this will take place?"

"Hunting Hills Country Club," Annie said. "They want to do it outdoors if they can. I guess Samantha has ordered eighty flats of chrysanthemums to make sure it's festive and hooked in a dozen RGS members to autumnize the gardens."

"Holy crap. I wish she'd talked to me. I've already been in contact with Henry Larsson to make sure the gardens include predominantly heirloom flowers—we want to make it authentic for the twenties, after all. If Samantha doesn't back off, I might have to wring her neck."

Cam knew that Henry actually handled Samantha well and would be diplomatic about whether her order fit or not. Maybe just the main garden would be heirloom and the rest of her plants could be spread around the grounds.

"The pro shop, bar, and tearoom are all booked in case of rain, and for dinner in any case," Annie said.

"You know our group. They were really only interested in supporting Samantha's cause if gardening could be a big focus," Cam admitted, "So outside, if at all possible . . . even in the second week in November."

The waiter brought their wine and poured, and when he left, Annie leaned in. "So? Idea?"

"It's not as big as I made it out to be," Cam said. "But you know how the story is set up to look like a jilted lover is to blame?"

"Yeah?"

"If Vivian is picked, I think we should have clues and a card ready to put her as the dame who left him. We could even have a second murder later in the night—as the number-two fund-raising person . . . and call him the smoking man."

"Oh, excellent! Now, even if I didn't already like her best, I want her picked!" Annie said.

"Then I think we're set!"

CHAPTER 3

The night of the party was a bit blustery, but the forecast said it would stay dry. The outer grounds were gorgeous, though Cam wasn't a fan of the meticulously trimmed hedges. The flowers brought it into a full state of fall glory, boasting every shade between pale yellow and deep red. Mums appeared to be the favorites of the groundskeeper of the country club, probably because they were reliably pretty and more dignified than asters, though Cam preferred the asters for the colors they offered. It was even mild, temperature-wise, so a game outside would be fairly comfortable. Cam wondered if Samantha Hollister had bribed the weather gods—she seemed connected to everyone else.

Cam had spent the afternoon helping her sister and brother-in-law. They were pros, but Petunia, Cam's sister, was six months pregnant, and snarky even without the extra passenger. Cam just thought things might flow more smoothly if they had an extra set of hands, so Petunia could take a break once the prep was done.

Nick was appreciative. Cam's brother-in-law looked like
a bit of a thug, prison tattoos, legitimately earned, and a
Jersey accent that screamed gangster, but he had a heart of
gold and always wanted what was truly best for Petunia,
rather than what Petunia claimed she wanted. Cam had
learned to appreciate his approach to her sister long ago.

There would be a choice between Aiguillette of Striped
Bass Joinville or Medallion of Spring Lamb Chasseur, and the
sides and salads were all prepped and ready. Nick had access
to the country club ovens for the occasion, so it would all go
smoothly once they arrived, which should be any minute now.

Cam, in the meantime, was checking that the grounds
where the party would be held were ready and that all the
game props were in place.

She circled the grounds, keeping a watchful eye for the
carefully chosen heirloom collection of flowers, first sweep-
ing through the garden where the pre-supper cocktail hour
would be held. There was a wall to one side of the garden
with a gorgeous blooming autumn clematis. The delicate
white flowers gave off a heavenly scent, so Cam forgave
them for not being heirloom, or even native. She and Henry
had agreed the majority of the flowers would be asters,
largely because Samantha had pressured them to focus on
red, white, and blue, and asters came in all those shades . . .
sort of. In other circumstances, Cam might have argued that
blue flowers were usually more purple than blue, as was true
for the aster, and the "red" was definitely more fuchsia, but
she wanted to minimize her headache and hadn't really
believed red, white, and blue was a priority, so she'd kept
those thoughts to herself.

She left the garden and wandered toward the first hole
of the golf course, noting anise hyssop to the sides. The
spiky flower clusters were pretty, but the decision had been
made by the golf course, not Cam. She thought it was
because they were relatively easy to maintain and looked

pretty late into the fall. She chuckled with amusement that most of Samantha's potted chrysanthemums had ended up also lining the fairway. They looked out of place with their red and pink pointed heads, but they were cheerful, none-theless. As she reached the tee, she switched from just look-ing to make sure things were attractive to running down her mental checklist for all the props and settings for the game that had to be in place. She thought they were ready.

Annie arrived not long after Cam had. She'd had to go home after her bakery day to change, but Cam was impressed. Annie wore a short, simple flapper dress, but it was silver and, therefore, elegant. She cursed her own fussy beaded number, which she was afraid to sit in until the last possible minute in case pieces of it went flying off in various directions.

"How's it look?" Annie asked.

"I assume you don't mean my floral checklist," Cam said. Annie tilted her head and raised a brow. "Other than that, props are in place. It looks pretty. I think we're set."

"No Rob tonight?"

"At a thousand dollars a plate? Hardly. He's glad, though. Virginia Tech had an away game last night, and he didn't get back into town until about three in the morning. He wouldn't have liked wearing a stuffy old suit." Rob was currently wind-ing down what had been a fairly exciting football season.

"Are Nick and Petunia here?"

Cam looked at her watch. "They should be."

"Excellent." Annie rubbed her hands together in a mad scientist fashion. Cam couldn't help but laugh. Annie fol-lowed Cam toward the kitchen to check.

The dining room looked gorgeous. Nick had planned a seven-course meal inspired by *The Great Gatsby* that would begin with cream of celery soup and toasties, along with celery olives and anchovy canapés. Even the decorations finalized by Joel Jaimeson looked sublime, much to Cam's irritation.

She scanned names on the place settings—seating had been preassigned based largely on donation and avoiding hassle. Four tables toward the front had been purchased outright for obscene amounts. It was what was expected, after all.

Ten tables of eight had been sold, the exclusivity allowing a premium donation request. Cam and Annie had figured the murder mystery to only have about twenty active players. Half the people present could be expected to pander so heavily to Koontz that they merely amounted to a cheering section, so that was fine. Twenty main players and twenty "citizen investigators" should make for a fun game. Joel hustled in then, fretting about something, so Cam scooted toward the kitchen, trying to look busy.

"It looks fabulous, Petunia!" Cam said as Petunia set out the salads on the last table.

Petunia rolled her eyes. "Keep that little twerp out of my way, will you? He keeps shifting things."

That was standard Petunia. But Joel tried her own patience, and Cam didn't have half of Petunia's anti-pretention bias, so Joel being the source of her irritation was hardly surprising.

Cam rolled her eyes, too, in solidarity—they were sisters, after all. Then she stuck her head in the kitchen to yell thanks to Nick before going out to the garden to greet guests.

"Do we have a clue on the winner yet?" Cam asked Annie as they went.

"Or loser . . . if you aren't keen on dying."

"It's not really dying."

"Oh, you know some of these people want . . . him or her . . . dead."

"Oh, come on," Cam said. She was sure Annie was just stalling. "You can tell me."

"No. Because then we'd have to kill *you*."

Cam huffed. "But I'm coordinating!"

"No. I'm the one in power for a change. Maybe these nuts will accuse *you* of murder."

Cam raised an eyebrow. It was true. These "nuts" had accused Annie of murder, but this wasn't really murder. It was a game with the purpose of raising money.

"My dad made me promise," Annie pleaded.

The dad card was something Cam understood. She'd played it herself, though Annie had played it with Cam's dad also—the two were close—but Cam decided not to pressure her friend further and let it go.

It was nerve-wracking, checking in all the VIPs. Cam had dealt with important people in the past, but usually they were either important in the domain of gardening, a field she knew was very narrow, and was rather expert herself, or else it was only a few VIPs at once.

This political fund-raiser had drawn people from across the state, across professions, and across class lines that Cam wasn't used to crossing.

She was used to the wealthy Roanoke Garden Society members, and her best friend was the daughter of a former senator of no small account, but here she encountered fur coats, elaborate jewels, and Rolex watches. She supposed it was standard for a country club—at least for a high-end party like this. But she thought new money seemed much more intent on being flashy about it than the typical bluebloods she was used to.

They looked fabulous in their wise-guy suits, fedoras, and flapper dresses, which added to how fancy everything felt.

She managed to check people in and point them toward

the grounds behind the pro shop, where hors d'oeuvres and wine were being served.

"Cam, honey. I can check people in."

Cam looked behind her to find Evangeline Patrick. She had a sneaking suspicion Evangeline preferred an official duty to socializing with this crowd, but that was okay. Mingling was a better position for damage control. Cam thanked Evangeline and left to look for Annie.

The asters smiled at her, and Cam looked more closely to see a mix of daisy poms and snapdragons filling in for some height variation. The only thing missing was roses, though transplanting those for a one-night event was cost-prohibitive. Cam thought the effect, while overdone, was still pretty.

She found Annie talking to a pair of businessmen. Cam wondered if she was being hit on and approached. The men were probably campaign staff for Jared Koontz and just coordinating, but Cam doubted it was where Annie wanted to be stuck, so she whispered in her ear.

"You can act like you're needed elsewhere if you want."

"Heavens, really?" Annie said out loud. "Then let's go."

They waved and left the two sycophants to their business.

"Who was that?" Cam asked.

Annie said, "I'm not sure. They were looking for Derrick Windermere."

They walked toward the growing crowd and made it all of ten feet before finding a familiar face.

"Daddy!" Cam was stunned to find the first real guest she ran into was her father. A beautiful, familiar woman was on his arm, or rather, he was on hers.

"Hiya, sunshine!"

"I didn't know you'd be here," Cam said.

She wasn't exactly disappointed. She loved her dad, and he was great company, but he somehow always became the planet around which middle-aged women orbited.

"Well, me neither," he said. "Not until Vi called. I didn't know this was the hoopla you've been complaining about."

Cam looked around, mortified at who might have heard, and she tried to express without words that her dad needed to be more careful, but he never took a hint. Thankfully, most people usually thought he was joking.

"You can't be Camellia! I don't believe it! Vivian Macy, do you remember me? Nelson graciously agreed to be my plus-one."

Now Cam placed her. The context of being with her dad had thrown off Cam's sense of who she might be. The city councilwoman's question seemed strange—Cam hardly needed to remember her. She was in the paper all the time. It was stranger, though, to see her dad was here on the arm of a politician.

"Councilwoman Macy! So nice to meet you! And this is my friend Annie Schulz, the primary coordinator."

"Please. Vivian. Until I have a title of three syllables or less, it's just too cumbersome."

They all laughed.

"And Annie. You know, the last time I saw you, you were obsessed with Hello Kitty." Vivian reached over to pat Annie's hand.

Cam smirked and filed it away. It wasn't very often new fodder to tease Annie with fell in her lap. Annie made a face Cam couldn't interpret.

"I'm sure this will be great fun," Vivian said.

At that, Cam's dad winked and led Vivian back out to a waiter who was circulating with a tray of wineglasses.

"I wonder how that happened," Cam said.

"I keep telling you. Your dad's a babe magnet. Sadly, though, I really can't watch him impress the crowd at large tonight—which he will. I'd like to get a feel for the bidding war. It was too close to call earlier, and I want to see how much attention I'll have to pay through dinner to who is going to get murdered later."

Cam stood, still wondering how her father ended up the date of the woman who would most likely be the next to announce she was running for a senate seat. Cam hadn't even known they knew each other. *Remember.* Had Cam met the woman in person before? She still couldn't shake the feeling that the councilwoman was more familiar than just her image from the newspapers. It was something about her voice and expressions. But if Cam had met her, she couldn't seem to pull the memory from her mind.

When Derrick Windermere arrived, Annie elbowed Cam as a way of announcing her return. They'd known the local financier would come with a big party—he'd paid for one of the full tables—but the sight of him was still a little alarming.

"This is hardly the venue for a harem," Annie whispered.

"I guess I forgot to clarify that on the invitations," Cam said.

"Well you clearly fell down on the job. *She's* not with him, is she?" Annie tilted her head.

Cam swiveled her head to see Jessica Benchly, a recent acquaintance of hers. She was noticeably pregnant, but had found a dress that flattered her.

"No. I think Jessica's done with poor companion choices," Cam said, remembering Jessica's unfortunate date and the murder fiasco they'd all been pulled into with the children's pageant the previous summer.

Cam enjoyed their sarcastic banter, but it wasn't thirty seconds before Annie whispered, "Daddio, two o'clock."

Since they'd already seen Cam's dad, that could only mean Annie's had just shown up.

"Need backup?" Cam asked.

"If you wouldn't mind."

"Where's Elle?" Elle was the senator's wife, and Cam had expected to see her on his arm.

"Finland?" Annie said. "Gone, anyway."

"During the election cycle?" Cam asked.

"Dad sent her. She makes him crazy with a bunch of stupid advice. When he was running, it was one thing—helped to look like he had a supportive wife, even if behind closed doors, she could be annoying. When he's not running, it's just easier to send her off."

It sounded crazy to Cam, but there wasn't time to ask for clarification as the senator and a tag-along crony had reached them.

"Sweetheart! It looks lovely! And Camellia. Thank you so much for helping my Annie pull this off."

Cam knew how badly Annie wanted to reclaim herself, but Cam stepped forward and gave Senator Schulz a small hug to make nice.

"I was happy to help. You know Annie's helped me a number of times. I was happy to do something for her for a change."

"Well Annie's got a good friend, don't you, pumpkin?"

"I do," Annie hugged her dad, but the eye roll couldn't have been clearer from Cam's vantage. Fortunately or unfortunately, the senator then seemed to be swarmed with a dozen others demanding his attention. Cam and Annie snuck away.

"Who are the other VIPs, pumpkin?" Cam said when they'd made their break.

"That's Goddess Pumpkin to you," Annie said.

They turned together so Annie could narrate. Derrick had broken free of his harem and was trailed by a trio of goons, loudly complaining about the whiskey quality.

"Should be top-shelf stuff for all the money I spent tonight!"

Joel Jaimeson seemed to be trying to edge in, perhaps to explain the goal of authenticity, which during prohibition would have been bathtub gin, but the more well-dressed of the cronies kept thwarting him.

They made their way to Senator Schulz.

"Joel's like a terrier, isn't he?" Annie leaned toward Cam and whispered.

"No offense meant to terriers, I'm sure."

"You're right. Strike that."

"So I know Derrick," Cam said, returning to sorting VIPs. "Do you know any others?"

"Slick guy is Melvin. Dad doesn't like him," Annie said.

"Melvin?"

"Big broker—investment banker or something."

"Okay. And the other two?"

"Not sure, they probably work with Derrick. And then him," Annie pointed. A stocky man eased in, the others parting for him, so obviously he was an important member of their little circle. "He was at Dad and Elle's wedding." She paused and frowned, then pointed across the patio to a woman with long dark hair. "With her. It wasn't a huge affair. I don't think Dad knows him, so he must know Elle."

The thick man shook the senator's hand. Cam could see they knew each other now. She also saw that whatever he said annoyed Senator Schulz. After that, Derrick whispered something to him and the thick man started to argue.

"Just go!" Derrick shouted.

The man scowled and left on some errand, possibly concocted by Derrick to get him out of the senator's way. He didn't look pleased.

Annie continued to narrate as Senator Schulz held court in the garden. Cam was chuckling before Annie had finished her presentation.

Annie glared at her. "And there are some media people who need attention. I think they're more your type than mine."

Cam got the hint. It was time to get back to work, and
the media was as good a place to start as any. She recognized Roger Griggs, editor of the *Roanoke Tribune*, and
Rob's boss. He was talking to someone else, which was just
as well. It left her free to focus on Toni Howe, a television
talk show host she had worked with in the past and enjoyed.
Cam was happy to approach her.

"Toni, it's nice to see you," Cam said.

"You, too, Cam. This should definitely make news, and
Mr. Windermere was generous enough to buy a media table."

"In addition to his own? That *was* generous." Cam had
wondered how they'd managed to all be at this exclusive,
expensive event. Windermere probably hoped to influence
the flow of information.

At the sound of his name, Derrick turned from some
other conversation, grinned at Cam, and bit Toni's earlobe.
"Can't be said I don't love the media," he said.

As soon as he left, Toni took a tissue and wiped her ear.

Cam gave her a questioning look, so Toni stepped closer.

"None of us could afford to be here without him, and it's
newsworthy. Unfortunately, I am additionally indentured.
He's signed as the primary sponsor of my show for the
spring season."

Cam felt bad for her. Toni was a decent person: respectable, ethical, and kind. Cam hated that the lech had his
thumb on her.

"I hope a much better sponsor comes along soon," Cam
whispered.

"I hear you have an in with Nelly's Nurseries," Toni said.

"So do you! Just call her. Use my name if it helps, but if
you promise to do a couple of gardening features, I'm sure
she'd be interested."

"I may have to do just that. Because I can't take *this*."
She eyed Derrick Windermere cautiously.

A triangle tinkled, and Cam was as startled as anybody

to realize it was suppertime. Samantha was gesturing with her arm, and the patrons were heading in to find their names among the place cards.

Supper was held in a large carpeted hall in the main building. The ceilings were high, and moonlight came in through the windows. Out-of-season hibiscus and exotic bird of paradise, which Cam thought must spend the evenings in a hothouse, lined the edges, but the rest of the decorations were strictly vintage.

Cam and Annie ducked all the way through. They were eating in the kitchen. She supposed some people might be offended not to merit the thousand-dollar seats when they'd planned the event. Joel Jaimeson was certainly out there, doing Samantha's bidding, no doubt. But it was a nice break for Cam and Annie, if they ignored Petunia's cursing, anyway.

"Tunia, couldn't somebody else have helped Nick tonight?" Cam asked.

"As a matter of fact, Nick and I are trying to set aside a little money for the baby. Paying somebody *else* to work doesn't help!"

"Sheesh, I know. I don't mean you can't work. I just thought long days can't be good for you."

"I don't need a lecture."

Annie touched Cam's arm to remind her Petunia would never be a person that could be reasoned with. She was a challenge to be gotten around. Cam would have to work with Nick to figure out how to trick Petunia into resting more.

Cam tried to casually clear some of the appetizer plates that had been returned to the kitchen between bites of her own food so Nick and Petunia would have a smaller job, but each time she did, Petunia glared. Finally, Annie gestured and Cam took Petunia's hand and led her out the servant's exit.

"So, how are you feeling?"

"Better than when I was throwing up."

"You were supposed to have an ultrasound, weren't you?"

"Last week," she admitted.

"Did you find out if I'm an auntie or an uncle?" Cam joked.

That finally got a laugh. "We don't want to know."

"Do you need any help with the nursery? Painting? Putting together furniture?"

"Well . . . I did have a stencil I wanted to do . . . You're more talented at that than I am."

"A painted stencil?"

"A trim, all the way around."

"I would be thrilled. How about I do it over Thanksgiving weekend? It's a long weekend, and if the fumes bother you, Daddy would love to have you there for a night or two." Nick and Petunia had a nice condominium, but it wasn't so much space that they could get very far away if there were paint fumes.

"Yeah. That's good."

Petunia didn't even notice when they went back inside that all the appetizer dishes had been put in the dishwasher.

"They want dessert soon," Nick said.

With dessert, Cam and Annie had to distribute game roles.

"Do you know who got top bid?" Cam asked.

"Yes," Annie said, but she walked out without elaborating.

Reentering the hubbub, Cam wondered if she'd blocked a lot of the tension the last time she was with the group. Waiters were pouring coffee and giving out chocolate mousse or custard, but there seemed to be crackling animosity all around.

Holden Hobbes spoke from a podium, and she felt sure that should calm most people. He directed them on what to do as they received their game roles, noting unless they had

a starred role, it would be best to finish dessert before opening their instructions. Cam cruised the perimeter, distribut-
ing envelopes as she went. She listened for arguing, and
finally heard muffled yet unhappy-sounding tones.

Prior to supper, she'd thought people were having fun.
Now she could feel the friction in the air. She tried to sense
the source and could have sworn it was with the harem,
though the supposed sultan was now nowhere in sight. She
thought Annie might have given him his role first, as he was
one of the top candidates to be murdered.

Cam could see a lot of people doing what she thought
they were supposed to. The trouble was, with so many people rushing off at once, she couldn't check off the list in her
head that this was all legitimate. She wasn't actually paranoid so much as, for a PR manager, *practicing* paranoia that
had served her well more than once.

Whatever the case, the dining room started to clear, and
Cam, left out of the loop by Annie's plan, guessed she might
be wisest just to follow the noise. She'd just have to see
where that took her.

As she started to move toward the door, a man she didn't
recognize rose, took a microphone, and said he had a treat
for everyone in the garden. For want of anything better to
do, Cam followed this last exodus.

The garden was lit with small lanterns, but a spotlight
shone on a low stage. It was clear where they were supposed
to focus their attention.

As they waited, Cam spotted her dad on the edges without Vivian. He looked around and then wandered off toward
the golf course. She thought the role-play instructions were
being followed. A few others were trickling off, some alone,
others in pairs or even small groups.

Evangeline Patrick, beautiful, and much younger than her
blue-blooded husband, sauntered out with the hair and
sequined dress of a 1920s mob moll. She played to the

audience beautifully as she slinked up to the stage. She glided up the few steps, thrust a shapely leg through a slit in her skirt, and began to belt out an impressive rendition of "Big Spender."

The audience was enthralled. Cam knew the song was written four decades after the party was meant to be set, but it was suited to the mood of the role play, the high-end classic event, and of course, the fact that it was a fund-raiser.

When Evangeline had reached the end of the song, right on cue, a loud crash rang out, drowning the last notes, at least for the back of the crowd.

Cam was confused, momentarily. The game was meant to have a gunshot, but when that followed, she let herself fall behind the players in the role play.

It didn't take long for a scream to bring the crowd running.

Cam followed Jared Koontz. It seemed the most logical step, since she was charged with the PR for this event and he was the star.

Halfway up the fairway for the first hole, they reached the crowd.

"Excuse me. Police," Jared said as he worked his way through the crowd. He had a pointed nose and prominent chin that, paired with his overacting, Cam thought gave the impression of Dudley Do-Right.

People parted and gave him room. This was, after all, meant to be his fund-raiser and he'd been highlighted as sheriff.

"Damn! That's realistic!" he said before falling back into his role. "Is there a doctor?" he whispered back to Cam.

Cam shook her head. "I'm sure it's safe to say he's dead, sir."

He was right about it looking realistic. Derrick Windermere had blood coming from his head and was staring at the trees above him. Cam thought Annie must have found a theater friend to help with makeup.

"Were there witnesses? Who saw this travesty of justice?"

Cam thought it was possible he'd watched too much John Wayne, then remembered a favorite uncle who loved John Wayne, and forgave him.

The strange thing was no one came forward. The crime was meant to have three witnesses, but they were being awfully closed-lipped.

Cam's phone buzzed.

"Yeah?"

"Where are you?" It was Annie.

"At the murder scene. Where are you?"

"You are *not* at the murder scene. Vivian Macy is sprawled here with three witnesses and nobody else."

"Vivian Macy is the victim?"

"By a landslide."

Cam squeezed her way through the crowd.

"Are you sure it wasn't Derrick Windermere?"

"Positive! I sorted the roles myself."

"Crap!"

"What?" Annie asked.

"We have the worst luck! Where are you?"

"Where are you?" Annie countered.

"First fairway," Cam said.

"Wrong nine—we're on the other side of the clubhouse."

Cam clinched her phone shut. "Turns out we have a second murder!" Cam shouted. "This one seems to have witnesses—maybe they will shed light on all of this. That way!" She pointed.

She knew for sure the one wouldn't solve the other, as this one was apparently real, but she had to get everyone away from the scene.

When she was alone with the real body, she stepped in to check for a pulse. Her stomach clenched. Nothing could be done for Derrick now, so she called Jake. Jake was Annie's boyfriend, but also a police detective Cam felt she could mostly trust. The last thing they needed was a panic.

As Cam waited, the sounds from the murder-mystery-solving part of the golf course indicated that the role play seemed to be progressing well. She could hear shouted answers and pleased murmurs when things made sense.

Finally, Jake arrived with his team to attend to the body of Derrick Windermere.

"So what happened, Cam?"

She explained the game, the crash, and the shots and how the rest of the crowd was off pursuing some fictional murder.

"Well, *this* man wasn't shot." Jake pointed out the dirt and shattered clay around his head. "Looks like he was assaulted by a pot of flowers."

"Chrysanthemums," Cam clarified.

Cam hadn't looked very closely at Derrick when she checked his pulse because it had made her nauseous, but where his head lay, off the main trail in the garden, it did indeed look like he'd been attacked by chrysanthemums. He'd just been hit hard enough that there was blood pooling by the side of his head.

"Killed with something on location. This might not be premeditated," Jake said, more to himself than to Cam. "Makes that party important," he said louder. "So were there any witnesses to this crime?"

"When Jared Koontz—he's playing sheriff for the game—asked for witnesses, nobody came forward. But I think only fictional witnesses—the people with game cards telling them what to say—would have thought they were supposed to. I have no clue if anybody actually saw it."

Jake shook his head. "You really tempted fate out here. Pretending murder? After all the real murder you've seen?"

"Look. You can be all high and mighty if you want. This was Annie's idea."

Cam knew that would shut him up, Annie being his girl-friend and all.

"Who would hide a murder in a murder game?" she asked. "Isn't that a bit obvious?"

"Maybe somebody wanting to camouflage the noise of it?" Jake said, brow raised.

Cam had to admit he was right. It had been a perfect setup. Even a dead body had been just part of the scenery to most of the witnesses.

"So who is he?" Jake asked, haltingly calling a truce.

"His name is Derrick Windermere. He's a robber baron of sorts. Made a fortune on foreclosures that he renovated and flipped, and then he does some investment stuff."

"So probably a well-liked guy, then?"

Cam actually snorted. Jake resorting to sarcasm was an amusing, if unhelpful, sign.

"Who around here would know the most about him?"

"Easy." Cam grinned. "Joel Jaimeson. He is Mr. Who's Who. You definitely need to ask him about pretty much everybody."

"And you're setting me up, why?"

"Not you. Him. I think he'll be helpful, and I would enjoy seeing him sit through hours of questioning."

"You have a mean streak," Jake said.

"I most certainly do not! I have a justice streak."

He laughed.

The medical and forensic guys butted in at that point with information Cam was sure she didn't want to know. She had no need to hear about wounds and blood. At the word "coagulation," she grimaced.

"Jake? Can I go now?"

"Sure. I know how to find you. Wait. Who was first on the scene?"

"There was a woman's scream from this direction, but I don't know who. And I don't know who showed up after that. It was a crowd before I got here. We all thought it was the game until Annie called me asking where we were."

"Seems like the kind of thing someone would admit, anyway," Jake said. "Thanks, Cam. Can you make sure nobody leaves?"

Crap. That was the last thing Cam wanted for the evening—an ending that everyone knew was a fiasco. Cam found her way back to the central garden. The mystery wasn't solved, but the crowd had returned to the clubhouse and seemed to be enjoying a round of collective reasoning with cocktails in hand. Nobody headed toward the exit, so Cam just hoped something might happen to change Jake's need to interview everyone.

Vivian Macy stood at the rear, covered in leaves and grinning. It was easy to see she'd been flattered to be murdered.

There should have been a second victim, though, and Cam couldn't figure out who he was. She actually stood on a bench to find Annie so she could ask. It took ages. Annie was at the back of the crowd, frantically making call after call. Cam made her way over.

"Where's murder victim number two?" she asked.

Annie looked up, eyes glistening. "Missing."

"Missing? What do you mean?"

"Gone. Poof. *Se fue.*" She followed the Spanish phrase that meant "it's gone" with a sniff.

"Geez, Annie. It's still fun with just one victim. But there's something I have to . . ."

"No. You don't get it. The second victim was supposed to be my dad!"

CHAPTER 4

Cam's breath caught. This couldn't be written off as some flake getting a better offer mid-game. This event had been Senator Schulz's baby, for starters. But there was no way even the worst emergency would cause him to leave without alerting Annie.

No matter what panic she felt at the apparent murder, Annie's emergency was personal, and she had to be strong and helpful. She stepped forward and hugged her friend. Annie was short enough to bury herself in Cam's chest, so Cam hugged with one arm, and with the other, she speed-dialed Jake.

"This is a bigger problem," she said when he answered.

"Bigger than dead?"

Annie's eyes grew wide as she overheard Jake, but she didn't interrupt.

"Yes. Annie's father has disappeared," Cam said.

"Disappeared? Like disappeared?"

"No call to Annie, no showing up where he was supposed to be. And this was his event."

As much of an ass as Jake could sometimes be when banging heads with Cam over a murder investigation, she knew he would put Annie first. He was a good guy—just annoyingly "by the book."

When she hung up, she explained to Annie about the body that had been found, then called Rob. Rob's boss had trumped him on the thousand-dollar media spot representing the *Roanoke Tribune*. Even Griggs probably wouldn't have been there without the funded media table so generously paid for by Derrick Windermere, though Cam was sure Derrick had had other motives besides informed citizens. But now that the supper was over, she doubted anybody would even notice if Rob showed up for a little moral support.

"Cam! Not over already?" Rob said when he answered.

"No, but we need you. Annie and I need you."

"Oh, man. What now?"

"Just come."

"Out the door already." It was true, too. She heard the obnoxious rumble of his Jeep starting.

She went back to hugging Annie. "Listen. I know this isn't ideal, but what if he just . . . tripped and hit his head or something? We should have somebody searching the grounds, right?"

Annie pulled away. "Oh, geez. I snotted on you. But . . . I guess maybe."

Cam went to the headwaiter. She didn't know whom to call, but he would. She explained her concern that Senator Schulz had been hurt and was out there somewhere.

"I make some calls, madam. Ten minutes, we have team looking." Cam couldn't identify his accent, but it didn't matter. He was being helpful.

"Thank you!"

* * *

When she returned to report to Annie, Jake had arrived. He was on his own. Clearly, the murder took precedence for the police force, but it was good to have a real cop involved.

"So where should he have been?" Jake asked.

Annie opened her iPhone and pressed a few buttons and then looked at a little map.

"Woods to the left of the second-hole tee, or that was his original note. When I tried to call with more information, he was gone."

"So let's go," he said.

Annie looked pleadingly at Cam.

"We can't both go," Cam said. "You two go. Annie, take a bunch of pictures. I probably can't help, but maybe something will jump out at me. And I should be *here* in case the club staff finds anything—so I can let you know."

Annie smiled, though her eyes were wet with tears.

Cam struggled to pay attention to the rest of the murder mystery. She had to text clues to a few "witnesses" for things that came out late in the game, so it was good she could take over for Annie. But the gravity of events was too much. Even when her dad laughingly admitted he was the murderer (as Vivian Macy's date), she still couldn't completely enjoy it.

Rob had arrived halfway into Cam's attempts at pretending nothing was wrong while keeping the game flowing. He stood with an arm around Cam's waist, lending support, but not asking much. Finally he nuzzled her neck.

"Where's Annie?"

"With Jake, trying to figure out what happened to her dad. He disappeared at around the time Derrick Windermere was murdered," Cam whispered.

Rob whistled. It pretty much said it all.

"And where is Griggs?"

Cam pointed. Rob's boss had followed the action of the game, rubbing elbows with the people he must have deemed most important, aside from Koontz. Koontz was clearly having a ball hamming it up. "We assigned him the role of reporter. He's been stuck to Koontz all night. We figured it was the best way to get a lot of coverage," she said.

"So he doesn't know there's been a murder?"

Rob's expression was that of a delighted child, and it finally brought a bit of lightness to all this. Rob, in spite of not being the reporter on scene, was going to get this scoop on his boss. He pulled out his smartphone and began drafting the briefest of story skeletons.

He paused to ask Cam a few questions, then let out a giggle that was probably inappropriate, but Cam understood. A homicide scoop was a big deal, and he'd managed it on the sly. Cam just hoped Griggs wasn't too bitter about it. If he was, Rob might be stuck with crappy assignments for months. Then again, a sports reporter's winter was all basketball and hockey anyway. There wasn't much that would change the majority of what Rob did.

A tap on her shoulder caused Cam to jump. The headwaiter had returned.

"Did you find anything?"

"Sadly, no. We can assure you we search all buildings on the grounds. But we don't have men for nighttime search of the grounds. A security team is looking at cameras and will tell you if anything is found, but I want to let you know about the buildings."

"I appreciate that. It isn't good news, but it also isn't bad news, so that helps."

Cam sighed when he left. "I guess I didn't think he'd be inside," she said to Rob. "But I should still let Annie know."

* * *

Rob went to the murder scene to see what he could find and returned a short while later with a police officer she didn't know. He whispered quietly that he was a police officer trained in high-profile kidnapping and would be coordinating with the FBI, but because of the nature of the senator's disappearance, they were making some exceptions in the case of the murder.

"We'd normally hold everybody here to question them, but we're worried about the safety of the senator and what the publicity might do. Do you have a complete list of everyone who is here?"

Cam assured him she did, and she made a copy of it for him immediately. He looked it over and nodded. "Best for the senator's safety if this is kept quiet tonight, okay?"

Cam not only agreed, she thought it was a miracle they managed to have the event end without any of the guests knowing about the real murder. One astute woman asked about the first body they'd found, and Cam explained there'd been a misunderstanding—that a few people had been pre-selected and wires had gotten crossed. Cam felt a little guilty of course—nobody deserved to die like that, but she thought avoiding hearing the news tonight would go a long way toward preserving the goodwill of the attendees. A lot of public relations was about timing. Hearing of the murder tonight would have soured the whole evening. Being asked questions tomorrow would have less of an effect, or at least that was what she hoped.

The officer nodded at her and left, leaving Rob and Cam out of earshot of anybody else.

"So how serious is this with Annie's dad?" Rob asked.

"He wouldn't have just left without letting Annie know," Cam said. "He is hurt, abducted, or worse."

"Is there anything we can do?"

"If I were you, as the only reporter left on site, I'd get back to the police for the murder investigation. Ask if there were signs of an additional struggle."

Rob kissed her cheek and rushed off the way she pointed. Cam realized she hadn't even said good-bye to her dad. He would know something was up, but she'd let him enjoy the rest of his night. Vivian Macy seemed charming, and Cam sort of liked the idea of her dad dating a future senator.

"Cam! Maybe you can tell me!"

The crowd was clearing, and Samantha rushed at Cam far too fast for the heels she was wearing, and nearly stumbled when she tried to stop.

"Tell you what?" Cam asked.

"I saw the police," she said. "It doesn't take a genius to tell me something happened."

Cam wondered if Samantha was slyly calling most of the party guests idiots, but decided that wasn't the most productive response. She also thought, with an event planner like Samantha, who'd already noticed something suspicious, that the truth was better than the quiet mix of lies and half-truths the rest of the guests had received.

"A couple things," Cam said. "Derrick Windermere is dead and Alden Schulz is missing."

Samantha's jaw dropped. "No!"

She began to tug Cam's arm, pulling her back into the pro shop, where she poured two measures of gin over ice. Thankfully, it was a tall enough glass that when Samantha handed Cam hers, Cam could walk behind the bar and add tonic. She wondered just how crucial Samantha Hollister's membership was to the country club that they would leave her in charge of a full bar.

"I can't believe Alden would kill somebody and take off like that!"

Cam heard a gasp behind her. It was an angle that hadn't

occurred to Cam, but was one that understandably devastated Annie.

"He did not do this, you old cow!" Annie shrieked. Tears spurted from her eyes. She tried to come forward, but Jake had her around the waist.

"Oh!" Samantha said. "I didn't mean . . . only it looks like . . ." she trailed off.

Jake kept a tight hold, but shared some news with Cam and Samantha. "There were signs of a struggle—a spot in the woods looked like somebody had been dragged away unwillingly. There were heel marks that led to the tire tracks for something wide—a truck or a van. Ms. Hollister," Jake said, his most polite deference on display. "Is there any way onto the grounds besides the main entrance?"

"Well, of course there is. A few of the holes on the golf course are unfenced. There are roads that run very close in several places. But it would be difficult to remain unnoticed for long—there are cameras everywhere."

"Cameras! That's helpful," Jake said. "Would you say all country club members know that?"

"Most," she said. "We've been told as a warning against hanky-panky on the course. Of course, some think that's an added thrill . . ."

Cam really didn't want to hear those details, but it was good to know there was a camera running most places.

"Would you mind taking a quick look at the guest list?" Jake asked. "If you could put a check by the members that would help."

"Sure. Why?" Samantha asked.

"My theory is that members might know better than to misbehave," Jake said.

"Oh, of course!" Samantha said. She began scanning the list.

Cam was glad Samantha hadn't taken Annie's insult to heart, but then there'd been a time when Cam liked Samantha a lot. And it was obvious Annie was upset. Rob came in as Samantha read and marked the list, checking about half the names, making question marks by half a dozen. Cam wondered what they meant. Were they former members? Inactive members? Eligible people who Samantha wasn't sure had joined or not? Whatever the case, Samantha was fairly quick at it and soon handed the list back to Jake.

"Thank you, ma'am. At this point, we should probably be on our way. Would you like us to help you lock up?"

"I can lock the door behind you," she said.

Cam wondered if she didn't have a secret guest tucked away somewhere—that was sort of Samantha's style—but it was none of her business.

"If you're sure," Cam said.

"Of course I am, hon. I'll be fine. You kids run along."

It wasn't as easy as all that. Cam grilled Jake first on how things were going, but he assured her the department's best man was on the kidnapping case and had coordinated with the murder investigation team.

"It's not normally how we do a murder investigation," Jake admitted, "but the safety of Senator Schulz has to take priority."

Cam was glad for that, thinking she had "Officer Experience" to thank, though she thought Jake might have bent the rules just a little for Annie if it had come to it.

They had four vehicles there, and Jake needed to check back with the police team, so musical cars was also a challenge.

"I don't think Annie should drive," Cam said.

"You're right," Jake said. "Annie, gimme your keys. I'll have my partner take the squad car, and I'll drive yours to your place. You go ahead with Cam. It might take me a little while to get out of here."

Annie looked grateful for the solution and handed her

keys to Jake. In Cam's car, Annie huddled a little, so Cam reached over and pulled her best friend toward her.

"What do they do when they kidnap someone?" Annie asked.

"Jake probably knows better than I do, but I think they usually want money." Cam left off the alternative of just wanting to torture somebody. She had no idea if there was residual anger about Alden Schulz's senate term, but it was certainly possible.

"My step-monster's out of the country," Annie said. "Who would they call?"

Annie's parents were divorced, and as so often happens with men of power, her dad had remarried a trophy wife.

"That's right. I guess either the kidnapper doesn't know, or Elle isn't the target. Say . . . do you have a key to his house?"

"Yeah."

"Maybe we should look for clues to see if this was personal. I mean, probably he just saw the murder, but maybe he was a target and there would be hints."

Annie sat up straighter and turned toward Cam.

"What about the guys? They're going to our place."

"There are a hundred good reasons you might go to your dad's. Maybe you're getting Cruella's itinerary so you can call her, or maybe there's a cat that needs tending."

Annie laughed at that. Cruella was a nickname Annie had coined for Elle, but Cam hadn't used it before.

"You know . . . there *is* a cat that will need tending."

"Is there?"

"I mean, Louise would take care of him, but I bet he would be happier with me at night if Dad and Elle are both gone."

"There we are then."

Cam had already turned around. Senator Schulz's house was back near the country club. Unfortunately, or possibly not, the maneuver took them past Rob, who turned around to follow them.

"Told you you were going to regret that special-order color," Annie said.

Cam wouldn't have changed the bright yellow of her Mustang for anything, but it was true she had the only one in town.

"It's better to have three of us," Cam said. "You look at computer files, and Rob and I will scan other stuff, then we'll get the cat. Maybe we'll even beat Jake back to our place."

Annie sighed as they pulled into the driveway.

They didn't get their chance to look around, however, as Cruella was pacing the living room.

CHAPTER 5

"Elle!" Annie shrieked when she stepped in, though it was much quieter than Elle's shriek. "I'm so sorry! I thought you were in Finland."

"That's next summer. I was in Milan, but I had a call from my brother to get back to the States. Why are you here?"

She was always a little terse, or at least she had been the times Cam had seen her before, though Cam knew those had been more formal events. Cam figured new wives within spitting distance of a daughter's age could be that way, and Annie had probably never done anything to try to smooth the relationship. She talked like it was an investment not worth making, as her dad would probably trade her in for a new model soon. It was just how Annie talked, but Cam thought she believed it to some extent.

"There was . . . something happened with Dad tonight," Annie said. "I came to see if there was an itinerary to call you."

"My cell wouldn't work?"

"Oh! Right. But I have a new cell, so I didn't have your

number in there . . ." Annie trailed off. Cam knew Annie was lying. There was no new cell, but there was also no reason Elle would know that.

"So?" Elle said.

"Dad was kidnapped."

"He was *what*?"

"Big fund-raiser dinner. There was a murder, and the police think maybe Dad saw it. There was a sign of a struggle and he disappeared."

"This happened tonight? A murder? And your father . . . kidnapped, you said?" Elle sounded panicked. "I thought he wasn't running for anything."

"He's not. It was for Jared Koontz."

"No!"

"Well I thought the same thing," Annie said. "But . . . is there a reason *you're* saying that?"

"Jared's just sort of a punk. I've known him for years. Do people take him seriously?"

Annie didn't have a response, and Elle just wore an expression that crossed confusion and disgust, so Cam butted in.

"Look, I'm sure the police will have more to tell you. Annie just thought you were gone and they wouldn't know how to reach you, so we were looking for your information. We should go."

"Right!" Annie said.

"If you must," Elle said, though Cam thought she was glad to see them leave.

Rob, fortunately, had not gone inside. It would have seemed like overkill to have three of them just to retrieve a phone number. They passed him where he stood listening from the porch. Without a word, they returned to their cars, turned around in the circle, then headed back to Cam's.

"I *know* she wasn't back when Dad left the house tonight," Annie said once they were driving.

"How would you know that?" Cam asked.

"Dad was in too good of a mood. He loves her, but this time of year, she's annoying—has an opinion about every political race, mostly ill-informed, or so he says, though you know *my* opinion on *his* political opinions—he'd just rather not deal with her. He would have been grouchier if she'd gotten home before he left for the fund-raiser."

"You don't think she had anything to do with this, do you?" Cam asked.

"Elle? Like what?" Annie said.

"I don't know. I've just done this murder thing before and don't believe in coincidences."

"Okay, stop there. My dad was *not* murdered!"

"Geez, Annie," Cam said. "I'm sorry! I totally didn't mean to imply that. But there *was* a murder."

Annie leaned back against the seat and closed her eyes. Cam knew she understood but was having trouble processing.

Jake met them as they arrived, and they all made their way into Cam's apartment. Cam was significantly neater than Annie. In Annie's apartment, the chance of finding a clear sitting surface for two wasn't bad, but finding seating for four was out of the question. Between baking, photography, and computer geeking, Annie just had too many hobbies to add cleaning to the list, and each hobby had an array of toys to top it off.

Cam, on the other hand, was a little OCD. She wasn't Felix Unger, but there was a really good chance you were safe following the five-second rule in her house. Every surface was washed at least weekly, which was far more often than every surface was used.

As they went in, Rob held Cam's elbow.

"So Mrs. Schulz probably doesn't know when Annie's lying," Rob whispered, "but I have this feeling that wasn't the full story."

"Not quite," Cam said. "It was intended to be the cover for Jake. I was going to help Annie look for clues about anybody who had it in for her dad."

Rob shook his head.

"Seriously. The police are going to look at the murder first. But what if it was a kidnapping first and the witness got killed?"

He stared, and for a moment, Cam felt some satisfaction that she'd been convincing, but then realized she had felt convinced, too, and she didn't want Annie's dad to be the real target. Especially if this was a crime worth killing over.

Cam and Rob joined Annie and Jake in Cam's living room. Annie had found a bottle of wine and some glasses, and Jake was pulling the cork.

"So where've y'all been?" Jake asked. His tone was casual, but Cam knew he was smart enough to know it hadn't been a snack run.

"I went to see if Cruella had left her itinerary," Annie said. "I figured, as Dad's wife, she deserved to know he was gone."

"Uh-huh," Jake said. Cam could tell he was certain that was only part of the story. Cam felt a little relieved he knew Annie that well, because she knew secrets always came out.

"She was *there*, though I could swear Dad said she would be gone all week, but there she was."

Jake frowned. "Does that mean something?"

Annie stopped and looked at him for a long moment, then at Cam. "I don't know," she said. "I mean, I would like to think it means she's a flake, but I've never thought that was one of her faults before. She said her brother called, but didn't say what about. I really hope it's not something bad."

"What could it be?" Jake asked.

"Getting rid of my dad!" Annie shouted. Her tears returned.

Jake stepped in to hold her, but she pushed him back, letting Cam grab her instead.

"She wouldn't hurt him," Cam said. "She'd know she'd get caught. If she had anything to do with it, he's okay."

Annie sniffed into Cam's chest. "You better be right, or I'll have to unleash the flying monkeys."

"Annie," Rob said. "It is probably just that he saw something."

"Freaking Derrick Windermere! Damn man probably deserved what he got. He put half this town out of business. Who'd hurt my dad over that?"

"Maybe they'll let him go if they know he agrees with them," Jake said.

"See, that's the trouble," Annie said. "Dad's feeling was it was just capitalism at work. It's the kind of thing he always shrugged his shoulders at."

Jake hung his head.

"Maybe it's somebody trying to hurt the party," Rob suggested.

"Or take it over," Cam countered. "Derrick and Senator Schulz were the party's old blood. Maybe they want to be the new power."

Though, strictly speaking, that wasn't true. Derrick was just the party's money. New or old had nothing to do with it.

"Can we please . . ." Annie said. "I can't think about all this tonight. Can we not speculate until we know something?"

Cam hugged Annie again, then Annie finally let Jake hug her as well and take her upstairs.

When they were alone, Cam and Rob could finally talk more freely.

"You think this is politics?" Rob asked.

"I think money is more likely," Cam said. "Windermere was a first-class ass. He really did reverse several fortunes."

"So you think Annie's dad is just a case of wrong place, wrong time?"

"I don't know. I wish I felt more confident about that."

"And this . . . Cruella?"

"Elle Chamberlain Schulz. Gold digger. I think Annie is her dad's primary heir, so Elle is better off with Senator Schulz alive than dead."

"Well, that's helpful."

"I hope so. I didn't want to bring it up with Annie, since I figured a sentence that included 'dead' would be a downer, regardless."

"I need to get this story in," Rob said.

"I know you do. I'm fine." Cam was familiar with newspaper deadlines by now, and understood Rob's compulsion to advance his career. She would do the same if she were the reporter.

"You can do it here, yes?"

"I could."

"You write and send. I'll take a bath and try to relax."

"Oh, right. Like I can write when you're wet and naked in the next room."

"Your incentive, hotshot, is if you finish in time, maybe we can go to sleep together. Your deadline is two?"

He nodded.

"Try to meet it an hour early."

The warm water was soothing, but Cam's brain was racing. She was trying to relive the party and all the encounters she'd seen with Derrick Windermere that implied bad blood. It was no small number. There was the man Annie said her dad couldn't stand following around behind Derrick, and the man Derrick had sent off for offending Senator Schulz, or so it had appeared. The harem had looked rather angry, and Toni Howe had been annoyed with him, too. Cam had thought at least Toni's situation had a reasonable solution on the horizon. Then there was what they had learned from Joel Jaimeson about him when they were planning the party—that Derrick had been milking fortunes from other people.

Nobody had displayed obvious bad blood toward Alden Schulz other than the man who'd been sent off and the other man, Melvin, whom Annie said her dad already disliked before the night began. Then again, Senator Schulz was a party patriarch, a person one didn't confront directly.

She realized, though, in addition to political animosity, that the event was a perfect opportunity for someone who had a personal issue to take advantage of the setup. She had no idea who Derrick Windermere might have offended personally—surely dozens of people.

She was just glad she wasn't stuck investigating this fiasco. She didn't want to dig around in the sleazebag's life. She would continue to help Annie, but that was about finding her dad. Being a murder witness was a "just in case" angle.

She faded off as she lay in the soothing water, and just before she fell asleep, it occurred to her that her father had been with someone who would have liked their event to end in tragedy. She hated to think it, but maybe he knew something.

Rob woke her up. She wasn't sure how much later it was, but the water was definitely tepid. He dried her and got her into bed, kissed her forehead, and that was the last she knew.

It was strange to wake up naked the next morning. It wasn't normally her thing, but at least she felt rested. The bath had done that much.

As she showered to prepare for her day, she tried to think of a way to spin this event. She would do her best to describe it as a tragedy, but RGS would not benefit from being mentioned, so she would leave them out of it.

She was just drying off as her phone buzzed.

"Tunia?" she answered.

"Cam! Get over here!"

"Why? What happened?"

"They're searching the van!"

"Slow down, Petunia. Who is?"

"The police!"

"The catering van? Why?"

"Somebody was kidnapped? They must think our van was used."

"Okay, calm down. You and Nick didn't kidnap Annie's dad, did you?"

"Don't be ridiculous."

"Then all looking in the van can do is clear you."

"But we cleaned it."

"Which is normal. You do use it to transport food. That's a normal and perfectly explainable practice."

"You're sure?"

"Positive."

Petunia seemed to breathe easier, but then gasped. "It was Annie's dad?"

"It was."

Petunia paused, and Cam thought she was wrestling with her dislike of public figures but fondness for Annie. "Tell her I'm sorry, okay?"

"I will. Thank you."

They hung up. Petunia's nerves were understandable. Six months earlier, Nick had been falsely accused of murder. Cam didn't see any way they could be accused of this. The evidence would clear them. The search must just be a precaution because the van was known to have been on location.

She debated going to the office after that but decided to work from home. She emailed the Roanoke Garden Society board to let them know where she was and how to reach her.

Next she followed through on the idea swimming in her head when she'd fallen asleep the night before. She retrieved her phone.

"Daddy?"

"Hiya, sunshine!"

"Have the police . . ." she stalled. This was the third time she'd asked her dad this question, and it wasn't getting any easier. For the first time, though, he seemed lost.

"Have the police what?"

"A couple of bad things happened last night. I'm surprised they haven't reached you."

"Again?"

Cam sighed. "Look. Could we meet for lunch?"

"Of course we can, but can you give me a hint?" She heard crumpling and then, "Wait, never mind. Murder, huh?"

Damn. That meant this news had made the papers already. Why was Rob so efficient? No wonder he had disappeared before she woke up.

"Yeah, and does it mention Annie's dad?"

"Should it?"

"He was kidnapped."

"Oh, dear. Sunshine, I think maybe I should pick up lunch and we should meet Annie. Do you know where she is?"

"She planned to work. The customer part is rough, but the baking part calms her. She said she'd go crazy sitting around waiting."

"Then we'll take lunch there. Meet you at noon?"

"Make it one. Annie sometimes has a busy lunchtime with all those nearby businesses."

"One it is, then!"

When Cam reached Sweet Surprise, her dad was working the counter. Annie was in back baking. She frowned at her dad.

"You said dealing with the customers might be hard. I'm not so senile I can't put a cupcake in a box and work a cash register."

Cam felt herself tear up and then scolded her own sentimentality. She loved that her dad thought of her best friend as his own daughter . . . only maybe with more TMI than he shared with his own daughters. This wasn't the first time he'd been there for Annie.

Cam walked behind the counter and kissed her dad, then proceeded to the back to find Annie pulling what appeared to be cheesecakes from the industrial oven.

"Hey."

"Have I ever told you how lucky you got in the dad department?" Annie said.

"I know. He's yours, too. As often as you need him."

"I seem to need him more than you do, lately."

"That's still less than Petunia, and he loves to help," Cam said.

Annie set the tray on a large marble slab.

"So? Cheesecake?"

"I'm trying to perfect a few flavors for the holidays. I've got a pumpkin, an eggnog, and that one," Annie pointed an accusatory finger at the cracked culprit, "is me trying to figure out some way to incorporate rum. I was thinking plum pudding for my inspiration."

"Why don't you just make . . . you know . . . plum pudding? Or Christmas pudding? I think I have my grandma's recipe."

"Really? See, family recipes aren't so big at my house. They tend to get burned in divorces."

Cam tried not to laugh. "I'll find it and give it to you for a starting place."

"Perfect! Now what did your dad bring for lunch?"

CHAPTER 6

The three sat around a table in Annie's back room. The bell would alert them if a customer came in, and Cam's dad leaped up each time it happened.

It frustrated Cam, as her real goal had been to question her dad and the stream was steady enough that he rarely sat, but it was still companionable. Finally, Annie broke onto the conversational freeway Cam felt they needed to approach.

"So you're dating power women now?" Annie teased.

"Shucks, Vivian and I have been friends for years."

"I don't remember her," Cam said.

"Sure you do, sunshine. Aunt Vi?"

"Aunt Vi?" Cam knew Aunt Vi was not an actual relation, but had in fact been her mother's college roommate. Cam hadn't seen her since she was in elementary school and never would have recognized the professional woman she saw the night before from the big hair and miniskirt of her memory. "Are you sure?"

Her dad laughed. "I didn't recognize her either. It's been

twenty years. I suppose being a lawyer will curb someone's style a little."

"Man, no kidding!" Cam scratched her head. "Wasn't she blonde?"

"I guess not naturally. It was different times. Your mother and I got married before . . . well . . . the silly hair and all. So we didn't get too caught up, though I remember shoulder pads that made Mom look like a linebacker."

Cam grinned. The eighties hadn't missed her mother entirely. Cam also remembered a fitness craze that involved Lycra and leotards and a tall-bangs thing her mother had tried for a while.

"So how did you and Aunt Vi reconnect?" Cam asked.

"Facebook!"

Cam almost dropped her sandwich. "I didn't know you were on Facebook."

"Well no. I can hardly have my daughters monitoring who I talk to."

"I'm his Facebook friend," Annie said.

Cam stood and let out a disgruntled noise.

"Annie doesn't care who I flirt with," her dad argued.

"It's true," Annie said. "I dig that your dad's a babe magnet."

"I wouldn't judge!" Cam said.

Annie dropped her head so she was looking at Cam through her eyebrows. The front bell dinged and Cam's dad rose. When he was out of earshot, Annie whispered.

"Let me do this. He has like forty friends and he doesn't want to worry what you think. I'll keep an eye."

Cam was still a little offended, but she supposed it made some sense. Annie cheered every time her dad got lucky, and Cam preferred not to think about it. But Annie would tell her if anything big happened, or if anybody who was a bad idea appeared in the mix.

She was just about to clarify that with Annie when her dad returned, looking pleased. "I gave her a sample of that pumpkin cheesecake and she ordered one for Thanksgiving."

Annie looked back at the cheesecakes. Two pieces were missing from one. Her jaw dropped.

"What?" her dad asked. "I tried it and it was fantastic!"

Annie rolled her eyes. "I can't leave you unsupervised!"

Her dad chuckled. Cam knew that he preferred to think of himself as a bit of a renegade.

She finally worked up the nerve to ask her dad about the night before—about what he saw and did, and how frequently he was with his date throughout the evening.

"Well, she was the victim! I hardly saw her once she got up from supper to powder her nose! Though we were both surrounded by people the whole time, if that's what you're asking."

It was, but now that he said it, Cam felt guilty for it. She hadn't been accusing *her dad*, but the question sounded like it.

"I'm sorry, Daddy. I just . . . from a motive perspective . . . Vi may run against Jared, and having his event go wrong . . . really wrong . . ."

"She's not running for that seat. She's going for the House of Delegates." He looked very proud.

"Really?"

"Not that she said anything about cronyism in the state Senate," he said.

Annie snorted. *Great.* Cam didn't need the two of them feeding off each other when she was trying to get to the bottom of something.

"You said she got up to powder her nose. When?"

"Dessert. Because I got to finish hers—she'd left it."

"And had she just gotten her role?"

"As a matter of fact, she had."

Annie made a frustrated noise. "That was us. We told her to use the excuse, but to get out to the murder scene."

Cam nodded. "Okay, so what about during the party—before supper. Did you and she ever talk to Derrick?"

"Not me. Though when I stopped to shake Alden's hand—you know, because of you girls—I did hear her scoff at him and say, 'You wish!'"

"At Derrick?"

Cam's dad nodded, looking proud again. Cam thought he hadn't quite processed the implications.

"Did she say what it was about?"

"Didn't ask. I figured it was politics."

"Okay. Did you see anything that might have been a clue about Annie's dad?" Cam asked.

"No . . . I did see him later, though, after supper. And I know what time it was. Or . . . well, I can tell you. Because I got a game hint: where I was supposed to go and what to say for the game. It came on my phone—the alibi I was supposed to be using."

He pulled his phone out and scanned his texts.

"Nine forty-two. So I saw him at maybe nine forty."

"Was he with anyone?" Annie asked.

"Not that I saw. He was on the phone and it didn't look game related."

"We can get that," Annie said. "Jake can look up who he talked to."

"And *where* was he?"

"Fairway of the first hole. I was at the tee."

"Fairway? That's where Derrick was."

"Well, I saw the crowd, but my first clue, officially, was on the other side of the clubhouse, so I quit following the crowd. Alden was a little farther down."

"So that means he was taken after the murder," Cam said.

"It would seem so."

"It also means he might have seen it," Annie said.

Cam wrote down the details. It wasn't much, but it was definitely more than what they'd known before. Not that Jake would have shared details with her, though maybe he would with Annie. It was *her* dad, after all, who was missing.

When lunch was over and they all rose and hugged, Annie asked Cam if she could stick around awhile.

"Sure. That fiasco last night was my big event, and a press release entirely devoid of the Roanoke Garden Society was my response. It's been sent to the watchdogs—apparently explosive political news has channels to go through that gardening news doesn't, even if there is a body involved. Plus, the office phones have been forwarded to my cell. If there's an emergency, I'll know."

They sent Cam's dad off, then Annie got behind the counter and began taking inventory, not meeting Cam's eyes.

"Did you know he was leaving her?" Annie said, without turning to Cam.

"He . . . your dad? Elle?"

Annie nodded. "He gave me several hints last night that it just wasn't working. I puzzled it out while I tried to sleep. You know politicians and euphemisms, but I'm sure that's what he meant. You don't think she'd . . ."

"Why didn't you tell me the hints last night?"

"I hadn't worked out that they *were* hints. Denial maybe?"

"Did you tell Jake?" Cam asked.

"I've barely seen him."

"Tell Jake. That might be important! Now *why* is he leaving her?"

"He didn't say it that clearly—just that it wasn't working."

"Infidelity? Annoying factor?"

"Seriously," Annie said. "I wish I knew."

"Well, tell Jake. He certainly has a lot better resources than I do. But I'll help however I can. Are you thinking of doing anything?"

"A couple of bugs?"

"Like . . . spying bugs?"

Annie nodded. "Phone, purse, kitchen."

"Isn't that illegal?"

"It's illegal in court, but I just want to know if that harpy had anything to do with my dad disappearing, so I can go kick her butt myself if she did."

Cam imagined she'd feel the same way—maybe more so. Cam actually *liked* her dad. But she looked at Annie, all of five feet, two inches. Still, Annie was pretty resourceful where gadgets were concerned. There was no reason to think gadgets of torture to get her revenge on Elle would be less likely than these bugs, though Annie-torture would probably include a lot of itching and embarrassment rather than pain.

"So what? We go then . . . you say you have something in a room . . . then plant it when she's not looking?"

"Yeah, but we gotta be prepared for her to come with me instead of you. We each need a few bugs on us."

"I'll need a lesson."

"Silly. Don't you ever just browse online for how all this stuff works? I used to try to make my own." Annie said it as if it were normal, but then she'd been taking things apart to see if she could get them back together since they were kids.

Cam was uncomfortable, but also a little thrilled at this espionage idea. Annie had helped her a lot. She'd paid the price for helping, over and above what could be expected. Besides, if she was honest, this investigation excited her.

Cam and Annie debated when they might actually miss seeing Elle altogether. Neither of them wanted to be stuck in a conversation. Annie thought Elle did a spinning class in the afternoon, so they decided to go right away, Annie coaching Cam on the finer points of bug planting on the way. Unfortunately, either the jet lag hadn't left her the energy for exercising or something was going on.

Now that it was light, Cam could see the state of the garden at the front of the house. She pointed out the rhododendrons, a pair of them, that were leaping from their edge. "Those should probably be trimmed or moved. Now is the time, right before we get a freeze."

"In case you hadn't noticed, Henry Larsson has had other things to do for a few weeks. I'm sure he's been contacted," Annie said. She rang the bell.

The housekeeper greeted them.

"Hi, Louise," Annie said. "I left something here that I hoped to pick up. Is Elle around? I don't want to bother her."

Louise, who had been the housekeeper as long as Cam had known Annie and had been gray-haired even in those days, got a dark look. "She won't go anywhere. It's like she's afraid I'll toss her things on the street," she whispered.

"Would you?" Annie whispered back with a playful grin.

"I'd like to some days, but it's not worth my job." Then, more loudly, she said, "Ms. Elle is up in the home gym if you need to see her. Can I get you girls some tea?"

"Oh, no thank you. We won't be long. I'm not sure if what I need would be in dad's study or up in the library. Cam, why don't you check the study?"

Cam nodded. She thought she knew what she needed to do. Annie climbed the stairs and Cam entered the big study near the front door, where Alden handled some portion of his local business when he wasn't in Richmond. Since his last term had ended a few years earlier, that had been often. Cam sat in his big leather chair and took off the piece of the phone she needed to remove in order to install the bug and fiddled the little thing into place.

"What do you think you're doing?"

Cam looked up to see Elle.

"Oh. Annie had some paperwork she thought her dad might have filed for her. I'm trying to figure out where he might have put it in here, and Annie is up checking the library."

"I mean to the phone."

"When we were little, he used to tape his combinations and stuff on the phone in different locations," she lied. "I just thought . . . in case it was in the file drawer."

"It has a key. And we keep the keys in the bedroom. What kind of papers are you looking for?"

"Her birth certificate. Annie has to renew her passport, so she needs it." It was a stupid answer, but Cam had to think on her feet, so it was all she could manage.

"And *she* doesn't have it? She's a big girl."

Elle looked disgusted, like Annie was an irresponsible child, which was stupid. Elle was probably only three years older than they were and had never supported herself a day in her life. Was it more irresponsible to store a document at a parent's home or to marry for money so you didn't have to get a job?

"Well what do you need it for besides getting a passport or driver's license? The last time Annie did those things, she was living at home." Cam knew her smile was sour.

"I'll be right back," Elle said.

Cam heard her climbing the stairs and let out a breath. On a whim, she darted across the entry to a similar "hers" study and tucked the other bug behind a gadget on a high shelf, then returned to the senator's study and noticed Louise watching her curiously.

"And what was that about, Miss Camellia?" she asked, her frame stiff.

Cam sighed. "Senator Schulz. We don't want to think Elle had anything to do with it, but we have to be sure."

Cam was surprised when Louise seemed to find merit in that and nodded then left.

Annie and Elle returned together, and Elle opened a drawer for them. Strangely, in a file marked "Birth Certificates" was their alibi. Elle handed the page to Annie, locked the drawer again, and stood. Cam was glad Annie could maintain a poker face, because she was sure she was confused.

"You two need anything else?"

"We should be asking you. Are you okay?" Cam asked.

"A little scared. I manage, though."

Cam couldn't help comparing Elle to Evangeline Patrick, the other trophy wife she knew. Evangeline was leagues ahead of Elle. For one thing, Evangeline was a sincerely nice person, and Cam thought she loved her husband a lot more than Elle seemed to. Elle was barely upset, or at least she wasn't showing it.

When they reached Annie's Beetle, Annie thrust the birth certificate at her. "Now you're stuck with it."

"What?"

"You know me. It would be lost forever at my place. I left it *there* so I knew where it was."

"It was the only thing I could think of. Elle was grilling me."

"Okay. It wasn't bad thinking, especially as it was really there. But you need to file it so I can come get it if I need it. I'm not nearly responsible enough to hang on to anything I need forever."

"Louise busted me, too."

"Man. Some spy you are."

"I just told her what we were doing . . . well not what, but why."

"She's probably been spying, too," Annie said.

"Should we talk to her?"

"Yeah, but at home. We'll stop by her place tonight. Take

her a bottle of bourbon. She'll talk happily then, and Elle won't know anything about it."

At the next stoplight, Cam noticed Annie's hands were shaking on the wheel.

"Hey, are you holding up okay?"

"It's just . . . I know I complain and everything . . . but this is my dad."

"I know. We'll find him, okay?"

Thankfully, home wasn't far away and Annie managed to get there without breaking down.

"Do you want company? Or would you rather be alone?" Cam asked.

"Company. Jake's coming over later, but not until six. I may go nuts if I have to be alone."

"My place or yours?"

"Mine. I need to bake."

That was normal for Annie—baking as therapy. So they filed up to Annie's chaotic apartment. She handed a bottle of wine to Cam to open and then started getting out ingredients for something fussy.

Cam pulled glasses from a cupboard and poured them each a glass of wine, and Annie strapped on an apron, a sign she intended to do this like a kamikaze.

They spent the next two hours baking and drinking wine, though Cam intentionally paced herself. She didn't want a headache and figured at least one of them ought to stay sober. Finally, Rob and Jake arrived together with takeout from a nearby Italian place.

"So how's the murder investigation going?" Cam asked.

"Well, I still have a job, which is good," Rob said.

"Griggs was ticked, then?"

"Wouldn't you be? Junior reporter scoops you on one of

the biggest stories of the year—one you were present for, and the punk has already scooped two murder stories this year?"

"When you say it like that . . ." Cam smiled a little, feeling proud.

"He found out by reading the article, too. It's not that I didn't try to let him know, but he must have gone for drinks with somebody after the fund-raiser, because I got Kathy when I filed the article."

Kathy was the assistant editor, and normally Rob didn't get along with her quite as well as he did with Griggs; she thought sports was a fluff topic. But on this, she'd probably been pleased to rush through an important piece while her boss was busy.

"I noticed there was no mention of the kidnapping."

"That cop asked me to keep that quiet—said it could put the senator in more danger if it became public."

Cam nodded. It was what they'd heard the night before, too, and what she expected was being weeded from her press releases.

"But Griggs got over being mad?" Cam asked.

"Yeah. He swore at me awhile, then confessed he was mad at himself."

"Was he willing to tell you what he saw?"

"He sure was. Got an eyeful."

Jake eyed Rob. Cam thought maybe Rob had waited to tell them when they were all together.

"Griggs thought it looked like Derrick was basically campaigning for Koontz. He went from table to table, group to group, always with the same couple of lines. He thought it seemed really important to Derrick that Koontz win. Pretty normal for a fund-raiser, if you ask me. But he also saw Derrick, and this is different from what we've heard, get into a fairly nasty argument with Melvin Entwhistle. They had words, Melvin walked away, and then Melvin came back a little while later with one of the women who'd been with

Derrick. Griggs thought maybe she'd been sent to appease Entwhistle."

"I'll bet," Annie said.

"Any other arguments?" Cam asked.

"Not that he noticed."

"Okay. How about you, Jake?"

Jake gave her a look to mind her own business, but he'd known her long enough to know that would never happen. Rob slurped his last strand of spaghetti.

"They figure it's either a political rival or one of the people he bilked."

"Genius. Who thought of those motives?" Cam asked. Annie swatted her, not appreciating the sarcasm, but Cam had thought those two angles were obvious the night before.

Rob eyed Cam, and she realized he knew more, but wasn't going to tell her in front of Jake. That probably meant he'd either been told in confidence, or he'd been told by his non-Jake police source—a guy in the forensics lab whom he preferred to keep secret from Jake. Otherwise, the guy would get reprimanded and Rob's source would dry up. She decided to tackle what they *could* talk about.

"So is there a list of people who lost their shirts to Windermere's business strategies?"

"Those financial records have been requested, but there are an awful lot of people to sort through," Jake said.

Cam sighed. "Okay, what about witnesses?"

"We'll start looking more tomorrow. Only thing we know is the screamer was a pregnant woman."

"Jessica," Cam said. She'd been the only noticeably pregnant woman at the party.

"Shoot," Annie said.

"What?"

"I keep ruining our leads. She's official, too. She was screaming for the game—an official witness. She probably didn't actually see anything."

"You don't plan to tell me anything else, do you?" Cam asked Jake.

"He's just doing his job," Rob said reasonably.

He wouldn't get away with the "just his job" card on that front, not with Annie as his girlfriend, but it could wait.

"How about the kidnapping then?" Cam said to Jake.

"They think I'm too close. They don't want me investigating it. Besides, Len is coordinating with Special Forces. FBI does kidnapping, especially with a public figure."

"Seriously?" Annie asked. She looked devastated.

"Hey, I'll still talk to the guys so I know everything they can share and will keep you in the loop."

"Jake?" Annie said. "Dad hinted last night that he was leaving Elle."

"Hinted?"

"You know Dad. He never says *anything* outright."

"I'll tell the guys. They'll listen to my input. They just won't let me be out in the field on it."

"Speaking of field," Annie said. "I bet Louise is home!"

"Louise?" Rob asked.

"She's been my dad's housekeeper since I was six. She's a gem and I love her, and Cam and I were going to ask her if she knew anything. Can we all go?"

"Ah! That Louise. I like her," Rob said.

"Won't she feel overwhelmed?" Jake asked.

"No, silly. You're my boyfriend. Rob is Cam's. She's known Cam and me forever, like family. It will be nice. She'll be glad to help us."

Cam wasn't sure she'd be *glad*, but she'd sort of forgotten their plans for Louise when they invited the boys over, and she really wasn't in the mood to wait. Besides, Louise was pretty unflappable. She'd even made the media feel stupid in her days as a senator's housekeeper.

They all went in Cam's car, since it was the most comfortable for four people. Louise obviously hadn't been home very long. She still had on her housekeeping dress. But she invited the four of them in, and when Annie handed her the bottle of bourbon, Cam explained. She hoped that in doing so, she could also avoid Louise mentioning her and Annie's trip to the house later in the conversation. Thankfully, Louise was quick on the uptake and used to Annie keeping a secret now and then.

"Louise, have you met Annie's boyfriend, Jake, and my boyfriend, Rob?" Cam asked.

"I think I remember Rob. You and he have been together quite some time, haven't you?"

"We have."

"Good to see you again. And it's nice to meet you, Jake."

"Jake is a police officer. He's not officially investigating Senator Schulz's disappearance because of his relationship with Annie, but we thought maybe you might be more comfortable thinking about all this at home with people who know you instead of at work when it's official."

"Well, yes. I suppose."

"Louise, I know it's horrible to think about," Annie said. Cam was glad she finally chimed in. "I don't think Elle would hurt Daddy."

"Well no. She's not . . ." Cam thought she was hesitant to say anything bad about her employer. The pause was fairly long, but then she looked at Annie and went on. " . . . not my cup of tea, but I always thought, to the extent she can, she loves him."

"Did you know Daddy planned to leave her?"

Louise looked very uncomfortable. "I might have guessed."

"Do you know why?"

"There were a lot of phone calls. Some were at strange hours," she said.

"Do you think she was having an affair?"

"Well I don't know about *that*, but I suspect your father

thought so. She refused to answer questions about it. I heard her say she'd clear it up."

"With her marriage on the line?" Annie asked. Her eyes were wide.

"Miss Annie, your daddy is not always so forthcoming. He *told her* he understood and he'd give her time to explain. You and I have known him a long time and know that means a day or two. But Miss Elle sees the world through rose-colored glasses. She probably wished so hard he meant weeks that she made herself believe it."

Cam had known people like that. They were frustrating to deal with, but she could see Elle being that way.

"So you don't think she knew he was leaving?"

"Well, it's possible I hinted that to her."

"How?" Annie asked.

"She called to speak with your father and he wasn't here. She said some things she thought I should do, and I disagreed and knew your father would, too. I refused. She threatened what she'd do when she got home, and I said something like . . . I wasn't sure she would be welcome. She just made me so mad. Of course, I got my punishment. She was home two days later, far earlier than scheduled. I don't know what she thought!"

Cam did. The woman heard she might be evicted and was planning to squat. Cam wondered if there'd even been a call from a brother. Coming home to squat, though, was a lot better than returning from Europe to kidnap or murder your husband. So in a way it was hopeful.

"Have you noticed anything strange around the house since Senator Schulz was taken?" Cam asked.

"Other than Miss Elle refusing to leave? Not really. I mean . . . your dad being taken, of course, but not before that."

"Would you mind . . . keeping an eye open for odd things?" Annie said.

"Of course not, sweetheart. You're like my own daughter,

and Senator Schulz has been good to me over the years. I'm happy to keep an eye out."

They all rose and Annie hugged Louise. Cam was surprised neither Jake nor Rob had more to add, but they'd gotten some decent information anyway.

"I think we should call it a night," Jake said when they arrived back at Cam's and Annie's apartments.

Cam agreed quickly, not because she was tired, but because she thought she and Rob might make more progress without a cop and a very upset girl in their midst; plus, she was still dying for his secret information.

They made it inside and Cam cracked a Diet Pepsi and handed Rob a beer.

"So can we compare notes?"

"We can. And for the record, I'm not sure these cases are related, but until we are sure they *aren't*, I think all the information should go in the same pool," Rob said.

"You're hot when you're in investigator mode."

"And you're distracting when you're in compliment mode. Let's do this first. Hopefully I can bank my hotness."

Cam smirked. It was even hotter that Rob was able to focus when it was called for, but yes, he could bank it.

"So," Rob started. "There was definitely DNA in Nick and Petunia's van, and also the van that delivered the wine and champagne. The only other vehicles in the back that night, where they were out of view and off camera, belonged to the country club and had so much DNA it would be impossible to sort."

"But those vehicles are probably how it was done—either that or a car off in another area that wasn't actually seen."

"That last is what they fear. And I think they will go through the other vehicles. They were just starting with those two."

"But you know Nick and Petunia didn't do this."

"I know. I'm not going to get on the other side of that argument again." Rob had once been convinced Nick was guilty of murder, and it had created a lot of problems for Rob and Cam.

"Good," Cam said.

"I'm hoping it just eliminates them once and for all."

"Well it should, since they didn't kidnap anyone."

"And then I know Jake has a list of all the investors who lost at least a hundred thousand dollars in the last year because of Windermere's shenanigans."

"Oh, that sounds promising!"

"Yes and no. I haven't had a chance to look at it. He's holding it close. But it's long—a lot of names."

"So a lot of murder suspects."

Cam wasn't sure how she felt about that. Unlike the past murders she'd learned about, no one she cared for this time was accused of the crime. It was nice in a way, just helping Rob for the sake of it and for her own curiosity. But unlike before, just throwing up a lot of doubt about who did it didn't help. What they needed were specific clues that might also point to a murderer, or more urgently, a kidnapper.

"Have they been looking at the kidnapping?"

"Station is pretty tight-lipped there. Like Jake said, they don't want it out for Senator Schulz's safety. I think they are waiting for a ransom call. Most kidnappers that are actually kidnappers do it for money. They should call within forty-eight hours and demand that."

"But that's bad. They haven't called," Cam said.

"Not that we *know of,* no."

"Are you suggesting they called Elle and she didn't go to the police?"

"Maybe. It would explain her refusal to leave home if they ordered it. But the police will have thought of that.

They've got an eye on her," Rob said. "He's a public figure, after all."

Cam wondered just how many bugs Elle had on her right now. The thought made her itchy.

CHAPTER 7

"Cam!" The urgent whispered yell woke Cam. She had to remove Rob's arm to slide out of bed, but she didn't hesitate. If Annie could be this frantic at this hour, when she was undoubtedly hungover, Cam could respond appropriately. She put on a robe and shut her door.

"What is it?"

"I need you to scan this. Fast!" Annie held a paper-clipped printout. It looked like a spreadsheet file.

"Why couldn't you . . ."

"I couldn't risk waking Jake. I can't have this!"

"Got it."

Cam turned on her laptop and plugged in the cable to her scanner, then scanned the pages. It took about three minutes, and Annie left without saying anything, hustling back up to her own apartment to return the contraband.

Cam, wide awake after the strange encounter, opened the first page of the document. Names and numbers. In dollars. All in the negative.

"Holy crap! Annie, you're a genius!"

"Why's she a genius?" Rob yawned, coming out of her room and wiping his face with a washcloth.

He leaned over her shoulder to see the list of people for whom Windermere had lost a lot of money.

"That little minx!" His smile was huge.

"I know, right? Bonus points for Annie!"

"We could stay busy with that all day!"

"I wish," Cam complained. She had a phone interview with the Richmond paper to discuss the press release she'd sent the day before. They had a political reporter very curious about the senate race, and she wanted a lot more details about the mood and content of the evening. Cam had some research to do, as she hadn't formerly understood much about the local political players and their histories with each other before their event planning had started a few weeks earlier, and she felt even more confused now.

"I'll make notes," Rob grinned. "Can you make a copy of that for me?"

"I can. But keep in mind this is an anonymous source. We don't want to get Annie in trouble."

"I know," he said. "But sheesh! Look at that list! It's a wonder this guy wasn't offed years ago."

It was true. That much money lost for that many people could not make him a popular man. Especially as he'd managed to amass a small fortune for himself in the process.

Work was painful, even from her kitchen table. There was nothing worse than trying to concentrate on something you really didn't care about when there was something else so pressing. As a distraction, she spent an hour in her garden splitting bulbs to try to relax her brain. It needed to be done in the fall for all the early spring flowers: tulips, daffodils, hyacinths. And it didn't take much thought. After that, she managed to come up with a list of people most likely to be Jared Koontz's political rivals—the kind of folks who would love to see some really bad publicity come to the campaign. So far, Rob's matter-of-fact article was the only one that had been published, so she doubted this potentially bad publicity was a murder motive. Then again, maybe someone was playing a longer game.

Her head had begun to throb at all the manipulations the politicians and their supporters employed. She wished cooperation were more common and that people could be polite even when disagreeing, like they had been when Holden Hobbes was senator. That thought inspired her. Holden could give her the lesson she needed in local politics. He hadn't been a player for years, but he was still very involved and knew everybody. She called him to make an appointment.

"Well you know, Cam, I don't typically engage in gossip," Holden said when Cam called.

"I don't want you to gossip, exactly. I'm just trying to understand the players so I can set the events from the other night in context. A reporter wants to talk to me and I don't want to be uninformed."

"All right, then. I'd be happy to meet you for coffee." She could hear his smile. She enjoyed the man. It was exactly why current politics were so disappointing. Politicians used to be the most polished of gentlemen. Now they were reality TV stars.

She drove her car downtown and parked halfway between City Bliss Café, where she was meeting Holden Hobbes, and the Patrick Henry hotel, where she would check in with work afterward.

Holden kissed her cheek when she entered and gestured toward one of the comfortable sofas. He already had two cups of coffee there waiting for them.

"Before you start in with your questions, Cam, is it true? Has Alden Schulz disappeared?"

"He has. Annie's worried sick but, supposedly for the senator's safety, we aren't supposed to spread the news."

"And you don't think he just went to the Dominican Republic or something to file for a quickie divorce?"

"What do you know about his marriage?"

"Just talk from petty women, so I have no idea if there is any truth behind it. But I thought I might throw out the idea, in case it was possible."

"He wouldn't have worried Annie like this. He would have called her."

"I suppose you're right, there. We try to give our children the best of us." He smiled and took a sip of his coffee, spooning in a little more sugar afterward.

"Can I ask you who these petty women were—in case they might have more actual information?"

"Ramona Pemberly and Madge Gant. Seemed to me Ramona was talking more and Madge was just gasping a lot."

Cam sighed. She didn't want to have to talk to Mrs. Pemberly. The woman was a menace. But despite being a menace, Cam thought she was also as up on her gossip as anybody in town—real gossip, not the sissy kind that needed a basis in fact.

She then asked Holden for his understanding of the current political players and their relationships. They spent a lovely lunch reviewing how he saw things. She was sure he was far too generous, though there were a couple of cases where he couldn't seem to keep his true opinions to himself. He was not a fan of Jared Koontz, whom he referred to as a "silver-spooned social climber," and he felt Chad Phillips, another "fast-rising star," was a liar and a cheat—his old party was turning out to be a sore disappointment to him for the current election cycle. She asked if he'd seen anything at the party, but as the MC, he'd had his own show to put on. He'd stayed on the patio and reviewed his notes when he wasn't speaking.

She then walked to the Patrick Henry, typed up her notes, and made her call. It felt like an awful lot of energy had gone into this one thing. That was sometimes how it was, but she didn't have to like it. She wrote a follow-up to her press release of the day before and sent it on to the papers she always communicated with, thinking at least she could enrich what they had, too, since she'd gone to all the effort.

Finally, at four, Annie stumbled into her office.

"So what did you find?" she asked, referring to the people who'd lost money.

"Got the lay of the political landscape, but that was all. I had a swamped day. Rob was working on your list, though. Should we meet him?"

"Definitely."

Cam called Rob and they decided on margaritas at five.

Annie gave a thumbs-up. "Then I just have time to shower. I'm stinky."

"You always smell like vanilla to me," Cam said.

"That was an explosion. It was bad. I dropped one of those bottles of the Mexican stuff onto my marble cooling sheet, glass and vanilla everywhere. And then I had to throw out the batch on top of it, but I'm sick about losing that vanilla. That stuff is expensive."

"I should go get cleaned up, too. I had a working lunch today, so I've earned leaving a little early."

The two headed out together.

El Palenque was nearly deserted at five o'clock. Cam knew it would fill up, and that if it had been a Friday, it would have been full by now, but it was a Tuesday, and so the waitress nearly tripped over herself to come serve them.

"I love this place," Annie said when the pitcher of margaritas arrived two minutes later, a good ten minutes ahead of Rob.

Cam filled their glasses and let Annie sip. She took a small one, then nibbled on chips and salsa before taking another. She knew they needed to pace themselves.

Rob walked in slower and more miserably than Cam expected. His frown caught Annie's attention and she asked who died.

He raised an eyebrow, because of course somebody had. It just wasn't somebody they cared all that much about. Cam decided to redirect.

"So what did you learn about the list?"

"You aren't going to like it," he said.

"I might," Annie said.

"No. I doubt that, too."

"Okay, can you stop being so cryptic? Is it the whole Roanoke Garden Society or something?" Cam asked.

"Not all of it."

"Drat!" Cam sat back and took a larger sip of margarita, then regretted it as brain freeze set in. "Ouch, ouch, ouch!" She held her forehead and tried to massage the roof of her mouth with her tongue, but it took a minute.

Rob set a printed copy of the list on the table, and Cam could see a couple of highlighted names. Neil Patrick was one. Alden Schulz was another.

"Damn!" Annie said.

"He could hardly murder someone if he was kidnapped!" Cam said.

"No, and I know he wouldn't anyway. But this *looks like* he might have murdered somebody and disappeared. It makes him look guilty."

"Do you know how bad this hurt your dad?" Rob asked.

"Says a hundred and fifty thousand."

"No, I mean . . . was that half his worth? Ten percent? One percent?"

"I don't know. If I were guessing, I'd say ten percent is closest. But we never talked money."

"So this hurt, but didn't ruin him?" Cam followed what Rob was getting at.

"I doubt it."

"Okay. I think what we want to figure out is who this really devastated. We're looking for somebody he pretty much wiped out," Cam said.

"Let's hope the police are that logical. The record isn't in their favor, though," Rob said.

"That's why you're on this," Cam said to Rob, then turned to Annie. "Would Elle think this was devastating?"

Annie raised her eyebrows. "So you think she might have done both crimes?"

"Worth going back to my place to listen after this pitcher. Rob can stop and buy the stuff to make these at home."

"Why do I have to stop at the store?" Rob asked.

"We'll wait here for takeout, but will need something to drink when we get home." Cam gave Rob a pleading look, hoping he'd read that she wanted to give Annie a chance to grieve or vent with just her best friend.

Rob shrugged and agreed, though he stayed seated for a few more questions.

"What about Mr. Patrick?" he asked.

"I think he's better off than Annie's dad. I mean, he lost more, but I still think this is only a small amount to him."

"Worth a trip to see your buddy Evangeline?"

"Yeah—she'll be at the Patrick Henry tomorrow, so I don't need to make a special trip."

"What does she *do* there?" Rob asked.

"For your information, a lot. She's smart. But largely, she focuses on their nonprofit stuff. The Patricks like to give back."

Rob looked skeptical, and Cam thought Annie would

have, too, except she was engaged in a text conversation with Jake.

"Phooey! I couldn't think of a reason to make him wait. So he's meeting us at your place, too."

"And no listening to illicit bugs when the cop is around?" Rob said.

Annie touched the tip of his nose with her index finger, which caused Rob to shake his head.

"So after we eat, you distract him, and Rob and I will listen," Cam said.

Annie wasn't paying attention, though. She had pushed a few buttons on her phone, so Cam and Rob waited to see what it was about as Annie put the telephone to her ear.

"Elle? This is Annie," she said into the phone. "I just wondered . . . they haven't called for a ransom or anything, have they?"

Cam could hear a screechy sound in the background, but not words.

"Will you please tell me if they do?"

She hung up.

"Sorry about that," Rob said.

Cam kicked him under the table. She had hoped not to get into the forty-eight hours thing with Annie, but Annie seemed to know instinctively.

"I just had to check. If it's not ransom, it's . . . bad, right?"

Cam reached over and took Annie's hand. "If they called, they might have told Elle not to tell anyone." She didn't want to agree with Annie, but disagreeing too strongly required lying, and she and Annie didn't do that.

Jake beat Cam and Annie to their place. He was waiting in Annie's apartment, as that was the one he had the key to, but he heard them trampling in and came down to join them.

"So what have you been up to?" he asked.

"I had a crazy day. Go ahead. Ask me about any Roanoke politician. I can tell you," Cam said.

"Not murder investigating?" he said cautiously.

Cam shook her head. "Boring old damage control. Holden Hobbes helped me prep for a press interview."

"Really? That might be useful," he said.

Cam was surprised at the response. She and Jake mostly liked each other, but when these investigations came into play, they didn't always see eye to eye. Jake preferred that Cam stay out of it, and it just wasn't in her to do it that way when people she knew were involved. She was glad that wasn't the case at the moment.

"So quiz me!" Cam said as she pulled plates out of the cupboard.

Rob arrived at about the third question and smirked as he made margaritas and listened. Jake had been *his* friend first, so it frustrated him even more than Annie when Cam and Jake didn't get along. Cam thought this was a nice change of pace.

After his fifth question, Cam hit her hand on the table, "Quid pro quo, Officer Moreno, has the investigative team looked into Mr. Windermere's harem?"

Rob laughed, but then turned to Jake with interest.

"As a matter of fact, they have. We heard about the discord, or unhappy vibe. But apparently, Windermere always brought a harem—not a literal harem, you understand. He was in the habit of making sure beautiful women were present at fund-raisers because the male donors tended to dig deeper into their pockets to impress. It was a fund-raising strategy of his. The discord was due to an internal bet between the women. They were competing over who could encourage the largest donation."

"Oh, man! I hate it when a sleazebag has a really good idea," Cam said.

"A good idea that probably didn't get him killed," Jake said.

When the conversation about the murder slowed down, Annie asked softly, "Any news about the kidnapping?"

Jake looked sad and hugged her. "No, but maybe I should ask some political questions there, too. Cam, did you learn anything about Alden's relationships?"

"Yeah, but other than a few cases of annoyance where he was backing one candidate versus another, nothing bad. He isn't running, so people treat him more like a father figure or adviser. They treat him respectfully."

"Some of those that want his support, though . . ." Annie said.

"Yeah, there are several. Some who think they deserve it, others who are delusional," Cam said, "At least according to Holden."

"But is that the kind of thing a person would be this extreme over? Kill the funder who won't back you and kidnap the politician who won't endorse you?" Annie asked.

"It's possible," Jake said. "Cam, can you make a list?"

"I can. In fact I did, for work notes. I'll print it for you." She opened her laptop.

When they were done, Annie pleaded exhaustion, and she and Jake headed out.

"Be careful not to be too nice or he's going to get suspicious," Rob whispered when Jake was already halfway up the stairs.

Cam laughed as they left, then led Rob back to her laptop so they could get set up to listen to what had been transmitted from the bugs in the Schulz house.

"Are you ready for a little excitement?" she asked.

"Excitement is my middle name," he said.

"Robert Excitement Columbus. Works for me!"

They sat and Cam tried to remember what Annie had showed her. The bugs had been nicked from Jake. Annie sort of figured minor theft with the goal of catching bad guys was almost her civic duty. But they were complicated gadgets, so Cam had to try a few things, remembering that Annie had said tutorials could be found online. With the help of YouTube, she found the file where the recordings had been stored.

There was an audio image they could see on the screen, and places on the bar that were brighter indicated voice activity, so those were the places they clicked to listen.

From one bug, presumably the phone in the study, they got only messages related to Senator Schulz. Elle didn't tell anyone he was missing, only that he would call back when he could. One person even asked if he'd really been taken, and she said she had no comment.

"Are the phone lines different in different parts of the house?" Rob asked.

"They must be."

"Did Annie get her bedroom phone?"

"Might have. Come to think of it, what we really need is her cell phone."

"I'm sure the police have that covered," Rob said. "They definitely would have known how the kidnappers would try to reach her."

Annie burst in then.

"Erm. Hello," Cam said.

"It's Louise! She just called me. She said she had a chance to look today. Dad's medication is all gone."

Cam and Rob looked at each other, then looked back at Annie.

"That's great, right? It means whoever has him doesn't mean to harm him," Cam said.

"I guess. But it also means whoever has him knows him. That creeps me out."

"Yeah, I can see that side. But maybe this is just . . . some battle of wills or something. Annie, it's good that they want to keep him healthy."

"I guess. I just had to share that."

"I'm glad you did," Cam said.

As soon as Annie had left again, Cam and Rob went back to browsing the bars on her computer screen for more voice moments.

They were almost done with the bedroom phone before they heard anything else interesting, and even then, it was more confusing than important. It was, however, something to add to the mystery list.

"Look, you gotta stop drivin' by here. People will get suspicious. Besides, there's not a falutin' thing I can do right now about that stupid money you owe, so you'll just have to keep your shorts on."

Cam noted Elle had the same Jersey accent Nick had, or maybe it was the Bronx. Either way, it was nothing compared with the man swearing at her. Unfortunately, swearing was about all he did besides some unclear ranting and telling her they needed to hurry and go. His words were hard to understand without the proper context. He didn't seem to like that a meeting couldn't be set up for whatever tryst he had in mind.

"You kiss your mother with that mouth? Look, Sully. Nothing I can do. With Alden missing, I'm being watched."

She hung up on him then, cutting off still more swearing.

Cam looked at Rob. "What do you make of that?"

"She sure pissed somebody off, someone who isn't her husband. And he wants both money and a meeting."

"What about 'Sully'?"

"Usually short for Sullivan, but we don't know if it's a first name, last name, or nickname."

"We should ask Annie to see if the name means anything to her," Cam said as she was writing it down.

The money issue nagged at her, but it nagged at her in a way she didn't want to address. It had sounded to her like he had money trouble that might be related to gambling debt—an issue that tied back to a man she was trying not to think about, so she squashed the thought. They listened to a couple more calls, but the most condemning of them was that Elle seemed to be trying to rush a plastic surgery appointment of some sort.

"Like those boobs could fall," Cam said.

"She's worried about him leaving. Wants to at least touch up if she's going to be single again."

"Repulsive, if you ask me," Cam said.

"I didn't need to ask you. We share the same opinion. Real is better than fake any day," Rob said.

He ran his hand up her side as he said it, hoping to cop a feel, but Cam was too ticklish. She squirmed out of the way.

"One more set of recordings. You ready?" She asked.

"As I'll ever be," he sighed.

The worst thing they heard, in fact the only thing other than a brief conversation between Elle and Louise and a talk show on the television, was what sounded like half a cell phone conversation.

"You can't call me here!"

"I understand, but you'll just have to wait!"

"I know. Two, maybe three days, but believe me. Just wait for *me* to call *you*."

Elle snarled when she hung up. It might have been the same person she'd talked to earlier, but since they couldn't hear the other person, they couldn't be sure. Cam thought Elle at least had something fishy going on. It was too bad this wasn't more of a lead than an indication to watch her. Something was going to happen, as soon as Elle thought the eyes weren't looking in her direction.

"While this all *might* be kidnapping or murder, I'm not completely convinced," Rob said.

Cam begrudgingly agreed, though she thought the case for an affair had a lot of merit.

CHAPTER 8

Cam slept poorly. She had way too much in her head. Tasks she couldn't forget kept popping into her mind, even though she'd made a perfectly good list to keep track of them.

Finally, about twenty minutes before her alarm made it mandatory, she climbed out of bed and turned on her coffeepot. She realized as she did so that the magical forty-eight hours had passed for Annie's dad, but she tried to convince herself the missing medication was a good sign. Annie would be devastated if that wasn't true, and Cam didn't want to watch her friend go through that.

Cam was on autopilot as she went through her morning routine. She poured coffee, took a shower, put in her contacts, then put on some makeup. But when she was done, she couldn't remember having done any of it. In fact, when she pulled her car into a parking spot near the Patrick Henry, she didn't even remember going out to her car. She was just suddenly there.

At least this was her chance to talk to Evangeline, who usually arrived early, often before her husband. Cam thought she was too social to get very much done when other people were present, so this was a strategy to have some time when being social wasn't an option. Cam felt a little guilty about stealing that time, until she got to Evangeline's office and found she wasn't there, but a light was on a few doors down.

"Mr. Patrick?" Cam called.

"Oh! Cammi. You startled me," he said when she reached his office.

She wondered if his hearing was going, as she hadn't made any effort to be quiet when she got there.

"Is Evangeline coming in this morning?"

"I'm afraid not. She seems to be a little under the weather."

"Oh, no. Nothing too serious, I hope."

"No, I don't think so. She can't even really put her finger on the symptoms. She just doesn't feel herself."

"Do you think she's well enough for a visitor?"

"She planned to sleep in, but if you waited until ten thirty or so, I'm sure she'd be delighted. She may even have slept off this . . . well . . . whatever it is."

He smiled and turned back to his paperwork, so Cam left him to it. She had a few tasks she could complete to kill the next hour and a half until she could go out to visit Evangeline, so she got to work, too.

The day was rainy and miserable, and Cam drove carefully because the wind seemed to be blowing things about and she didn't want them to scratch the finish on her car. She made it out to La Fontaine, the Patricks' house, without incident, and hid her head under a jacket as she ran for the front door. Thankfully, the porch was covered.

"Mademoiselle Harris!" Giselle, the housekeeper, greeted Cam with her faux French accent. "'ow lovely to see you."

"Sorry to just drop in, dripping even. I was hoping Evangeline felt well enough for a visitor?"

"Oh, well I hope so, as she already has one. But he should be gone in the next fifteen or twenty minutes. Should I let her know you're waiting?"

"No, don't disturb her. I'm not expected and don't want to interrupt other business. It's just . . . Mr. Patrick said she didn't feel well."

"Yes, I suspect she led him to believe that. She is planning a surprise, I think. Of course I'm just guessing, based on the guest, but sometimes husbands and wives need to be a little bit sneaky to do things for each other." She smiled.

"I can just use my laptop in the study, if that's okay," Cam said.

"Of course it is. You know your way around."

It was true. Cam had spent a lot of time there, not all of it pleasant. There'd been two murders at the home the previous year as part of a big event the Roanoke Garden Society was hosting. Still, the house had also been home base for the RGS for a while, so she was very comfortable there. And she had an ulterior motive she could act on, so long as she was going to be left alone in the study for a while.

She went in the study and set up her laptop, then scanned the room for a spot where investment records might be hiding. She tried to tune her ears so she'd hear if anyone was coming, then carefully began opening file drawers.

Somebody very meticulous—Evangeline, if Cam was to judge by the handwriting, had set up the system. It was very clear where files pertaining to home repair, purchases, charity, insurance, and pet care were. The absence of investments, given the organization, told Cam she was just in the wrong drawer, so she went to the next one.

This drawer was full of various folders, and all of them indeed seemed investment related.

"Bingo," she whispered, and began thumbing through.

There were prospectuses and quarterly reports, but the most important information she gleaned was that all of it seemed to be coordinated through a company called Entwhistle Investment, a large local firm Cam thought was run by the same Entwhistle who had been at the fund-raiser. She didn't have time to look through everything, but she couldn't see any part of the portfolio the company hadn't handled.

She slid the drawer shut and went out to fetch a cup of tea to drink while she worked. In the entryway before Cam ever reached the kitchen, Evangeline was saying good-bye to a man in a very expensive suit. He looked familiar. Cam squinted at him and knew he'd been at the fund-raiser, but it took a minute to realize who he was. Melvin, the man Senator Schulz didn't care for.

"Cam! How long have you been here?" Evangeline said when she turned around and spotted her.

"Just about ten minutes. I hoped to talk to you, but I didn't want to interrupt."

"Oh. Well, I appreciate that." Evangeline wasn't exactly terse, but it also wasn't the friendly tone she usually used. It must have been a big surprise she was planning.

"Was he at the fund-raiser the other night?" she asked as Evangeline shut the door.

"He was. That's Melvin Entwhistle."

"Oh! Now that I hear the name, I remember him being on the guest list."

It seemed auspicious that his name was also on the files Cam had just been looking at. The rule of three meant he had to be important in some way. So Evangeline had a project going that required her investment banker, and her husband didn't know about it. She wondered if Evangeline was liquidating something so she had cash for a gift, or if she was making a surprise investment. She suspected the former, but realized it was none of her business, so she didn't let on that she knew what the man's field was.

"So would you like tea while we talk?" Evangeline asked.

"That would be perfect."

Evangeline took the time to let Giselle know what they wanted and then led Cam to the library.

"Are you investigating murders again, Cam?" Evangeline teased.

Cam felt a little guilty that that seemed to be the only time she came to visit with Evangeline, though of course that wasn't true—they had work they did together often. But this scenario still felt strangely familiar.

"I'm more interested in the kidnapping, honestly. But it's possible the two are related." Cam had told her employers earlier about the kidnapping and the importance for discretion.

"I wondered. It seemed like too much for two big things to happen at the same time unless they were related."

"The police think maybe one of them was the target and the other an unfortunate witness."

Evangeline nodded.

"And if Derrick Windermere was the target, there is a long list of investors who lost their shirts with him. Did you know Mr. Patrick was on that list?"

"I did. Melvin was beside himself when he came to explain what had happened with that investment."

"Was he? Does Mr. Entwhistle handle other clients who lost a lot in that deal?"

"I imagine so. He was quite persuasive when he asked us to invest—said it was a great opportunity. I doubt we'd be the only people he'd do that with."

"Interesting."

"Of course, Melvin's very good at what he does. He always tells us to keep our portfolio diverse, so it wasn't as bad as it might have been. And I think the loss was nothing compared to some of Derrick's shadier deals. I mean, this was just an effort to get a green energy company off the ground. He has development projects that are much longer shots than that."

"But you haven't been invested in any of those?"

"No. With Neil's age, Melvin strongly recommends we don't take huge risks. He has younger clients who might, but we tend to want financial security."

"So do you think somebody who lost a lot on a Windermere project might have killed him?"

"Money is a powerful motivator," she said.

Cam was thinking reputation might be even more powerful. Windermere had bilked a lot of rich people out of a lot of money, but he'd used Melvin Entwhistle, a trusted local investment banker who had formerly had an impeccable reputation, to do it. Griggs had seen an argument between Windermere and Entwhistle that night. But for Cam's own interests, Entwhistle didn't seem like the kind of man who would kidnap a former senator.

Still, she liked it as a lead and decided to pass it on.

"How well do you understand our local politics?"

"Oh, there I'm only a pretender." She lowered her voice to a whisper. "Actually, I'm a Democrat. So I just keep my mouth shut."

Cam laughed. She happened to be an independent, but could see why a Democrat would keep her opinion to herself in the social circles Evangeline circulated in.

"Just from observation, can you see any reason, political or otherwise, for getting Alden Schulz out of the way for a while?"

"The only political angle I can think of is removing support from Jared, and his primary rival is probably going to be Chad Phillips—I could see a motive there."

"Was he at the fund-raiser?"

"Heavens, no. He couldn't be seen promoting Jared when he plans to run. There were some Chad supporters there—Melvin, even, but I suspect they want to play nice on both sides so they aren't stuck with no influence after the election."

That was one of the reasons Cam hated politics.

"What about Vivian Macy?" she asked.

"See, she can afford to be there. She knows there's no overlap in support at all between Jared and herself. I think she was there to needle him."

"You may be right, there. I've heard Chad Phillips's name, but hadn't realized he was interested in the same seat." That wasn't strictly true, but Cam liked to let people she talked to feel like they were the experts.

"And he would have loved Alden's support, but I think Jared did an internship for Alden or something—there's a personal connection."

"So Senator Schulz never would have supported Chad anyway?"

"Probably not, at least not against Jared—unless of course, the man made some huge, scandalous mistake. But Chad may not know that. Alden supported him for county commissioner, after all. And Chad strikes me as the kind of man who doesn't always do all his homework. Relies on charm, so he may not know Alden's commitment to Jared."

That gave Cam a lot of food for thought, so she thanked Evangeline and decided while she was out this direction, she would brave checking in with Samantha, too. She could use a debriefing of the event as her excuse, since the fundraiser had been Samantha's baby.

Cam hadn't been to Samantha's house since the day she'd rescued her from the most bizarre situation she'd ever encountered. She felt sure she was having a PTSD episode when she knocked on the door, in spite of the gorgeous display of helenium lining the walk—their orange and yellow heads dancing in the breeze. Normally, without her impending visit playing on her nerves, Cam would have found them quite cheerful, since the sun was peeking through the clouds and the rain was finally evaporating. Thankfully, Samantha looked pleased to see her.

"Well, come in! Come in! You got that car you were saving for!"

"I did. The pageant this summer gave me the rest of my down payment so I could finally buy it."

"It's lovely—looks fast!"

Cam laughed. "Want a ride?"

"Oh, maybe sometime, but today is too miserable. You come in and have some lunch. Francine?"

The housekeeper poked her head out of the kitchen.

"Cam is joining me for lunch. Could you set an extra place?"

"Yes, ma'am," Francine said.

Cam noticed nobody had waited for her answer, but it was okay. She had to eat. What she wasn't looking forward to was the subject of murder. She'd accused Samantha of murder not long ago, so she thought admitting she was looking into another one was going to bring up a lot of old baggage for the two of them.

Samantha was the most connected person she knew, though, so if anyone could help her sort out the players, especially the financial ones, it was Samantha.

"This is the most awkward conversation," Cam said. "But I think I should just dive in. I'm not sure how I'll manage it otherwise."

"Well, okay."

"I'm trying really hard to help Annie find her dad, and I need some help figuring out the politics and finances of the people involved."

"Now why would that be the most awkward conversation you've ever had?" Samantha asked, pouring sweet tea.

Cam couldn't believe Samantha wasn't leaping to conclusions about Cam as an investigator, but since she wasn't,

Cam wasn't going to point it out. She felt like she'd just dodged a bullet.

"Who do you see who might want Alden Schulz out of the way?" Cam asked.

"Oh. Well, you know he has no shortage of enemies."

Cam remembered this from an earlier investigation. Alden had been the hinge vote for a very important land bill that had angered much of the Roanoke Garden Society.

"But you and he were both supporting Jared Koontz, so surely some of the water has finally passed under the bridge?"

"Cam, I'm a practical woman. Alden still has a lot of popularity with the public, and I knew his endorsement would help Jared, whom I like quite well. I was willing to put old disagreements aside, and I think at least some of the people who felt angry before will have done the same."

"So you think people who like and support Jared are unlikely to be involved in the senator's disappearance, because he endorsed Jared."

"That's exactly what I think."

"And you think there were people there Sunday who don't support Jared?"

"Oh, of course there were—spies trying to get a feel for his campaign and support system. Take that Vivian Macy, for instance. That woman was strictly scanning the competition."

"She isn't running against him," Cam said.

"Oh, not yet."

"No. My dad said she's interested in the House of Delegates first."

"Did he now?"

Cam wondered if she would regret her candor. It wasn't like Vi had made a public announcement. But maybe it would get Samantha to stop focusing on someone who Cam felt sure wasn't responsible.

"You know . . . if I had the guest list, I bet I could high-light about a quarter of the people who weren't real supporters."

"Would you? I have it on my laptop. Would you mind?"

"Not at all."

Cam opened her laptop to the document and began reading through names, highlighting them brightly when Samantha indicated she was sure they didn't really support Jared, and more often highlighting entries dimly when she said it was possible.

When they reached Griggs's name, Cam was reminded of something. "You know, it was so generous of Mr. Windermere to pay for that media table."

"Well, he didn't do it directly—Chrysanthemum Holdings needed the deduction, I'm sure. And I have a bone to pick with them."

"Chrysanthemum Holdings?"

"It's an investment firm, real estate mostly, but they put a hold on their check that paid for that media table, if you can believe that!"

"Oh! Maybe it has to do with Mr. Windermere's death."

"It may, but they committed and used those spots, so J will get that money!"

Her ferocity startled Cam. She preferred to get back to what they'd been doing, as it seemed more productive. She pointed at the entry Samantha had stopped on. "Mike Sullivan?" Cam stared at the name.

"Oh, no, honey. That's Derrick's son-in-law. I don't know his relationship to Jared, but his presence was about his family connection."

It was probably nothing. Sullivan wasn't such an unusual name. And the context she'd heard it in before didn't seem to fit the son-in-law of somebody who was as wealthy and well connected as Derrick. The Sully she had heard about was tangled up with the senator's wife . . . though if this

Mike Sullivan was in fact helping Elle with a kidnapping because he knew he'd be at the event, that was another matter altogether.

"Do you know what he does? I just think I've heard the name before."

"That would have to be another Mike Sullivan. This one is really a nobody. I know how hard it's been for Derrick to have his daughter married to someone with such poor prospects."

So poor he might run cons? Cam wondered. *Like kidnapping.*

Whom did she know who might be acquainted with the who's who of Roanoke lowlifes?

The answer came to her unwillingly. She knew a couple of people, but she preferred not to entangle them in yet another project. And it was probably smart for her to just stay away from at least one of them. Dylan Markham was a tall handsome thug whom Cam seemed to be too drawn to for a girl with a longtime boyfriend. But he certainly knew a lot of unsavory people.

Cam was relieved at how well the visit had gone. What's more, she remembered there was a time when she had enjoyed Samantha's company. Cam drove back to her office to get the rest of her day's tasks done. She'd generated a lot more questions than she'd answered, but at least they were questions that felt a lot more important than the ones she'd been stuck with before. She called Annie.

"Want to come over for dinner and I can share what I've gotten today?"

"No. I'm a better cook, so you can come to my place. Besides. I just put it in the oven."

"You did?"

"Seafood enchiladas. New recipe."

When Annie was stressed, she cooked, so Cam shouldn't have been surprised.

"Can I bring anything?"

"Line of Chippendales dancers?"

"That bad, huh? I'll see what I can do."

CHAPTER 9

Annie's apartment was a disaster. She'd clearly been cooking since she got home from work. Not just enchiladas, but homemade salsa, guacamole, and if Cam wasn't mistaken, flan.

"Is it bad to love it when you're stressed out?" Cam asked.

"Yes. Yes it is," Annie said, then she stuck her finger in Cam's mouth. It was coated in guacamole. "That okay?"

"Could maybe use a little more heat," Cam said.

"Little more heat? From you? That bland, eh?"

"No. It's good. Maybe you're just making progress with my taste buds." Annie had always teased her about preferring bland food.

"We can only hope."

Cam rolled her eyes, set the bottle of wine she'd brought on the counter, and got out the corkscrew. "Are the boys coming?"

"No. Mine's not anyway. Haven't talked to yours."

Cam's phone buzzed and she wondered if Rob's ears had been burning, but it was Petunia.

"Cam! They found . . . it's a . . . something matching!"

"Whoa, slow down, Petunia. Who found what?"

"The police! A DNA match. But it's not a match. It's . . . something related to the senator in our van!"

"I don't get it. He was never . . . wait a minute. Oh, geez. Why didn't we think of this? Petunia, calm down. It's Annie. They found DNA from Annie in your van. We can go down and prove it and you'll be in the clear."

"Really?"

"Really. I promise we'll take care of it tonight."

"Thank goodness! Why do all these people you work with always cause us trouble?"

"I'm sorry, Tunia. Really I am. I'm sure that's what it's about, though."

She hung up.

"Let me guess," Annie said. "Partial DNA match for my dad in the Spoons van?"

"That's what it sounds like. Petunia's not the world's most articulate person when she panics."

"This can rest for half an hour after I pull it out. We'll go then."

Cam nodded and called Jake to give him a heads-up as to what they were doing and why.

"Those idiots. I told them they would probably get something like that," he said. "Len Sullivan can be the densest detective on the planet sometimes."

"Sullivan?"

"You know him?"

"No. I haven't known a Sullivan since college, but suddenly they're popping up everywhere."

"Yeah, they're like a bad penny—keep turning up to annoy you," Jake said. "He's the kidnapping pro, though, so we need him."

They hung up and Cam looked at Annie.

"Are we having a Sullivan infestation?" she asked.

Annie hear an idea she really preferred debunked. "You know . . . Derrick was sponsoring Toni Howe's television program."

"Toni from the pageant?"

"Yeah. She didn't seem very happy about it."

"Can't say I blame her."

"You don't think she'd . . ."

"Off him without securing another sponsor? Heck, no."

Cam breathed easier. It was what she'd hoped to hear. "For my next two ideas, I need your help," she said.

"Okay?"

"First, we thought maybe that message from Elle sounded like the guy was a little desperate to see her—not just like . . . for love, but desperate maybe for money, too. Like maybe there's a gambling issue?" She still wasn't comfortable sharing it, but putting the thoughts into words for Annie was safer than it would have been with Rob.

"Okay."

"And we happen to know a couple of people in town who are involved in that gambling circuit." Cam couldn't believe she hadn't talked herself out of pursuing this route.

"You're afraid to talk to Dylan by yourself."

"A little."

"Probably wise. You can't be trusted."

Cam rolled her eyes, but it was only habit. She was a little worried that where Dylan was concerned, it might be true.

Cam opened her phone and felt guilty to still have him on speed dial from when she'd worked with him during the summer. It was good she had the number now, of course, but nothing about Dylan and her having contact was actually good. Except maybe the steamy kiss he'd given her when he'd been pumped up on pain pills, but she tried to think about that as little as possible.

"Miss Harris? I'm surprised to hear from you," he answered the phone.

"I'm surprised to be calling," she said. "But I'm involved in another investigation, and it turns out I could use your knowledge of the local gambling community."

"And here I thought you missed me."

She didn't respond to that. Couldn't respond. Everything about him made her blush, and Annie was watching her carefully.

"Do you know anything about someone called Sully?"

"I might. What's in it for me?"

"Look, Annie's dad has been kidnapped, and this Sully character might be involved."

"Annie's? You coulda just said so. I like Annie. Yeah, listen. I don't want to get into it here. I could stop by later and tell you, though."

That was the last thing Cam wanted, but she could hear enough noise in the background to tell he was someplace he probably didn't feel comfortable talking, so she agreed and then begged Annie not to leave her side until it was done.

"You're a big chicken," Annie said.

"I am not. I have no intention of . . . anything . . . I'm just attracted . . . I don't want to be alone with him!"

Annie sighed. "Poor Cam."

Dylan knocked just after ten. Cam was wondering where Rob was, as he usually called or dropped in. Annie had been grumbling about bakers having early hours and had just threatened to leave, so Cam was feeling lucky that Annie was still there and Rob wasn't.

"Come in. Thank you."

His look burned her face. Something about him had always made her feel like a middle school girl.

"Can I get you something to drink?" she asked.

"Wouldn't say no to a beer."

"Wine okay?"

He shrugged, so Cam got him a glass from the second bottle she and Annie had opened, but barely dented.

"So you know a Sully, in the gambling circle?" Cam said as she handed Dylan his wine. Dylan sprawled across her futon and seemed impossibly long. Arms went one way and legs another to take over the room. Annie was on her only other chair, so Cam retrieved her own wine and stood.

"Yeah. Odd guy, really. Well, not odd. Big teddy bear. But sometimes he acts like he's rolling. Sometimes he's broke. But the fat part—when he has a lot of cash—doesn't seem to have anything to do with winning. I've never heard of him winning more than a few hands, but he loves to gamble. Always comes back."

"Might that be because his wife is loaded, but doesn't give him access all the time?" Cam asked.

"That would make sense, actually, but I don't know him that well."

"Do you know his whole name?"

"No, but Sullivan is the last name."

"Mike?"

"Maybe."

"But he's not a cop?"

"Geez, I hope not! Not that I ever have the kind of money to gamble with that crowd—it's the high-end group. But some of them also gamble with my group, so I tend bar for the big games. That would be bad to have a cop around."

"Jake said there was an Officer Sullivan investigating Annie's dad's disappearance. We just wanted to make sure there wasn't a conflict of interest."

"They could always be cousins or something," Dylan said.

Cam had thought the same thing, but was relieved to get some doubt that the Sully they were worried about might be a cop—a dirty cop in charge of this investigation would be hard to deal with. It seemed much more likely he was just a gambler and the son-in-law of the murder victim.

"Do you . . . have a physical description?" Cam asked.

"Sure. Sully is sorta thick—in the shoulders, I mean. Black hair, or almost. Gray eyes, I think—not dark, anyway. Wears suits, but sloppy—open shirt, no tie."

"Wait. C'mere," Annie said, crooking her finger at Dylan to follow.

She went over to Cam's laptop and pulled up a program, then gave Dylan a lot of choices that reminded Cam strangely of an eye exam. "Is this closer, or is this?"

In the end, they had a picture Dylan said wasn't quite right, but someone who saw both the photo and the man would think they looked similar.

Dylan stood and walked toward the door, Cam following him. On a table where she kept her mail in a basket was a newspaper.

"Hey, I know that guy, too."

It was the political section and the article was the announcement that Chad Phillips intended to run in the primaries against Jared Koontz. The picture was of Chad, a man Cam hadn't ever actually met.

"Do you? How?"

"Well, he's way out of my league. High-stakes card games and stuff. But he's got a sort of reputation. Golden fingers."

"Gold finger? Seriously?"

"Not like the James Bond thing—it's not a nickname. Just something they say about him."

"But he's a serious player in the gambling circles?"

"Yeah. I've bartended at some of those. Otherwise, I probably wouldn't know. Like I said. Way out of my league."

"That helps," Annie said, picking up the paper. "Thank you!"

"Hey, I did this for you," Dylan said to Annie. "I was going to trade a favor to Cam for it, but for you, free of charge."

Annie grinned. "Right."

Cam wanted to elbow her, but it would have been too obvious. It was best that Dylan just leave, which thankfully, he did.

"I've seen him," Annie said after Dylan left. She was pointing at the computer composite.

"Of course. He was at the fund-raiser. You said he was at your dad's wedding?"

"I think that's the Sully Elle was yelling at, but I can't remember any more. I'm exhausted. And I have to get up early, so I'll sleep on it. This helps, though."

CHAPTER 10

Cam's next day fell into the realm of almost normal. She went to work and did her thing, feeling like all she could do was pass the information she'd learned on to Jake. She didn't feel much closer to catching the kidnapper or finding Senator Schulz, and she felt guilty about that, but then the police seemed to be spinning their wheels, too.

Annie called at noon and requested a powwow with Jake and Rob after work. She said Jake had something big to talk about, and Annie hoped a solution was in sight.

They met at Martin's on First. It was a sports bar and there was commentary running about the BCS—the college football conference—and which teams were likely to win each conference. It would be easy enough to tune out for everyone but Rob. As a sports reporter, he just had a harder time ignoring the games and statistics displayed on screen. With that in mind, Cam made him sit with his back to the nearest screen and kept a loving hand on the back of his neck just to remind him where his focus belonged. Facing away from the TV, the gang could hold his attention, especially given Jake's intense expression. It was unusual for Jake to get there first, and it looked a lot like he had bad news.

"Uh-oh," Cam said as she sat Rob down and scooted up beside him. Annie was apparently running late, though they generally referred to that as Annie time.

"I think we've got a dirty-cop problem."

Cam wasn't sure what to say to that, but Rob, the reporter, was always ready to plow ahead.

"How dirty?"

"Covering evidence dirty. There was a lead that one of the guys told me about—something from the cell phone records. He was going to show me to see if it rang any bells or if it overlapped with the murder, but the sheet from the cell phone company is gone."

"You can just request that again, right? It's not like it erases the information," Rob said.

"It takes a few days, but the real problem is if we have trouble inside, I'm worried about this getting solved."

"Is that enough to say it's a dirty cop?" Rob asked. "Maybe it's because of the kidnapping protocol."

"Well, that could be, but we also got the tapes from the country club, and all but the main party in the garden is blank. The security guard said it looked like they were all erased, but they missed this one because of the back-up process."

"So can we see what happened to Annie's dad?" Cam said.

Rob shook his head, but Jake froze momentarily.

Annie must have just walked through the door, as Jake and Rob both looked like they'd seen a ghost.

"There's bad news about my dad, isn't there?"

"Sort of," Jake said. "I just suspect one of the cops on

the case might be hiding stuff, and I'm worried, as it's the guy running the kidnapping investigation."

"So what do we do about it?" Cam said.

"We? Nothing,"

"Come on, Jake," Rob said. "We've shown we're good at this. Wouldn't it be better to work *with* us for a change?"

Jake looked uncomfortable at the request, but finally nodded. "Okay, but at the first solid indication that there is a dirty cop tampering with evidence, I have to report what I've found, and I can't give any of you credit, or I get in trouble for endangering civilians."

"Have we succeeded in making a sneak out of you?" Annie said. She wore a brave face, but Cam knew it was a front. This was bad news and Annie was scared.

"So we're a team?" Cam asked.

Jake squinted. "I guess. I just wish I knew how this was supposed to go. He is the one coordinating with the FBI, and I've never done it."

"Maybe this will help. We will share what *we've* got," Cam said.

"You know I can't officially endorse you investigating, right?"

"It's Annie's dad!"

"Besides," Rob said. "We sort of dig this investigative stuff." He took a large drink from his beer and grinned.

Jake shook his head. "You two are incorrigible."

"Good thing they are," Annie said.

Jake put his arm around Annie and kissed her temple, then turned back to Cam and Rob.

"So what do you have?" Jake asked, looking at Cam.

"Annie heard from Louise who overheard an argument when Elle was on the phone. She yelled at a guy named Sully, and it sounded like it was maybe about money."

"Overheard?"

"She's the housekeeper." There was no way Cam was

confessing to literally bugging the house, especially as the equipment had been "borrowed" from Jake in the first place.

She didn't think Jake believed her, but it didn't matter. He had the information now.

"And Annie and I asked someone in the gambling circuit locally about a Sully. And Annie used a computer program to put this together." She set the composite picture on the table.

"I recognize that guy," Jake said. "I have to break up some high-stakes poker now and then, and he's there."

"His name is Mike Sullivan. And not only was Sully talking to Elle, he's the son-in-law of Derrick Windermere."

"Sullivan. Sully. Crap," Jake said.

"You got there, did you?" Cam asked.

"A motive for our dirty cop. The officer coordinating the kidnapping? He's a guy by the name of Len Sullivan. Dollars to doughnuts these two are brothers or something. Len looks a lot like that."

"That was sort of what we guessed when you said the name Sullivan to me earlier," Cam said. "It sounds like a motive to hide evidence."

"But Len's not a bad guy. Maybe he just wanted to take care of this himself—go directly to this other . . . Sully . . . and find out what he could. I don't know how we missed a son-in-law on our murder suspect list, though."

Annie's phone buzzed. She looked at the screen in confusion, but answered.

"Hello? Wait . . . Dad? Slow down!"

And then the call was cut off.

"Shoot!"

"Your dad called?"

"Yeah. He sounded . . . well . . . out of breath, and a little confused."

"Let's get that to the station and see if they can tell anything about the call," Jake said.

Annie nodded and the two of them rushed out.

"This will be weird, won't it?" Rob said.

"What will?"

"Working *with* Jake for a change."

Cam laughed. It definitely would. She wondered if she and Jake would get along better or worse. They were both control freaks, so she worried this cooperation might turn out to be anything but.

"Speaking of Jake," Rob said. "He told me a little from canvassing the party guests . . ."

Cam figured he'd go on, but he was lost in thought. "And?" she probed.

"And it's a quagmire. Everybody has theories and there is no shortage of dislike for Windermere, but there are too many things to make a pattern out of."

"What do you think our next steps are?" Cam asked.

"Well, I'd think talking to Elle might be smart. She is a central piece here—connected to this Sully character. Maybe she can clear this all up."

"Or we'd be alerting her to cover up something worse."

"You still think she did this?" Rob asked.

"It doesn't make sense, really, except if she's involved with this Sully, who is also related to the other case. But if he is involved in a murder . . . that really puts Senator Schulz in danger."

"Think about the murder method, though . . . flowerpot. Who would think that would actually kill someone?" Maybe he really was just a witness and he wasn't meant to end up dead."

"A witness who happened to be his father-in-law? No. If Sully did this, he'd know his father-in-law could ID him."

Rob sighed.

It turned out the phone call from Annie's dad had come from a prepaid phone, so there was no way to trace it, but Jake was very keen on another visit to Elle after what they'd learned. The four of them set out in Cam's car again, and drove to the Schulzes'.

Annie rang the bell and nobody answered. It was after Louise had gone home, so they waited a few minutes and rang again. Finally, Annie got impatient and pulled out her key.

The house was silent once Annie had disarmed the alarm.

"Guess we have a search opportunity, even if there's nobody to question," she said. She sounded nervous, though. Cam thought the same idea had crossed Annie's mind as had crossed her own—what if Elle had been taken, too?

"Annie, we can't . . ." Jake began.

"Jake, this is my father's house and there is an open invitation," she snapped, revealing her worry. Then she took a breath and tried to get back to herself. "I respect Elle . . ."

Cam coughed at that, which brought an evil grin from Annie. Cam was glad Annie took strength from Cam's display of support.

"So I don't do it when she's here," Annie continued, "but I know my dad would want me to look for clues."

Cam knew it was part bravado and all justification, but that was okay with her. She thought it was definitely possible there were clues in the house somewhere, and finding them would be good, whether they were only looking for clues about Senator Schulz or he and his wife, both. And at least Jake seemed to mostly buy the argument, though he said he couldn't participate without the appearance of impropriety.

Annie pointed Jake to the kitchen and told him to get them all a snack while the rest of them snooped properly, then headed straight for the stairs. Cam followed her.

"Cam?" Rob said, seeking instruction.

"Start with the study—her study." She pointed at the room, though it was hardly necessary. The his and hers décors couldn't have been more different.

Jake went to the kitchen, as directed, but shouted every

once in a while about how uncomfortable he was about the whole thing.

"What did your buddy say? Have they even been here?" Rob shouted from the study.

Cam could swear she heard, "Damn rookies," from the kitchen as she went back to climbing the stairs.

Cam had to jog to catch Annie, but she was in the room where Cam suspected she'd be: Elle's bedroom.

"Anything telling from Cruella?" she asked.

"Not sure yet. I don't know what I'm looking for."

"She and your dad don't share a room?"

"Sort of. I think there's a his, hers, and theirs. There are three bedrooms they use, anyway. I've never asked, but I remember my mom saying Dad snored, so if I didn't think things were weird, I might blame that."

Snoring kept Cam awake, too. Thankfully, Rob only did it when he had a cold, but she'd had a college roommate who snored, so she knew if she had the option, she'd sleep elsewhere, too.

"Have you told your mom about any of this?" Cam asked.

"Mom is singularly uninterested in anything to do with Dad."

"But this has to do with you, too. Your dad is missing and you're her daughter."

Annie sighed. "I guess."

"Call her."

"Yeah, but then she might *come here*. You know . . . to be supportive."

Cam knew the deal. It was almost funny, actually. Annie and her dad didn't agree on anything, but could have fun and enjoy each other's company. Annie and her mom agreed on almost everything but had a very hard time sharing space. Her mom just tried to take over on the problem solving, even when there weren't any real problems to solve.

"You still should tell her. Maybe before you call her come

up with a reason she'd be in the way that doesn't sound offensive," Cam suggested.

"Like that she'd be a suspect."

"Yeah, work with that."

"So what are we looking for?" Annie asked.

"Evidence that Elle would want your dad gone? A connection to Derrick Windermere? Maybe a connection to Melvin Entwhistle?"

"What about evidence she's flown the coop?" Annie said.

"Like gone nuts? Or left town?"

"Both? But what I have is a missing toothbrush, makeup bag. I'm sure there should be more in here."

Cam followed Annie into the bathroom.

"Yeah, that sounds fishy. Why would she leave when her husband was missing if she had nothing to do with it?"

"Exactly. Maybe to meet this *Sully*."

"So how would we confirm it?" Cam asked. It seemed like a toothbrush was only minorly damning. She'd known people, herself included, who took their toothbrush in their purse if they had a long day and wanted to be fresh after a meal or snack. Then again, Elle didn't exactly seem like the kind of woman who had an evening filled with meetings very often. She didn't work. She might have appointments related to the investigation, or maybe along the line of the one she'd found Evangeline in that morning. But Cam thought those were more likely to be during the day.

"Call Louise. This is weird," Cam said. "Find out when she left and when she said she'd be back."

Annie nodded and Cam opened a closet. There was an unzipped suitcase in it, possibly because a smaller one had been removed from the inside. Her own nested that way, and she thought that was pretty normal.

When Annie came back she looked dejected.

"Elle sent her home at two. She said she had a guest coming and wanted some privacy."

"But then she left? Definitely suspicious."

"Okay. Don't imagine for a minute I'm sympathizing with Elle, but . . . what if her guest took her?"

"Might have, but they seemed to take a bag for her, too. It looks to me like the small suitcase is gone from this set. You've noticed the toothbrush. It would be impossible to sort if clothes were gone with all this, but there seems to have been stuff packed for her to go somewhere, at least overnight."

"Yeah. I agree there. She wasn't taken by someone who doesn't care. But then again, neither was Dad, if you think about his medication being gone."

"You think . . . what? Someone took them to sit in a room and work it out?"

"Maybe." Annie sounded like she knew she shouldn't believe it, but wanted to.

"What about his call?"

"He got away for a minute. I hope they didn't hurt him when they got him again."

"I hope so, too."

They walked down the stairs with their arms around each other. It didn't seem like there was going to be any further information up there, so they wanted to see if Rob or Jake had found anything. Annie gave them the news.

"Annie, I have to let the detectives know," Jake said.

"In a minute? When we have a chance to sort things out a little?" Annie begged.

Jake nodded.

When they all gathered again in the kitchen, Rob held out a folder. "Contradictory, unfortunately, but helpful."

Cam took it. She had to be fast to beat Jake's grab, but she got there first, probably because Annie was scolding him about the lameness of the bag of chips he'd found as a snack.

It was an investment portfolio. Melvin Entwhistle was

the financial adviser, but it looked like, other than normal market fluctuations, Senator Schulz hadn't lost anything. He apparently hadn't been pulled into the scheme that Derrick Windermere had cooked up.

But Cam was confused. She'd seen his name on the list, and Annie said he didn't like Entwhistle.

"Do you remember your dad ever talking about Derrick Windermere?" Cam asked.

"Do you know how much attention I pay to the names my dad drops?" Annie said.

Cam had figured as much. Annie hated name-droppers. But the list she couldn't mention in front of Jake bugged her. She flipped over the page.

"This is Elle's." She pointed out the name on the top of the statement. "I think we need to talk to Melvin. Obviously a bunch of his clients lost huge amounts of money. Your step-monster didn't. Why?"

"Why wouldn't Elle save her husband if she knew something? It changes all this a little, doesn't it? Maybe whoever did this was the person behind Derrick's scam, and they took your dad to keep Elle quiet," Rob said.

"Well, that's not good. That kind of person might hurt Dad," Annie said.

Cam knew that upset Annie, even if it was true. But in her mind, finding Annie's dad was more important than putting things in a happy light at the moment, and this definitely sounded like a motive to kidnap him.

"Okay, Annie, calm down. We're only generating suspects. That just increases our need to talk to Melvin, right? I nominate Jake."

"Won't do any good. The man is very tight-lipped," Jake said. "I already talked to him about the party. He acted completely clueless. Claimed he only knew Windermere professionally and hadn't even talked to him that night, which I know from Rob is a lie."

"I have an idea," Cam said.

"Of course you do," Jake said. He didn't try to hide his annoyance.

"Evangeline Patrick met with him just yesterday—I saw him. I bet she'd be willing to meet with him again, and make it worth his while to answer some questions."

"Why would you think that?"

"Because she's a good person—ethical. She would want him to answer and be willing to withhold her business if he wouldn't when Annie's dad has his life on the line."

"I really don't think it's a good idea to involve more civilians," Jake said.

"Oh, come on. It's a great idea. If he didn't *do* this thing, he will answer. And if he doesn't answer, we'll know he's involved."

"And then Evangeline's life is in danger, too."

"Not if she plays dumb, which I know she's smart enough to do," Cam said.

"Come on, Jake. What other lead do we have?" Rob asked.

But Cam thought it was Annie's teary look that made him give in.

"Fine. Evangeline is, indeed, a great person to try to approach Entwhistle, since he stonewalled the police. I have to call this in about Elle, though. In fact I'm doing it right now."

They knew he was right, so nobody argued. But they weren't dropping the other angle they had.

"I can call Evangeline tonight. Hopefully, she can set it up for tomorrow," Cam said.

Rob winked at Cam. She knew it was about outplaying the cop. Life, to Rob, was mostly a game, and the best player always deserved credit.

"I have a few more drawers in here," Rob said, pointing back at Elle's study.

"I can look in Dad's," Annie said. "Then Cam and I can check the rest of this floor."

"What about your dad's bedroom?" Cam said.

"Would *you* want to check *your* dad's bedroom?" Annie said.

"Fair point, but I don't think it should go unchecked." Cam thought it sounded downright awkward, but somebody had to. "I'll do it. You and Rob cover the rest of this floor when you're done."

Annie shrugged and headed for her dad's study, shouting hints at Jake about where the good snacks were.

If she were honest, Cam wasn't all that comfortable poking into Senator Schulz's things, either. She and Annie had been best friends since middle school, but the senator had always seemed sort of untouchable, even if he greeted her kindly when he saw her. The conversations Cam had had with him always felt formal, as if she were interviewing to be a friend for his daughter. In fact, when Annie was present, she usually blew up over it. She didn't want a screener for her friends and she didn't choose who she spent time with by how well they did this or that.

Still, Cam figured she was probably the best person to do this, as she had known the senator the longest, other than Annie, and would be most likely to recognize anything unusual. And she understood Annie's hesitation on the matter. There were things you didn't want to know about your own parents.

His bedroom was immaculate. If Cam didn't know he had a housekeeper, she would have questioned his relationship with Annie, a notorious slob. It was decorated with deep gold walls and bronze fabrics, all with subtle navy and deep red undertones. It was definitely a man's room.

Cam wasn't sure what she was looking for, so she began opening drawers near the bed, always fearing the sex toys it was rumored some people kept there. But his drawers seemed pretty normal. There was a mystery novel she'd heard of. Nail clippers. A little fabric bag she thought had rice in it that she knew could be heated in the microwave to apply to sore muscles.

On the other side were a notebook, an old-fashioned Rolodex, and pens and business cards. This was clearly the work side of the bed. She opened the notebook to see if she could learn anything that way.

She thought it was like deciphering another person's shorthand. There were words, but also a lot of symbols, though not symbols she'd ever learned. She knew a few medical ones from friends and a lot of editing ones from working with the press, but these were probably legal marks. Alden Schulz had been a lawyer before he was a politician, and she guessed that was where the extras had come from.

Finally, she figured out that it was a record of suspicions of infidelity. There were times and dates and notes such as "spa" and "gym." Things Cam thought Elle had said she was doing and about which there was evidence to the contrary. It wasn't a ton of occasions, but enough that it seemed reasonable he'd been suspicious of his wife. She couldn't think of what else she'd find in the bedroom that would be more informative. This wasn't the place he'd store information on political rivals. She wondered if he had hired an investigator to check out Elle. He had the means, and if she had been in his shoes, that's what she would have done, assuming there was an infidelity clause in the premarital agreement, which surely there was.

She gave a cursory look through the rest of the room, but it really seemed like more of a movie set of a man's bedroom than an actual place that was used.

She went back down to ask Annie if she'd found anything like that—either evidence of a PI or a copy of a premarital agreement.

"I bet it's in his safe-deposit box," Annie said. "That isn't the kind of thing you leave lying around when your wife has full access to everything."

"Does he keep an office anywhere else?" Cam asked.

"Not anymore."

"And how do we get access to the safe-deposit box?"

Jake sighed. He didn't like where this was headed. "No way short of a subpoena. They're pretty ironclad that way."

"And what do we need for a subpoena?" Annie asked.

"More than you have now."

"But we need to find Elle to find my dad."

"So maybe we figure out who might lead us to Elle," Jake said.

"And our most logical clue is Mike Sully," Annie said. "How do we do that?"

Jake shrugged and walked outside. Cam got the distinct impression that their options were only marginally legal. Jake would help, but he would follow their lead, rather than directing them to do something illegal.

Rob made sure Jake was out of earshot, then spoke. "We figure out where he is and what he's driving and put a GPS device on his car. That way, we can check anywhere he goes, especially if he makes some unusual stops."

"How hard is that?" Annie asked.

"Not hard at all if we can find him. Let's hope he goes home tonight."

Rob used a newspaper search engine for public records. There were three vehicles registered to the Mike Sullivan they finally decided was the right one, and that night when they drove past the address listed, two of the cars were parked outside his home. Cam kept watch, feeling like a secret agent, as Rob attached the GPS tags to each in the wheel well, a trick he had learned from shadowing Jake. They then returned to Annie and Cam's house.

"Just a matter of time."

"Unless he's using the missing one, which you know he is," Annie said dryly. "So what's the plan tomorrow?"

"We talk to Melvin with Evangeline's help, and we look into whether Chad Phillips had any connection to either victim," Cam said.

"And is Evangeline on board?" Annie asked.

"I left her a message. I assume she will be, but she's been out this evening, so I still need to talk to her. You don't have any more of those bugs left, do you?"

"I'll drop a couple in your purse when I leave for work tomorrow."

Cam wondered if that meant Annie would have to nick them overnight or if she just had them upstairs. It was one of those questions she preferred not to know the answer to.

She didn't have any doubts about Evangeline participating. It was the kind of thing she seemed to enjoy, but Cam had tried to call her three times now and hadn't gotten an answer. She wondered if Evangeline had forgotten her cell phone somewhere so she couldn't get to it. She couldn't think of another reason the woman wouldn't respond.

CHAPTER 11

Cam still hadn't heard from Evangeline when she headed to work the next morning and so was a little surprised to be practically assaulted when she got to her office. Evangeline, in spite of the two of them being there alone, was whispering.

"Sorry I didn't call you back. I just don't want to worry Neil, but I'm happy to help. What do you need me to do?"

Cam remembered that Neil had high blood pressure and so she understood Evangeline's concern. She suggested they go get coffee and a pastry while Cam filled Evangeline in, just in case someone else arrived while they were discussing it.

Evangeline grabbed her coat and purse and then held Cam's arm as they went down the elevator. The nearest coffee shop, aside from the one in their building, which seemed too public, was just a short walk, so they waited until they were there, had ordered, and finally had a chance to sit before they got down to business.

"So you don't actually think Melvin is involved, do you?" Evangeline asked when Cam had finished her story.

"We don't know. He may be. But it's helpful to double-check if he's not, too. This hint we got suggests he's not—that he got used, and Elle Schulz knew some reason not to trust the deal."

"Elle? Not Alden?"

"No. I guess Alden doesn't actually like the man much, so he lost quite a bit, but through another broker."

"Oh! I'd forgotten about that—I mean, I wasn't here for the falling out, but Neil told me it had happened. So Elle knew something and didn't help him? Her husband?"

"I know it doesn't make sense. We want to know if Melvin knew *why* Elle backed out. That might be our clue as to who is really behind everything."

"And what is it you want me to do?" Evangeline asked.

"Maybe ask him about the loss? Not accusingly, but like you need to understand it."

"For tax purposes!" Evangeline said.

"Perfect! But maybe play dumb and pretend you don't know anything yet. Claim you just happened across the loss."

"That should be easy."

"Oh, stop it. You're one of the smartest people I know," Cam said.

"A lot of people can't get past the beauty queen stuff. They want to believe I'm stupid, so when I act like it, they're satisfied rather than surprised."

"That may be, but that works in our favor. And for the record, I know better."

"Well, thank you for that."

"Remember, we want it to seem as natural as possible."

Evangeline called to make the appointment with Melvin, but had to leave a message.

Cam thanked her. "Just call me if there's anything. Wait!" She dug in her purse. "Are you comfortable carrying this?"

"What is it?"

"It's a bug. Rob and I can listen . . . maybe even from just around the corner."

"You don't think this will be dangerous?"

"No. We *think* he got used, remember? And if so, then he should want to help you out. But it's possible he's guilty, and if he is, then it's also possible he's dangerous."

Evangeline glared at the bug like it might bite her. "How do I use this thing?"

"Just put it somewhere that reception should be pretty good. If you had a lapel pocket, that would work. Or if you put it in your purse, leave your purse open and set it between you."

Evangeline gingerly took the device and put it in the front pocket of her purse. "I suppose."

"And if you could call me and tell me the meeting time so we know when to listen . . ."

Cam walked Evangeline back to the office, gave her a hug, and headed for home. She had a few work ends to tie up for the day, but she could do them from there and was ready to be away from people for a while. Before she began, though, she needed to talk to Joel Jaimeson.

"Cam? What a lovely surprise."

Joel sounded as sincere and annoying as he always did, but Cam knew she had to keep on task.

"Joel, how are you? I just had a few questions for you about the other night. I'm sure you heard . . ."

"It's tragic! Mr. Windermere was such a great philanthropist."

Cam couldn't classify political donations as philanthropy, but she didn't argue. There was no point.

"Listen. This is strange, but . . . you didn't lend anybody your phone that night, did you?"

"As a matter of fact, I did . . . Alden Schulz!"

"Senator Schulz? Why would he need your phone? He had his own."

"Oh, no. The man who asked for it specifically told me he didn't—he lost it."

"What man was that?"

"He didn't say," Joel said, sounding peeved to be questioned.

"Would it be possible to see your phone?" Cam asked.

"Of course not, silly. It disappeared when the senator did."

Cam sighed and hung up.

She sat down to work, but her phone buzzed just as she settled down in front of her computer. "Cam? Jake found Mike Sullivan." It was Rob. "He's following him. And . . . um, I'm following Jake."

"I take it Jake doesn't know you're following him?"

"That's true."

"Take me, too. He expects these shenanigans from me."

"Can't. I'm tailing the old-fashioned way."

"In the Jeep? Yeah, that's inconspicuous."

"Look, it's a fluke I even heard. I stopped at the police station to talk to him when the call came over a radio that one of the units had spotted him. Guess he ended up on the official radar after all. Jake sprinted out, so I followed."

"Good thing I put a GPS tracker in your phone."

"You did not!"

"I did. It was Annie's idea. And it's not activated, but this is exactly why. You get yourself into trouble!"

"Only when I'm with you."

That was true, but Cam didn't want to admit it. "I put one on mine, too. We seem to be in this crime-solving business now, and I just thought it would be safer. You get back to keeping an eye. I'll get Annie and we'll follow."

She hung up before he could make his case for them not to follow him, then speed-dialed Annie, glad it was about closing time for Sweet Surprise.

Cam explained the mission, and Annie immediately agreed. "And you're not going to believe what I found out," she said.

"What?"

"No time! I'll pick you up in five. I just need to lock the doors. My car is a lot stealthier than yours."

Cam would have argued, except it was true. A tiny green Bug was not nearly as conspicuous as a specially ordered bright yellow Mustang, if only because half the time it was hidden by bigger cars.

Cam changed into jeans and a T-shirt, then as she waited, worked her phone to pick up the GPS signal on Rob's. She hoped Evangeline wouldn't need them during this bad-guy chase, but surely Melvin wouldn't be able to meet for at least a few hours.

When Annie screeched into the driveway, Cam hopped in the car and began giving a stream of directions. Annie was infinitely easier to direct than Rob, who wanted three-blocks warning for turns and if she changed her mind, started ranting that she didn't know where she was going. Annie would turn on a dime and was fond of saying, "There's no shame in a U-turn." There had been moments Cam had been tempted to point out that in fact sometimes it was against the law, but today wasn't one of those days.

Unfortunately, when they reached the small apartment building where "Mike" had been headed, it turned out it was a friend of Mike's who was using his vehicle. Cam and Annie were bolder than Rob, or rather, had the option to get a lot closer in their less conspicuous car. They passed Rob, who'd parked half a block back, pulled into a street spot much nearer to Jake, and got out so they could listen.

"Do you know where we could find Mr. Sullivan?" Jake asked.

"He left town for a few days. Asked me to stay. I'm watch-ing his cats."

"He lives here?"

The man stuttered for a minute. "Well, sometimes."

"Would you mind if we came in and had a look?" Jake asked.

"Yeah, uh . . . I'd be happy to let you if it was my place and all. But it's not. I'd have to ask Sully, and I don't expect to hear from him for a couple days."

"So I need to get a warrant?"

"Yeah, I guess I'd have to let you in then, right?"

"That's right. Then it's the law."

The guy looked uncomfortable, but Jake pressed on.

"Do you know this woman?" he held out a picture.

"Ellie. Sure."

"How do you know her?"

"Knew her since we were kids. She and Mike lived around the corner—she's closer to my age, so we went to school together."

"She and Mike lived together as kids?"

"Yeah, and Lenny, and their parents. Ellie's the baby sister, isn't she?"

"That was my news I forgot to tell you," Annie whispered. "I found some wedding pictures at Dad's place."

"Sister? I thought her maiden name was Chamberlain," Jake said, voicing Cam's question.

The man shrugged. "It's his sister. I don't know why the names are different."

Cam tried to assess how that changed the situation. Was it any better to have your brother kidnap your husband than your lover? Possibly, but the degree of difference was pretty minor in relation to the act of kidnapping somebody. It eliminated the likelihood they were having an affair, though.

Jake left after that. Cam wasn't sure if Rob followed, because Annie flatly refused to get back in her car.

"Jake may not be able to go in there, but we can," Annie said.

"Annie, that's breaking and entering!"

"Not if we show up with a half case of beer pretending we want to party with Mike."

Cam stared at her. "Holy crap, Annie. Do you know how dangerous that is?"

"If by dangerous, you mean brilliant!"

Annie finally hopped in the car, but only to go as far as a corner market. She ran in, Cam trailing. They discussed beer and decided on something just a little exotic. They bought a half case of Molson and then got back in the car.

"I can't believe you want to do this."

"Tell Rob to come as backup—to knock in about twenty minutes and start a fight so we have a reason to leave."

"If I call him now, he'll start the fight immediately."

"Okay, draft a text that you can send in about fifteen minutes."

"You've gotten more devious since you started dating a cop, you know?"

"Well, yeah. I look at it as a challenge."

Cam rolled her eyes, but somehow had never been able to resist these risky ideas of Annie's.

Cam's phone vibrated when they pulled back into the apartment complex, but she chose to silence it instead of telling Rob what they were doing just yet. She didn't want to argue. An apology after the fact was always easier.

Annie gave her an evil smile and led her up the stairs to the apartment. The mailboxes said Sullivan was in number eight, so they knocked.

The man they'd seen earlier opened the door, and Annie, bold as brass, just walked in.

"Sully around?"

"No. Who are you?"

"Fiona. This is Ursula. He said to stop by with some beer sometime, so we're stopping."

"He's not here."

Annie got really close to him. "Do *you* want a beer?"

Without waiting for an answer, she set the half case on a coffee table, opened it, and sat back with a beer on the sofa, throwing her feet up next to the box.

"Er . . . I guess. But I really can't let you stay long."

"Why not? Is your girlfriend coming over?" Annie asked, sounding like she was actually interested.

Cam thought she might as well join the act. Standing there gawking, she was only going to interfere with Annie's plan, whatever that was. She strolled over, grabbed a beer, and then sat in a chair.

"So do you live here?" she asked.

"No. Sully's out of town. He asked me to stay to watch the . . ." He looked at the beer longingly and seemed to give up his hesitation, so he grabbed one and sat.

At that, the end of the guy's sentence jumped in Cam's lap. A big black cat so heavy it felt like it almost crushed her.

"Well, hello."

"That's Frank, and Joe is around here somewhere."

Annie snorted. "Who woulda thunk Sully was a Hardy Boys fan?"

"I think he inherited them from a girlfriend, but he likes them. They're good cats."

Frank had begun kneading Cam's legs and she was glad she had on jeans instead of the linen slacks she'd worn earlier. When she scratched his ears he settled right in.

"I should use the loo before I get buried in cat, too," Annie said.

"It's on the end," he said.

"We didn't catch your name," Cam said.

"Leo. And I think you're the first Ursula I've ever met."

"There aren't a lot of us," Cam said, cursing Annie for giving her such an odd name. "Does Sully have any snacks or anything?" She was unsure what someone in this situation would really say. She'd never been in the habit of dropping in on people, let alone friends of friends.

"I think there's chips and salsa or something. You want some?"

"If you wouldn't mind."

When he left the room she spent the better part of a minute trying to figure out how to encourage the cat to jump off her without offending it too badly, but then she opened a couple of drawers. Finding nothing, she turned to the one bookshelf. There was a framed picture of three people who Cam now believed to be the Sullivan-Chamberlain siblings. They were at a marina in front of a fancy boat. It was a large sailboat and it didn't look like their positioning was accidental. She pulled her phone out and snapped a picture of the picture and then sent the text she'd drafted for Rob.

Annie finally came back. Cam was shocked Leo hadn't noticed her missing so long.

"Anything?" Annie mouthed.

"Maybe," Cam whispered, sitting down again and calling the cat back to her lap.

Leo came back in with the chips and salsa and cracked himself a second beer.

"So how do you know Sully?" Annie asked conversationally.

"Same neighborhood. We've been friends for years. How do you know him?"

"Betting party from the Kentucky Derby last year," Annie said. Cam wondered how she came up with these things off the cuff, but this one backfired.

"He went to the *actual* Derby." Leo frowned.

"Well, yeah. I did, too," Annie said, not missing a beat, but Cam thought she had aroused suspicion. A betting party would not be confused with the actual Derby. He probably wouldn't confront them, but she was very glad Rob was on the way. As soon as they left, Mike would be getting a call.

She didn't believe for a minute Leo didn't know how to reach him—cats or no cats, Leo was here to keep an eye on things.

Thankfully, much faster than expected, there was a pounding on the door.

"Is she here?" Rob shouted.

Cam squealed, half acting, but half to head off any name Rob might use.

"Oh, honey, I'm sorry. We didn't mean to disappear without telling you!"

"And you're here doing what? Yukking it up with . . . who're you?"

"Leo Portnoy."

Leo stuck out his hand and Rob scowled. "I told you we had to be at the club at nine and look at you. It'll take at least two hours to whip you into shape. And you," he turned to Annie. "Xavier has been looking for you. He's going to be ticked."

"Yeah, well Xavier should pay better attention if he doesn't want me to go looking for a party," Annie sassed.

Rob glared again, grabbed the beer, and tugged Cam's arm, then gestured for Annie to leave ahead of them. Leo just looked stunned.

They met back at Cam's place, Cam and Annie gleeful, Rob alternating between angry and amused. Annie poked him and said "Xavier" several times, and that finally got him to lighten up. When he took the half case of beer, less about four, and put it in Cam's refrigerator, he was chuckling.

"Anybody need one?"

"Yes," Cam shouted.

Annie nodded, but looked a little surprised that it had been Cam who had responded so quickly.

When Rob joined them, Annie looked at him. "So why did they think that was Sully?"

"That was his car—the one that wasn't home that night, obviously. They spotted it parked at the airport and watched it."

"So he might actually be out of the country or something, and this Leo was just picking up his car?"

Rob shrugged.

"If I had just committed murder, I'd probably get out of town," Cam said. "Maybe he really did off Derrick Windermere . . . Hey, wait a minute. Isn't this the guy who is supposed to be Derrick's son-in-law?"

"Yeah."

"Why doesn't he live with his wife—in a nice house?"

Rob shrugged and changed subjects. "You know, I tried to see Chad Phillips earlier today. See what he thought about all this."

"Tried?" Cam asked.

"He has a nasty-tempered receptionist. Best I could manage was the front office, where I met this woman, Lorraine Patterson, and two guys."

"Do you think they'd talk?"

"Doubt it."

Cam pulled her phone out of her pocket to sit and looked at the blinking screen.

"Shoot!"

"What?"

"Shoot, shoot, shoot! Evangeline! We forgot to listen. Geez. I hope it went okay."

"Well maybe it's still going on," Annie said. "We weren't gone that long."

Cam listened to the message, hoping that was true, then scrambled to her computer to tune in to the frequency of the bug. Rob and Annie followed her as she set up at her table and fiddled.

"Let me do that." Annie scooted Cam aside.

Annie was much more proficient at these spy gadgets than she was. Cam thought she probably played games with

Jake using them, but she was afraid to ask in case she got more information than she was hoping for.

"There!" Annie said, as voices came over the computer.

". . . tied up. You know he's completely helpless."

"That's horrible. Wasn't there anything you could do?" Cam recognized Evangeline's voice. She sounded panicked.

"You'll suffer the same," he said. Or that's what Cam thought he said. There was a lot of loud crinkling, and Cam wondered if there were papers being shuffled next to the bug.

She turned to look at Annie and Rob. "We have to help her!"

"Where is she?" Rob asked.

"Her message said at the office. We can be there in five minutes. Hurry!"

The Jeep was the most conveniently parked, so they piled in and Rob drove as fast as was safe to the Patrick Henry. He parked in the loading zone, and Cam rushed to the stairs, unwilling to wait for the elevator. Rob was right on her heels with Annie bringing up the rear.

When she got to the second floor and burst into the office, she realized she hadn't come up with a reason to be there. It wasn't that she wanted Evangeline to be in trouble, but she really hoped she didn't need to explain.

Evangeline and Melvin sat in the conference room, which was off to the left, and had a full view of the panicked trio.

"Cam!" Evangeline said.

"Sorry! Running late! I forgot the tickets in my office," she said.

"And it took three of you to fetch them?" Melvin observed.

"Erm. We're on foot, and I guess we didn't think about it," Cam said. "Evangeline, could I have a word?"

Melvin frowned.

Evangeline came out and Cam whispered, "Is everything okay?"

"It was until you three burst in acting so strangely. He's been perfectly reasonable."

"And you don't need us to stay?"

"I think that would be pretty awkward now, you running late and all."

"So now Melvin knows we're investigating," Rob said back at Cam's place. "Jake's going to be ticked."

"Not necessarily. I don't think he did it," Annie said.

"Why not?"

"I just don't, but I'm going to go stay at my dad's. With Elle gone, I can turn it over with a fine-tooth comb and I *will* find something. I'll look for stuff on Melvin, on Sully, on Elle, on anybody else there might have been bad blood with."

"I'll come, too," Cam said.

"No. You and Rob should work on the murder, because if it really was about that and Dad was just in the wrong place at the wrong time, then we need to solve the murder to find him."

Cam was worried about sending Annie off alone, but she agreed that if they followed both paths at once they should get there faster.

CHAPTER 12

"So who are all the murder suspects?" Rob asked when it was just the two of them.

They had gone into Cam's kitchen, Cam fetching each of them a beer. Rob sat with a notebook. Cam stood to pace while she thought.

"Melvin Entwhistle, for reputation smearing. Chad Phillips, as a political rival of Jared. He might have resented Jared getting both men's support."

"Vivian Macy has political reasons, too," Rob said.

"I don't think so. Did you know she was my mom's college roommate?"

"She was? How did I not hear this before?"

"I didn't know about it until the fund-raiser, and things have been a little crazy since then. Dad thinks a lot of her, and he said she's running for the State House, not Senate, so she wasn't intending to run against Jared. She just wanted the lay of the land."

"What about Jared?" Rob asked.

"Jared? Why?"

"Maybe he'd just learned his number-one supporter was going to have some embarrassing skeletons come out dancing. Hey, wait. Let me see something."

Rob logged on to Cam's computer and went to his email.

"Remember the missing security tapes?"

"Yeah."

"Well, the one that wasn't missing . . . my informant sent me a copy—not official, of course, but so we could watch," Rob said.

"Nice!"

Rob opened the file and they began watching the garden reception in double time. A short way in, they slowed it down to get a closer look. The man who'd annoyed Senator Schulz had gotten a major lecture from Derrick Windermere and then stormed off.

"Thanks to you and Annie," Rob said, "we now know this guy, Mike Sullivan, is also Senator Schulz's brother-in-law. He's connected to both victims."

"Do we think he has a motivation to kill Derrick?"

Rob scratched his head. "Well, there's no shortage of in-law jokes. But why does Mike have an apartment with some guy staying at it when he should also have a house with Windermere's daughter?"

"Maybe things are strained at home? Let's see if there's anyone else."

They watched the rest of the tape and saw one more argument between Derrick Windermere and a man they didn't know, a man who, strangely, at the end of the tape was the same man they saw borrow Joel Jaimeson's phone. Cam didn't know who he was, but his hat was nautical, which reminded her of another detail.

"The boat!"

Rob looked at her like she'd grown a second head.

"When I was thinking on my feet, wandering around

Mike's place, there was a picture of Mike, Elle, and what's-his-face—the cop who's their brother. It was in front of a boat."

"And a boat . . . this time of year might be very private," Rob said.

Cam grinned. "We can hope."

Cam plugged in the cable between her phone and computer and transferred the picture over so they could enlarge it. It was too bad it hadn't been taken with one of Annie's good cameras—the enlarged picture was grainy, but Rob had some photo manipulation skills. Reporters occasionally had to work with what they had rather than what they wanted, so he knew how to select smaller pieces of the picture and sharpen them into focus.

The sailboat was white, as were ninety-nine percent of all sailboats, but it had royal blue piping in a double line up the sides, and the rim around the top was the same blue. Most telling, though, was the name written in a nice cursive on the side. *Coraline.*

"Are you sure that shouldn't be *Caroline*?" Rob asked when Cam said it.

"I don't think so; look at the 'a's. But I've heard the name."

"Probably not that common on boats," Rob grinned.

"No. Especially when we have a pretty good idea who might own it. What we need to figure out is where they moor it."

"This would be a lot faster if we brought Jake on board. He has access to more search routes than we do."

"Try yours first. Then we will bring him in. I'd just rather not have this battle until we have something bigger to dangle as success."

"He said he wanted our help," Rob argued.

"Do you really think that includes going inside Sully's apartment?"

Rob grinned again. "Probably not. Why do you follow her impulses?"

"Can you resist her ideas, hotshot?"

"I guess not."

"Right. Add a twenty-year friendship on top of that."

He shook his head, but Cam knew he understood the truth of it. Annie was a force of nature when she wanted to do something.

Rob fiddled on the computer for a while and started throwing out factual nuggets. Apparently, the Sullivan-Chamberlain family were boating enthusiasts with a few different boats, and nothing unofficial noted which one was kept where.

"If they have a couple of boats, shouldn't we check them all?" Cam asked.

"We should check the ones registered to Mike and Elle."

"Elle has a boat?"

"She does. Registered to her maiden name, with no connection at all to her husband."

"Well, that's curious," Cam said. "I guess maybe she's a 'mine and ours' girl. I know she'd pitch a fit if Senator Schulz had something *she* didn't know about."

"We don't know he doesn't know about it."

"Oh, stop being all technical. I want to be mad at her."

Rob ignored her. "From what I could tell, they lease slots in Newport News, Virginia Beach, and Baltimore."

"Baltimore?"

"I really doubt that's quite as sleepy, even this time of year, so we'll put that last on our list."

"Geez. Both of the others are more than four hours away."

"Which is probably why Sully flew. Good thing tomorrow's Friday, I guess. If we have weekend plans, I need to figure out how to cover Saturday's football games. Then we'll get a good night's sleep and go."

Cam looked at her watch. It was past midnight, so she

wasn't sure what he meant by "good night's sleep," but she agreed. It seemed like something they couldn't pass up.

"And what about Jake?" she asked.

"He should come, too. If they do have Annie's dad, we'll need a real cop."

They could have just taken one car to Newport News, but when they looked at the distance and the possibility there would be some hustling to do, they decided two was wiser. It was a bit of a wonder that Cam and Annie each convinced their partners she should drive, but there was no way Cam was riding that far in Rob's uncomfortable Jeep. She thought Jake had given in to Annie on a gas mileage argument.

They finally got on the road just before two. They couldn't leave earlier because Jake had to scramble a bit to come up with something to do that was legitimate work. He figured he could pretend it was the murder he was looking at, rather than the kidnapping, for about two hours of his shift.

Newport News was on a peninsula, so there were a dozen marinas, but Rob, using a smartphone mapping device, found the one they were looking for while Cam drove, rain pelting the car. When he showed her how private the marina was, she understood why the Sullivan family had chosen it.

It was dark when they reached Newport News, and the rain hadn't let up. They were eager to get on with their investigation, but felt it might be wiser to get hotel rooms and have dinner, then get an early start the next morning. Cam could see the charm of Newport News, though with everyone's nerves so frayed, the evening wasn't the great time it might have been under other circumstances.

* * *

In the morning, they found the smaller sub-peninsula, though Cam doubted that was the technical term. It was surrounded by park preserves and a handful of marinas that looked a lot more private than those on the other side of the peninsula. Most of the other marinas looked either high-end or else very public. The cluster in the park looked like it would draw privacy seekers.

Finding the boat was another matter. There was a man in a little shop at the entry to the marina who came out to watch them pass, flagging the cars to stop. He clearly kept an eye on things. They parked across the street at a small lot to discuss their options.

"Wonder if he's always there," Cam said.

"I don't know. This doesn't look like a high-end place necessarily, but you'd think the risk at night of somebody doing something sneaky would be worse, so I bet he is," Rob said.

"He doesn't look above bribery," Annie said.

"You think we should bribe him?" Cam asked.

"No. I think if Sully wanted him away for an hour, he would make himself scarce. He could figure what he didn't know wouldn't hurt him. Especially as Sully keeps a boat here."

"I thought it was Elle who kept her boat here," Cam said.

"Does it matter? Legitimate person gives someone some cash to take a break. Did he look above that?"

Cam had to admit he didn't. "So what do we do?"

"You two," Jake said, pointing at Cam and Rob, "go in and ask if he's got any rentals. Keep him occupied for a long time, and Annie and I will walk back there. Then you two come out and get in separate cars and drive a little ways down the road, find parking spots, and head back on foot to meet us, but stay in the trees."

"You've been taking your Annie lessons, haven't you?" Cam said.

"I'm a trained cop," Jake argued.

"Who just came up with a brilliantly sneaky, non-cop plan," Rob said. "Busted."

Annie grinned proudly.

"So we're in," Rob said. "Annie, gimme your keys."

Her grin disappeared but she cooperated. Cam took Rob's hand and they headed for the shack while Annie and Jake waited until they'd rounded the front of the little building.

The inside of the shack didn't have much to it, thankfully, including an absence of windows overlooking the direction they'd parked. Cam let Rob do the talking, since she was a bad liar. She could spin the heck out of something, but to do that, there had to be a seed of truth. While Rob didn't lie a lot, either, he was a reporter who'd had some experience in telling stories to get the cooperation of a source, though admittedly it wasn't much practice, given that sports reporting rarely called for deep-cover investigation.

"Hey there. We're here for the weekend and wanted to rent a boat. We wondered if anyone around here . . ." Rob said.

"Mister, this is a private marina. There isn't anyone here who does that unless you find it through an advertisement, and then the owner lets me know."

"So you don't have a listing of anyone willing?"

"I don't have the time to act like a rental clerk. People just check in with me to pick up keys if they do it."

"And you don't have any keys?" Cam asked.

She knew how it would sound. It would give him the idea they were joy riders wanting to make a deal.

"No! This isn't really the season for it."

Cam leaned in and tried to give him a flirty smile. "Don't you have any names we could call or something? Just to see?"

"Miss, the ocean is choppy, storms all the time. I assure you, you don't want to go out there right now."

Rob rubbed Cam's back as if she were actually getting upset. "Listen, man. My girl really had her heart set on a boat ride."

"Well, you'll have to go around the peninsula and see if the public places have anything. Because I don't."

Cam crossed her arms and pouted, but Rob put his arm around her and led her back out.

"Nicely played," he whispered as they crossed the lot to the two cars.

Cam led Rob up the road and found a parking lot for hiking trails through the preserve. They were supposed to have gotten a sticker, but she wondered how widely patrolled it was this time of year. Whatever the case, they didn't have time to deal with that. She just hoped they wouldn't get caught. They hurried back up the road on foot and then used the cover of trees to pass the man's little shack so they could track down Annie and Jake.

The lot looked fairly deserted. Cam figured November was indeed a bad season for sailing. Or maybe it was just that it was the weekend before Thanksgiving.

"Do you see them?" Cam asked.

"Not yet. I'm not sure if we should be obvious so they call us over or if they'll figure out a way to flag us."

"Well, *we* are closer to this guy's line of vision, aren't we?"

Rob frowned and looked around. "Depends how far out they are. That shack had a seaside window, so if they aren't right near shore, he can see their part of the dock. In fact maybe we should have distracted him longer."

"It's done now. I guess we walk the shoreline in his blind spot."

"Good thinking." Rob draped his arm over her and they walked.

Cam thought it would have actually been sort of a romantic place, had they wound up here under different circumstances. It didn't take long before they saw Annie frantically waving her arms. Jake was down the dock talking on his cell phone.

"Uh-oh," Cam said before she grabbed Rob's hand and hurried toward Annie.

"What happened?" Cam said.

"Sully. Dead!"

"Dead on the boat?"

Annie looked like she might throw up, and it occurred to Cam that in spite of the seeming murder flurry they'd dealt with in the last year, this was the first body Annie had found. In fact, Cam didn't think she'd even seen any of the others. She hugged her friend. The first body *she'd* seen had disturbed her a lot. And she definitely wasn't going to go aboard the boat to look at this one. They had Jake with them. It was a police matter now.

Unfortunately, as a police matter, it involved a lot of sitting and waiting once Cam had reassured Annie that there was no sign of her dad and that Sully's death wasn't necessarily related to the kidnapping. Jake directed Cam and Rob back to the hotel. They hadn't seen anything and Jake pretended that he and Annie had been on a romantic weekend when he heard a rumor about a case he'd been working on and decided to follow it up. Rob was strangely at peace with the arrangement, as it allowed him to watch a pair of football games on television and write an article on the Virginia Tech one.

Cam didn't know how the local police hadn't been suspicious about their presence, but they seemed just as happy to pass the murder on to another jurisdiction. Cam knew it made for better press to say it was part of some out-of-town investigation that just happened to drift their way than to worry the locals that one of their own was up to murder, especially in a town with a lot of tourism.

"So another favorite suspect down the drain," Cam complained when the four of them were sitting in a pub in Newport later eating fish-and-chips.

"And a delay in the next stop," Annie grumbled. Cam could tell she was more worried than ever.

The local police had insisted the scene couldn't be completely secured and processed for at least twenty-four hours, and Jake's captain had insisted he stay there until the Roanoke team arrived to work with the locals and ensure there was indeed no local connection.

"So what did you tell him about why you were here?" Cam asked.

"Well after the romantic weekend bit, I mentioned that we learned Sully, a suspect for Windermere's murder, had a boat here, so I thought I should look. The captain knew there was evidence of bad blood and that Sully had disappeared before we could even question him, so since we were here anyway, I couldn't not check it out."

"Did he buy it?" Rob asked.

"Don't know, but it seems pretty obviously related, so he's not griping about it."

"So have you guys heard anything in your investigation that would point toward why Sullivan was killed?" Cam asked.

Jake looked really uncomfortable, so Annie spoke up.

"He was hit in the head with a sort of anchor—something from the boat. It's possible my dad hit him when he escaped."

Cam felt her stomach drop. "You really think he was there?"

"They're checking for DNA. He might have been. I mean, that's why we were there, right? And Dad did call."

"But then he got cut off."

"So maybe Sully's partner caught him."

"Somebody here?" Cam asked.

"We're checking to see if he had local friends," Jake said. "It's possible. Or maybe there was more muscle involved and they took him in one of the other family boats."

"So Elle might have him?" Annie asked.

"We don't know, Annie. I've told you everything as I've learned it. Maybe," Jake said.

Annie pushed her food away, and Cam understood why she wasn't hungry.

"Wait a minute," Cam said. "Could you tell how long ago he died?"

"A day or less, I'd say," Jake said. "He still had rigor mortis, which works its way out after about twenty-four hours."

"So Annie, it couldn't have been when your dad called. That was longer ago. He escaped before this happened."

Annie threw herself across the vinyl seat at Cam. "Thank you!"

"He still might have been here," Jake said.

"But someone else killed Sully. That's the big thing," Annie said.

"But who else would kill Sully?" Rob asked.

"If it isn't related to the kidnapping," Cam said, "maybe it's related to the murder and I have an idea there, too. Let me out."

Rob frowned at her as she left the table, but she didn't want to let this thought get cold. She found Dylan on her speed dial.

"Bad timing, Cam. What do you need?"

"Mike Sullivan is dead."

"What?"

It sounded like Dylan changed locations as suddenly the clamor quieted.

"He was found in Newport News, dead on a boat. Have

you seen any arguments he was involved in or do you know of any enemies he might have?"

"He was sort of out of my . . . wait a minute . . . yeah. I actually saw him punch somebody last week. The guy in the newspaper when I was at your place. It was the same night, actually. Maybe I should have thought to call you."

Cam wasn't sure that would have been a good idea. "Chad Phillips? Are you sure?"

"Yeah. They shouted a little and then Sully decked him."

"Do you know what about?"

"Wasn't cards. They'd been talking nicely earlier, then Mike played cards with some other guys. Chad was doing the televised horse race thing. Then Sully hauled off and clocked him."

"So somebody in the card game told him something that made him angry with Chad?"

"You're good at this. Makes total sense."

"Do you remember anybody else in that card game?"

"You going to send the cops to talk to them?"

"Just Jake. He can be subtle if they need him to."

"That's not how I remember it," Dylan said.

"You were a suspect. These guys aren't. He'll meet them for a beer out of uniform or something."

"Okay. You just make sure that's it."

"Promise."

He shared two names and described two more people he didn't know.

"Thanks, Dylan! That helps a ton."

"Yeah, that's me. Mr. Police Helper."

Cam snorted and closed her phone.

When she reported back to the gang what she'd learned, she wished she could avoid Rob's gaze. He knew about the mutual attraction between her and Dylan. Rob also knew she had chosen him, but he obviously didn't like that she still knew how to reach Dylan if she needed to. Annie knew, too, but was too good a friend to be obvious about it. Only Jake was oblivious.

"A pretty serious argument, it sounds like. I definitely want to get back and talk to them. But we have Virginia Beach to check, and I can't leave here until probably late tomorrow," Jake said.

"Let Rob and me go to Virginia Beach," Cam said. She wanted to check it out, but also wanted a chance to make things right with Rob.

"I don't think that's a good idea," Jake said.

"Please," Annie said. "I don't want them to get too far ahead of us."

Jake sighed and shrugged, and Cam and Rob went to pack their things into Cam's car. It was an awkward silence, but Cam could tell Rob wanted to set things right as badly as she did. He was just waiting for her to explain away what she'd done. If only it were that easy.

CHAPTER 13

Cam let Rob drive. She hadn't done that in her car very often. She loved her Mustang and hated gender stereotypes about driving, but she wanted to be able to concentrate on how she explained things. And honestly, if Rob was paying attention to the road, he had less spare brain to focus on his next argument as she made her point. They were both wordsmiths for a living, but Cam didn't care for confrontation. Rob didn't savor it, but he was better at it than she was.

"I wouldn't have called him if it weren't Annie's dad, Rob. This isn't a normal situation."

"Why couldn't you just tell Jake to call him?"

"Because I know him well enough to know he wouldn't talk to Jake without some smoothing first."

"And see, that's what I hate about it. My girlfriend is smoothing things with some guy."

"It's not like that. Not even a little bit. Before this search started, I hadn't talked to him since July."

"But you didn't delete his number either."

"No. And I'm glad I didn't. We needed it."

"And today wasn't the first time you talked to him about it."

She could tell he knew. Not that she wanted lies between them, but the fact that she hadn't told him would be an additional problem.

"Second. But same issue. He's the only person I know in that gambling circle."

"Besides Benny."

It was sort of true. Benny Larsson, who worked as a gardener—assistant to his father—for much of the Roanoke Garden Society was connected to this same group. But Benny had only ever dealt with the small-money crowd as far as Cam could tell. Dylan knew a larger variety. Part of her debated whether to claim she'd tried Benny first, but she respected Rob too much. She tried to explain the different circles to Rob, but he was too annoyed at the moment, so she tried another tactic.

"Rob, I've known Senator Schulz since I was in high school. And Annie has been my best friend longer than that. I get that you're mad I called Dylan, but I called him for the very best reason and I swear to you I won't call him for any lesser reason. I just had some instinct after those summer murders that I might need a friend in low places at some point in the future, and I'm glad I had the contact. It helped."

Rob let out a loud sigh. He was nothing if not fair. He knew the truth of what she said, at least that it was important. He might or might not believe the "no other contact" piece, but Cam thought he would get past that if their time in Virginia Beach was either productive or romantic. *Both* would give them the shot of adrenaline needed to change the mood.

There were two clusters of marinas near Virginia Beach—one just south of downtown that was a public hub and a center of tourism, and then a set north of the city that was more resorty—the upper-crust people seemed to frequent the more classy cluster of marinas.

"I think if this is Elle's boat, she'd be at one of these better ones," Cam said.

"I wrote the name of the marina down night before last. Look on my phone."

Cam did so. "I didn't realize it had the marina."

"I'm just clever that way. Even had the slot number."

She pulled up the file and looked, then googled the marina. It was right where she'd guessed, on the channel between Chesapeake Bay and Broad Bay. It was a simple matter to traverse the two large roads between the freeway from Newport News and the cluster of marinas on the channel.

Unfortunately, when they got there and parked, the marina slot was empty.

"Is there a boat parked at Senator Schulz's house?" Rob asked.

"Not that I saw. I didn't go in the garage, but I bet Annie did."

She called Annie to double-check, as it seemed important.

"I didn't even know they *had* a boat. Dad is more a golf guy."

"Then this boat has been moved, sold, or otherwise hidden. The good news is I bet that means this is our boat."

Cam dialed Jake without waiting. She and Rob would be on a wild-goose chase looking for a boat with no location, but if the police were looking for it, that was another matter. She thought it might be found fairly easily. It certainly wasn't the kind of weather somebody would be out sailing around in.

"You don't think they have a friend or something they could just borrow a slot from?" Rob asked.

"Yes. But finding that would be a needle in a haystack."

"Should we just wander the docks looking for the name?"

"Is this one the *Coraline*?" Cam asked.

"Yeah. Sully's boat was smaller than that picture you

had. And I'm pretty sure the article that included the *Coraline* said Virginia Beach," Rob said.

"So we even know what it looks like. Sure. Let's get a coffee or something and wander up and down. Maybe we'll spot it."

"Do you think this will be even more private than the Newport News dock?"

"The setup is different. This is a more touristy area. The specific docks might be gated, but the bigger docks won't be."

"You know about this boating life?" Rob asked.

"Not really. I mean just from visiting Baltimore, or coming here when I was a kid. We did that sometimes for festivals. We were usually down in the public area, though."

Driving into the parking lot was a little encouraging. They couldn't get onto the exact docks with most of the nicer boats, but they could walk by close enough to see all of them pretty well, and the private docks could be accessed, if necessary, by climbing a low fence and jumping down a level. It wasn't what the resort encouraged, but it would be pretty easy if they saw a boat they thought was the *Coraline*. They wandered slowly, Rob using a zoom feature on his camera when necessary to see the name of a couple of boats that looked close to what they were looking for.

They didn't see the *Coraline* in the marina they were in, but decided to check one just up the river. It was less fancy and more crowded, so Cam doubted it would have the boat they sought, but it was worth looking in case the police took too long. It was just getting to be dusk when Rob pointed something out.

"Far dock. Lights. That means people, right?"

Cam nodded and picked up her pace. She and Rob could walk pretty fast when they were motivated.

"What do you think?" he asked when they got closer. He handed her his camera so she could zoom.

"Looks a lot like the boat we're looking for, even if we can't see the name."

"How far a drop do you think that is?" he asked.

"Five feet, maybe?"

"Thought so." Without waiting for any other response, he'd climbed the fence and dropped below. "Come on. Quick."

Cam wasn't sure why she could walk into a gangster's lair with Annie but trespassing on a boat dock with Rob made her so nervous, but she swallowed it and swung her leg over, then lowered herself until she reached Rob's waiting arms. She was too high for him to really hold her and balance, but he helped her drop slowly and land lightly.

"Duck!" he said.

The two of them ducked behind a large boat and just sat for a while, then they worked their way around and ducked again so they were hidden from most of the shore by a behemoth of a boat.

"Okay, we get close enough to see the name. If it's not it, we leave again like nothing happened. If it is, do you want to go on?"

"We have to. Annie's dad might be there."

"But whoever is holding him might be armed," he said.

"That's true. I guess we need to figure out a way to find out who's on board."

"You act like you're in trouble—get on another boat, scream for help. I'll go on."

"So the big thug can come out and find out I'm not really in trouble?" Cam said.

"You're right. Switch that."

"I don't want them coming after you either."

"Can you think of another plan?"

"Not really." They moved closer and confirmed it was indeed the *Coraline*.

With that, they looked for a suitable boat that Rob could

pretend he was trying to man—to call for help from. It wasn't hard. There was a boat two boats over tall enough that if he stood high, he could see onto the *Coraline*'s deck.

Rob made his way to the boat, looked to either side, and began to climb onto it while Cam made her way quietly down the dock, past the *Coraline* and near a boat moored to the last bit of dock at the end. She gave Rob a final thumbs-up before ducking behind the boat. Then Rob began to call for help.

"Anybody know anything about boats? Could somebody give me a hand? Hello? Anybody?" He repeated himself several times, shouting for assistance, and finally Cam saw a head pop up from the lower deck of the *Coraline*. She watched him climb the stairs; he had silver hair and looked familiar.

Cam stood, unable to help herself, and dashed out from her hiding spot.

"Senator Schulz?"

He turned, surprised. "Cam? What are you doing here?"

Cam saw Rob frown and climb down from the boat he'd been on.

"Are you safe?"

"Well, yes. I seem to be."

"Annie is worried sick."

"Mike didn't call her? He said he would."

"Mike?"

"Oh, it's a long story. Funny, actually. Elle's brother nabbed me to force us to talk through our problems, but I didn't know what it was about. I escaped, but then was caught again and he explained. He said he'd call Annie and let her know I was safe."

"He didn't get to it, apparently. He's dead," Rob said.

Elle, who must have followed her husband up from below deck, screamed.

"Dead? No! What happened?"

"Somebody found him at his boat in Newport News and killed him. Neither Cam nor I saw, so we don't know how."

Senator Schulz turned to console his sobbing wife.

"Why don't you two come on board and tell us what you know?" he asked.

Cam thought she could provide some answers himself, so she was happy to have a conversation as soon as Annie knew her dad was okay. She called her friend.

"Annie, your dad is here—he's in Virginia Beach on Elle's boat. They're just talking here—they were supposed to work on their relationship, and Mike was supposed to call you to tell you he was okay."

"But didn't get the chance," Annie finished.

"Exactly."

"Let me talk to him."

Cam handed her phone to Senator Schulz. She could hear Annie lecturing him from five feet away and she felt a little embarrassed, but she understood. If her dad had worried her like that and he'd actually been fine, she would have been angry, too. She caught, from what the senator said, that prior to Elle getting there, Mike hadn't been comfortable calling Annie, as he wasn't sure if Annie might send rescue right away, and if Elle wasn't there yet, the whole plan would be undermined. Mike had promised him, though, that he would call and let people know. He just hadn't gotten the chance. Cam doubted Annie liked that much, but at least it answered one of her own questions.

The cabin of the sailboat was nice and warm. A generator of some sort must have been running, and it felt quite cozy. A bottle of wine sat on the table with two glasses. Elle sank to the bench of the little table, but Cam forgave her the lack of hospitality. Learning her brother had been killed must have been shocking.

At the same time, Cam felt pretty sure Elle had master-minded this kidnapping thing, so she was fairly annoyed.

"Elle, how long ago did you plan this?"

"I didn't . . . oh. You mean the kidnapping?"

"Yes."

"It was Mikey's idea. I just had to make Alden listen."

Mikey. That had to be the brother version, as opposed to the angry "Sully."

"Alden had seen me behaving secretively. He was con-vinced I was having an affair. Really, I was just trying to help Mikey with some trouble he was having. Alden doesn't . . . well . . . Mikey always got into a lot of trouble and Alden felt it was his own making. I was sneaking because I didn't think Alden would approve of me helping my brother. But then he thought something far worse. I just had to get the chance to explain—have Mikey help me explain. So Mikey found out about the fund-raiser and put some of his associates into action. He was at the party and could com-municate when Alden was off alone so they could get him. He had a couple of friends turn off the security cameras at the club, then Mikey called Alden. He told him I was home— that I needed to talk and I would be brief—and to meet him at the golf course. I knew it would take a lot more than that, of course, but Alden didn't know I knew. So when he came out to the golf course to meet me, they grabbed him."

"Why do something so extreme, though? And the cameras. You know those could have helped solve the murder."

"Murder?" Senator Schulz asked. He apparently still hadn't been given the whole story.

Elle patted him on the arm. "Len handled it, honey—they knew you were already gone so were not involved and that you were doing something important." She turned back to Cam. "We hardly knew there was going to be a murder . . ."

"I'm curious about something," Rob said. "Why is your maiden name different from your brothers' last name?"

Elle actually gave a weak laugh. "My mother expressing her latent feminism, I suppose. She was done having children at two, and Daddy really wanted a daughter. She said she'd only have another if the baby could carry her name instead of his."

"Wouldn't Len be Sully, too?" he asked.

"Oh, no. Len's a pussycat. Always has been. No need to scream at him, and somehow Sully only comes out when I'm mad."

Cam frowned. This answered a couple of questions, but not the important ones. "Were you hurt at all, Senator?"

"Oh, no. Shaken up a bit, but they were decent enough, other than not telling me what it was about. I thought the thing about Elle was just a trick until she got there. So I was under the impression they wanted a ransom or something. That's why I tried to escape."

"See, Mike had a few things to tie up before he could meet them, and I had even more—you know, I'd barely arrived back in the country and then there was that murder and the police watching me," Elle said. "Len let me know when it was safe to go."

"Do you know what Mike was winding up?" Cam asked.

"Disentangling the mess I'd been helping him with, I thought."

"Do you know why he might have been fighting with Chad Phillips?"

"I know there was no love lost between them. In fact, Mikey was really angry about something when he recaptured Alden and brought him to me, but he didn't say what it was about. Do you think Chad had something to do with . . . with . . ."

"All we know is somebody saw them arguing. Mike actually took a swing at him. The police are looking at him, but no—nobody knows if the two things have anything to do with each other."

Elle wiped her eyes and blew her nose, and the senator stood to get two more wineglasses, pouring Cam and Rob each some without asking.

"I'm very sorry Annie's been so worried."

"We've *all* been worried. The police are looking for you."

"I didn't know about that part. And I thought she would feel better that I called."

Elle sighed like there was something she wanted to say but couldn't share.

"You got cut off, though. It was obvious you'd been captured again—or at least she thought so."

The senator stared at his hands for a while. "I just wish I hadn't gotten so tangled in appearances. If I'd just asked Elle what was going on instead of making assumptions . . ."

"Well, that might have avoided a lot, yes," Cam said. She didn't feel like letting him completely off the hook. "But this stuff with Mike . . . and maybe Chad, or whatever it is . . . that seems separate. You don't think Mike had anything to do with what happened to Derrick Windermere, do you?" Cam asked Elle.

"The murder? Heavens, no! I mean, I don't think Mikey liked Derrick. As fathers-in-law go, Derrick was a real jerk, but with Chad, it was a punch in the nose, right? That's more Mikey's style."

"And kidnapping," Cam said.

"He wouldn't do that for anybody but me. I was just so sad. And I'm his baby sister."

Cam wasn't sure she or Petunia would do anything quite that extreme, but that was hardly the point. And maybe there was some extra force behind a sister convincing a brother. She took a sip of the wine as she thought about it and tried to think of what else she had to ask the senator.

"Oh! Elle! Melvin Entwhistle recently lost a bunch of people a pile of money because of Derrick. Annie noticed you pulled out. How did you know to do that?"

"How would you know about that?" Elle asked.

"The police are looking at the money loss as a motive," Cam said. It wasn't the answer to the question, but it was a true statement.

"It was a conversation Mikey overheard between his wife and her father. He wouldn't tell me what they said, but he told me to get out."

"You didn't pass that on to your husband?"

"I couldn't put Alden in that danger. It would be insider trading!"

"But not when you did it?"

"Well . . . yes, but nobody was going to notice my twenty thousand in the grand scheme of things."

Senator Schulz was looking at his wife funny, and Cam felt Rob's hand on her leg.

"We should probably go, then," she said. "Do you two have a ride?"

"If something has happened to Mikey, then we don't. He was coming for us tomorrow afternoon," Elle said.

"Do you want to ride with us?" Cam asked.

"Why don't you just take me into town and I'll rent a car. I can get a phone there, too, to make some calls and clear up any misunderstandings. Then we can still stay our last night here, and we'll all be more comfortable," Senator Schulz said.

It sounded like a better solution, so Cam was glad for it. She and Rob gave Senator Schulz a ride to a car rental place and then debated staying the night or driving back to Roanoke.

"Let's find a little bed and breakfast and celebrate success with this kidnapping case," Rob said.

It sounded pretty heavenly, so that's just what they did.

CHAPTER 14

The drive home the next day was cold but sunny. Cam was careful of icy spots, as it was barely above freezing, but it sure was pretty. They passed a large field with patches of monkshood and witch hazel. They were both nice flowers, large but also useful, though potentially unruly to raise. The witch hazel was about twice the height of a normal person. She wondered if the person who owned the field might have aspirations as an apothecary. The side of the road, under the trees, was alive with turtlehead—the pretty purple flowers on the dark green foliage would last until the first hard freeze. It was always one of the last flowers to leave for the winter.

"So how do you think this . . . what's her name, anyway? The woman who was Derrick's daughter and Mike's wife. How do you think she's coping?" Rob asked.

Leave it to him to think of a psych angle, Cam thought.

"Probably not very well."

"She's the only person we know connected to both murders, right?"

"Well not exactly. They worked together," Cam said. "Both men were part of the power in Roanoke, even if one of them was from the underworld side of it. And because the two were related, there are probably tons of people connected to both of them."

"Worth talking to her, though," Rob said. "I mean the police have talked to her plenty, but we haven't."

"Spit it out, Rob. What are you thinking?" They'd had a lovely evening the night before. A wonderful dinner of soft-shell crab, ending with crème brûlée. She didn't want him to get cryptic now and ruin her memory of that.

"I just think that whoever committed these murders, *she* may be at the center of the reason."

Rob pulled out his smartphone and clicked through a few folders.

"Her name is Vera. Vera Windermere-Sullivan. Hyphenated."

"That's quite a commitment there. Gives her a six-syllable last name. You'd think she'd pick one or the other," Cam said.

"Yeah. I agree. She's making a statement of it. I wonder how *she* got along with her dad."

"It looks like she didn't want to give up the Windermere influence, but she wasn't willing to just stay a Windermere in spite of . . . how did Samantha put it? Marrying a nobody? I agree with you that there's some sort of power struggle."

Rob grinned. "I like it when you buy my conspiracy theories."

Cam rolled her eyes. She had been doing that a lot more since she'd found herself investigating the occasional murder.

Cam texted Annie when they were approaching Roanoke, so when she got home, she found her best friend pacing her living room and cursing her dad.

"I can't believe he'd worry me like that."

"It was lousy of him, but at least he's okay."

Annie came over and hugged her. "Thank you so much for finding him. Man, if I can find a curse for Elle . . . A voodoo doll! That's what I need."

"Now, don't quote me later. She's still Cruella and all. But I think she was desperate to save her marriage. She'd been helping her brother in secret, and your dad thought she was sneaking around having an affair and wouldn't let her explain. She was trying to get him alone so he had to listen."

Annie scowled. "Sounds like a stupid idea I'd have."

Cam smiled, glad she hadn't had to be the one to point that out.

"So where's Jake?"

"He got a call when we were still in Newport News—new lead on the murder, so they let us come back last night."

"New lead is good."

Annie shrugged. "He's being sort of a butt about it. He won't tell me anything."

"Rob will get it out of him."

She had dropped off Rob at his apartment before she came home, so she called him to alert him that Jake was following a new lead. When she hung up, she grinned at Annie.

"We'll know soon."

"Soon" was overly optimistic. In fact, Rob wasn't the one to tell them what it was at all. As suppertime approached, Cam's dad called and invited her over.

"Annie's here, too . . ." she began.

"Bring her. The more brains we have on this, the better."

That worried her. Her dad needed something solved, and his issues, at least the sort he wanted both Cam and Annie in on, were never easy ones.

"So . . . your dad hasn't had problems for a while," Annie said as they drove to his house.

"I was thinking the same. I'm not looking forward to it, but he's been a real trooper for all of us lately."

"Especially me," Annie said quietly, "and he's not even officially mine."

"Sure he is. He thinks of you as his. And sometimes that degree removed is helpful. I sure prefer *you* counseling him on his love life."

Annie giggled. "Oh, and that's a good set of stories!"

Cam covered one ear. She would have covered both if she hadn't been driving. "I don't want to know."

"Oh, don't be stuffy."

"Annie, he's my dad! Do you want to know about your dad?"

"Yeah, no . . . Okay. I'll keep his secrets. My dad is all uptight, though."

"He's married to a woman who is less than forty. I suspect he has something going on . . ."

"Power," Annie interrupted.

"Well, maybe. But . . . would you marry a much older man if there wasn't . . . you know . . ."

"No, but you forget who you're talking to. I find all that power stuff irritating. It's like there's some third person . . . or . . . maybe it's a committee . . . in the relationship with you. If you aren't the person with the power, then you don't have any . . . um . . . power. But if you *are* the person with power, you have no idea if they care about you or if it's all about the power. See?"

"I get it. Or I get how you see it. I don't think, say . . . with Evangeline and Mr. Patrick it's that way. She said she was tired of all the stupid games men her age played. She wanted someone past that."

"Yeah, I bet Mr. Patrick is a tiger in the sack, too."

Cam snorted at that. It wasn't something she wanted to think about one of her employers, but he was such a darned cute little old man that it was also a funny thing to imagine. Just not in a lot of detail.

Cam's dad's house was unassuming, but a decent size. Its only real decadence was a very well-attended garden. It was something her mother, the woman who had taught Cam her love of gardening, had developed over decades and Cam now helped her dad maintain. Currently it hosted the cheery asters her mom had always favored, along with the fabulous gold and orange hearts of the crimson glory, which was climbing a trellis her dad had built. Additionally, on the porch was a very strange flowering plant that looked like a cross between an orchid and a dragon.

"Nice," Annie said as they passed it.

"Yeah. I don't know what that's about. It appeared about a week ago, but it's definitely looking worse for its time here."

"You should ask him. Make sure it's not a sign of dementia," Annie said.

Cam punched her softly. Her dad was not remotely near dementia.

"My girls!" he said when they went in. He hugged first Cam, then Annie. "Come see what I made!"

He led them to the dining room. There was a pan in the center filled with cannoli.

"Are we having dinner first or just dessert?" Cam asked.

"I made minestrone, too, but that isn't as impressive."

Annie nodded. "And it's best to be warned not to eat too much dinner when there's such a killer dessert waiting."

Cam thought her dad would have laughed at that, but instead his face fell.

"What's up?" she asked.

"Let me get the soup. I'll tell you while we eat."

Cam helped him bring out the bowls of soup and a sliced baguette, along with a bottle of Chianti.

"When did we become Italian?" Cam asked.

"Vivian has been teaching me."

"She's Italian?"

"No, but it's fun to cook." Then his face darkened again, so as soon as they'd all sat down, Cam looked at him intently.

"Spill," she said.

"I was at Vivian's earlier. She and I made the cannoli together, actually. And . . . well, the police came by. And they questioned her for a long time. And they asked her to come to the station tomorrow . . . said she should plan on spending the day. They had a ton of questions."

"About what?"

"I guess Derrick Windermere. They found a lot of files on his computer that looked like he'd been harassing her. Threatening letters. Obscene emails. He was being horrible."

"That's awful. Why would he do that?"

"He was trying to convince her not to run. She has a lot of ideas for cracking down on fraud. That's what she said was his reason. You know her degree was in tax law, so she knows a lot of tricks those cheaters use."

"So the police think she might have been trying to stop him?"

"Something like that. I mean, they know where she was. She was the center of attention that whole time at the party. But they think maybe she could have hired someone."

"Well that stinks."

"See, sunshine . . . the trouble is . . . I know she didn't do it. But I know it looks bad. And . . ." he paused.

"You really like her, don't you?" Annie said.

"I do. I know I go out on dates a lot. But it's been a long time since I've had this much fun. I just really enjoy her company and I hate to see her facing this alone."

"So what do you want me to do?" Cam asked.

"Maybe just work a little of that magic like you did the time Annie got accused. Or last time, with that friend of yours . . ."

"You'll notice that didn't go so well," Cam said.

"But you figured out the truth."

Cam sipped at her soup, wondering how she'd somehow ended up being thought of as a private investigator by the people in her life—even her dad. She could see it was important to him, so she thought she could try.

"Do you know if Vivian knows Mike Sullivan?"

"Who?"

"He was Derrick Windermere's son-in-law and he's dead now, too."

"What?"

"If I'm going to look into this, Mike Sullivan's murder might be the easiest way to cancel Vivian out. Because I can't imagine the two murders aren't connected, so if she doesn't have anything to do with Mike . . ."

"We can sure ask her. She's never mentioned him to me."

"Is she home tonight?"

"She is. I could invite her over here to join us for the cannoli. I just wanted to talk to you about it first."

"That's a good idea. Call her, and I'll see if I can think of anything else."

Her dad left the table to call Vivian, and Annie frowned. "Why would she be coming out as a suspect this far after the fact?"

Cam shrugged. "Dad said the police were looking at Derrick's computer."

"Shouldn't they have started there?"

"Maybe it was encrypted or something, so they needed a hacker or expert."

"I think there must be another reason."

"You want to ask Jake about it?"

"Oh, that'll be popular . . . right after Rob has been grilling him about . . . oh wait . . . this must be it . . . the clue he was following up on. Call Rob!"

Cam shook her head, wondering why it had taken the cogs so long to fall into place.

Her dad came back. "She'll be here in half an hour."

Cam debated whether she should find out what information Rob had before or after talking to Vivian, but she finally decided to wait. She didn't want to risk setting Jake off if Rob and Jake were currently working together. She helped clean up the soup bowls and tried to be supportive of her dad while they waited.

When she finished with the dishes, she came out of the kitchen to find Annie and her dad playing Boggle. They played so dirty words counted twice, which was pretty funny.

"So, Dad, what's with the dragon plant on your porch?"

"Oh! I was going to ask you about that. It's Vivian's and it's having some trouble. I told her you could give it a look and nurse it back to health."

"It's tropical—Asian, I think. I've never seen one before."

"But you have that fancy degree . . ."

"If I was giving a guess, it probably doesn't want to be outside in the winter. It's used to tropical climates. Maybe I should see if the Patricks could keep it in the summer greenhouse while we figure it out. Or maybe Henry knows something. He has a lot of eccentric clients. Maybe he's cared for them before."

"Oh, now there's a good idea! She'll be glad. She really likes it. Her daughter sent it to her, so it has sentimental value. I guess they took a trip to Nepal several years ago and this reminded them both of that."

"I guess I can see that. Nepal, I think, means it wants a lot of moisture—super humid. But the summer greenhouse should do it. I'll take it over there tomorrow, but for now we should probably bring it in. It won't like these near-freezing temperatures."

As they were moving the plant into the house, Vivian arrived. It seemed strange to see her in jeans and a T-shirt, but as it was Sunday evening, it shouldn't have. It was just that the councilwoman was nearly always dressed like a professional.

"Cam, so good to see you," she said.

"And you remember Hello Kitty," Cam gestured at Annie, who punched her in the arm.

"Ha! Any word on your father?" Vivian asked.

"Yes, actually," Cam said. "Turns out his wife kidnapped him so he'd hear her out about an affair she wasn't having."

"What a clever girl. Could have let you in on it though, I imagine," she said to Annie.

"Yeah. No kidding," Annie mumbled.

Vivian reached out and touched Annie's shoulder in sympathy. Cam had noticed she was a touchy lady and wondered if that helped people feel close to her. It probably did. Cam wasn't particularly touchy, but she could see how it might work, especially for a political candidate.

"Should we get that cannoli on?" Cam said. "It looks amazing!"

They all followed her back to the table and Cam fetched coffee. The plates, forks, and cannoli were already waiting on the table.

Vivian touched the fan of forks. "Cannoli are for fingers. We won't need any of these."

"There's caramel sauce in there, too," her dad said, grinning like the Cheshire Cat.

Cam gave a shocked expression. "What, like a real restaurant?"

"It is, actually," Vivian said. "I met a couple last winter while I was vacationing, and they run a restaurant in New York City. They gave me the recipe if I swore I'd never open my own restaurant."

"I had to swear, too, before Vi would teach me," her dad said.

Cam spotted Annie giving her dad a thumbs-up, signaling her approval that the two were well matched, and if Cam were honest, they were. Cam could think of women he'd dated who'd been significantly more annoying. She also liked the idea that Vivian had been friends with her mom. She would respect their history and could share memories of her mom with him.

She had to yank herself out of her thoughts before she had them married off or something. If this woman was under investigation for murder, things could actually go very wrong.

"Vivian, do you know someone called Mike Sullivan?"

She frowned. "I know two Mike Sullivans. I assume you mean the local one?"

"Yes."

"He volunteered for my campaign last summer. I had to fire him because he was trying to embezzle money from me."

"Uh-oh."

"Uh-oh, what?"

"Well . . . Mike was found dead yesterday."

Vivian's hand fell to her lap. "Dead? Where? How?"

"We don't know the how, but we were trying to track down Senator Schulz on a boat in Newport News. Annie and Jake—her boyfriend, who also happens to be a police officer—were the ones who found him."

"How awful! Oh, honey, what a miserable thing to see."

Annie was unusually solemn, and Cam thought again how disturbing it must have been for her.

"You saw something about how he was killed, didn't you, Annie?" Cam asked gently.

"There was blood, so Jake turned me around and told me not to look. I didn't mind cooperating for a change. He called the police to come check instead of checking himself, but I think he got hit in the head with a boat anchor or something."

Vivian sucked in her breath.

Cam looked at her dad, who seemed to be very uncomfortable. She tried to scramble for a line of questioning that would lead to some other angle to investigate.

"How did you end up . . . with him working for you in the first place?"

"I get volunteers all the time. There's a skills assessment, and when people have expertise in certain areas, my staff manager asks them to do their volunteering in that domain."

"What did he have in his background that would lead you to put him in contact with money?"

"He claimed to be an investment banker. My staff manager confirmed employment at a local firm. It turns out he was actually in a more routine job—a midlevel administration person. But all she confirmed was where. Believe me—we won't be doing that again."

"I bet it was Windermere's company," Annie said. "If *you* had a daughter married to someone like that, you might try to give him a respectable job for her sake."

Vivian frowned. "He was Derrick Windermere's son-in-law? That rat! He may have been trying to infiltrate my campaign for more than just money!"

"He was probably trying to get information for Derrick and the money was his own little side idea," Cam said. "It seems he has a gambling problem. Had," she corrected. "Had a gambling problem."

So much for proving Vivian had no motive for murder number two. Both of these men had made her life miserable, one of them for quite a while, apparently.

"Why did they have it in for you? Both of them?"

"Derrick and I have butted heads for several years over his lack of ethics. I tried to convince him to fly right, but never seemed to get anywhere. He really didn't savor seeing me in government. I think at a city level he wasn't too worried, but at the state level, I can go after people like him. I have my doubts, now that you mention gambling, that the issue with Mike was personal—it would make sense if he were working for Derrick."

"I guess maybe that's enough for me to start with," Cam

said. It was a lie—it seemed like almost nothing, at least nothing good, but she didn't want to panic anyone.

"Start? Start what?"

"Um . . . er . . ."

"Cam has solved a couple of murders recently," Annie said. "She just looks into some of the angles the police ignore."

"Oh. Well, I don't know if that sounds safe," Vivian said.

"We'll be really careful," Cam said.

"You do that, sunshine," her dad added. He came over and gave her a hug and a kiss on the cheek, and then Cam and Annie headed to Cam's car.

"You've got nothing, don't you?" Annie asked once they were driving.

"Nothing at all."

"It's too bad. She's a nice lady."

Cam nodded.

"And your dad really likes her."

Cam let out a sigh. "Why do these things happen to us?"

"I don't know, but I'm sure there are other people who wanted to be rid of both of those guys."

"I have to think Vera Windermere-Sullivan is the linch-pin," Cam added. "I wonder how we get to her."

The senator and his wife were due home that night, so Annie headed to his house to give him a tongue-thrashing about worrying her so badly. Undoubtedly, she hoped some of the thrashing would land on Elle, too, though more indirectly. Cam waited for Rob. She wanted to share details with him because the two of them worked off each other well. She'd just traded shoes for fuzzy slippers when he arrived.

"Productive day?" he asked with a raised eyebrow. He always said Cam didn't give in to comfort enough, but he was clearly a little alarmed when she did.

"My dad has asked me to look into this murder."

"What? Oh!"

It was what she loved about him. He was quick on the uptake. She didn't need to explain the connection to Vivian. He'd been getting the evidence updates all afternoon and knew who the new prime suspect was. And he knew she'd gone to the fund-raiser with Cam's dad.

"Is it that serious?"

"Seems to be. I think there's also . . . she was a friend of my mom's, so he might have wanted to help her anyway, but you can tell he really likes her."

"Wow. Because the evidence is . . ."

"She's connected to both men. She told me how."

"You've talked to her?"

"Just ate cannoli with her, actually."

"Are you sure that's safe?"

"Are you serious? Look, we know she didn't physically do either crime. She was in the middle of a herd of people for the first and with my dad here in Roanoke for the second. And . . . she was my mom's friend! Aunt Vi! She wouldn't hurt me. Especially if I'm trying to help her, but even if I wasn't . . ."

"Okay, okay. I just don't get how you keep getting sucked into these things."

"You do, too."

"I'm a reporter. I'm just doing my job."

"You're a sports reporter. Your job is covering Virginia Tech, or the Redskins, or the Senators . . . or whatever that hockey team is . . ."

"The Capitals."

"Yeah. Dumb name."

"I didn't pick it. Red Wings all the way, baby."

Cam rolled her eyes. He was being silly, but he definitely could do a good impression of a mindless sports fan.

"My point is you report on games, not murder. You don't have any more business doing this than I do."

"We've done pretty well with it, though," he said.

She went over and hugged him. "So here we go again, hmm?"

He kissed her temple and sighed. She knew she had him. "Did you have dinner?"

"Sandwich," he said.

She fetched a bowl of grapes and a couple of beers and sat down on the futon with him.

"So let's think this through."

Cam shared what she had learned from Vivian at her dad's house, and Rob shared a few other details that Vivian must not have thought to bring up.

"You know they've subpoenaed her computer and phone records."

"Seriously? What do they hope to get?"

"Jake's not talking. They must have some reason to suspect her."

"Yeah, I'll believe that when they prove it. I don't think that's the right direction," Cam said. "Anything else?"

"Potentially big. That company that paid for the media table—the one that was arranged by Derrick Windermere?"

"Chrysanthemum Holdings, yeah?"

"The other partner—Treemore? Something like that. Anyway, there was a suit filed to have Windermere declared incompetent so the other partner could take over. Looks fishy enough that their books have been subpoenaed, too."

"Treemore. I've never heard of them."

"No, the searching I've done looks like it's just a dummy company for some other one."

"How many dead ends are we going to hit?" Cam asked.

"I'm not sure it's dead. It's just above my pay grade," Rob said. "We should work on something more manageable. Any suggestions?"

"How do we get close to Vera Windermere-Sullivan?" Cam said.

"Funeral for her dad is tomorrow," Rob answered.

"Oh, that sounds tasteless."

"It sounds like where we can assess who's sad and who's just being seen. Maybe there will even be someone there who's a little smug. Or someone obviously missing."

"Okay, then. He was a miserable man, so I suppose being tacky by going doesn't bother me all that much," Cam said. "Say . . . was there a life insurance policy?"

"There was, actually. Rather sizable."

"And the beneficiary?"

"Police have sealed the information. They know, but they aren't telling."

"You mean Jake won't give a hint?"

"I think it's being contested pending the investigation anyway, so he can't."

Cam pulled out her phone and called Annie, who didn't answer. She was probably mid-rant at her dad, so Cam left a message.

"Big life insurance policy on Derrick. Police aren't saying who gets the money . . . but maybe one could be persuaded."

"You're terrible," Rob said when she clicked her phone shut.

"No. I'm efficient."

"Very." He pulled her closer.

CHAPTER 15

Cam thought she'd never seen such a pretentious funeral. Even dead, the guy was obnoxious. The flowers were so thick and pungent Cam almost felt nauseated, and *she* was a flower enthusiast. There was a string of black limousines six deep, as if his immediate family couldn't stand to be in the same car with each other. The church was filled with blaring organ music. The harem from the fund-raiser had hardly bothered to make themselves appear more appropriate. And the orations given by supposed loved ones sounded bought and paid for. At least it was very interesting people-watching.

Derrick's ex-wife sat with their daughter, Vera, whom Cam recognized from the fund-raiser. Both looked like a studied example of grief, sniffing and holding each other, but Cam wasn't buying it. She could understand an ex-wife being supportive of her child, but given what she knew about Derrick and that this woman had gotten away from him some time ago, real grief didn't make sense. Unless of course she was sad she wasn't still married to him because now the bastard was gone and she wouldn't get any of his money.

That was another issue—Derrick had an estate besides the life insurance policy. Cam wondered what it was worth. He had lived like a very wealthy man, but his livelihood had required that he look successful. She wondered if he really was. She decided maybe the ex-wife was a good person to approach at the reception.

His current wife was so surrounded with people it was hard to actually see her face. Her hat also had a veil to it. Cam wondered if she was hiding her dry eyes. Why hadn't this woman been looked at more seriously? Wasn't it always the wife?

Rob elbowed her, pulling her from her thoughts. He pointed to a trio of people coming in.

"Who are they?" she whispered.

"That is what we in the sporting world call organized gambling."

"Oh! Wait a minute. That guy was the guy with the phone."

"What phone?"

"Joel's phone, remember? So who are they?"

"The guy at the back is Big Al."

"That's a bit of a stereotype on naming, don't you think?"

"I think he likes to play on it. He keeps clean, at least on paper, but everyone who gambles in this town knows he's behind it."

"And who are the other guys?"

"Now that I see him in context, rather than on a little screen with a naval hat, the suit is Dave Barrett. He's a lawyer, and I think he knows how to keep them walking the 'can't get caught' line. I don't know the third."

"The lawyer for a gambling ring borrowed and kept the phone of a staff member. And they're here paying respects to Derrick Windermere. Interesting."

"Not really. Derrick was just a white-collar version of what they do."

Cam thought that was probably true, but in her mind, white-collar and blue-collar gamblers didn't play together. "Maybe gambling is behind the murder."

Cam was surprised how many faces she recognized as she looked through the crowd. A number of them had been at the fund-raiser. Even Samantha was there, sitting with Jared Koontz, of all people. When Joel Jaimeson stopped to greet her, Cam almost hid. They had to be quiet then, as the events of the funeral began in earnest. Other than the people she recognized, it looked a little like a who's who of seedy society. Cam was surprised people like this were so prevalent in Roanoke. There were a lot of furs and six-inch heels, which seemed very over-the-top for a somber occasion, and there were a few men with oversize rings and flashy suits. They were not the mourning funeral-goers she would have expected at a classier man's funeral, or even a humbler man's. No, Derrick Windermere, if he had had a hand in planning this, wanted everyone to think he was loaded.

Thankfully, the service wasn't overly long. And thankfully, though for an entirely different reason, the reception was across the parking lot at a hotel conference room. The same sort of decorations graced the place, and Cam thought some local florist had made thousands from this man's death. The estimated profit was almost enough to suspect a murder motive. She whispered that to Rob and saw his mouth twitch.

"There she is. We're going in," Rob said. "You're point." He put a hand on her back and followed her silently.

"Do we know her name?" Cam whispered behind Derrick's former wife.

"Charlotte? Charlene? Something like that."

Cam didn't want to get it wrong, so she went with the ever-reliable "Mrs. Windermere."

"Mrs. Windermere, I'm so sorry for your loss."

The woman had chocolate hair and eyes that were almost black. She appraised Cam a moment.

"Why thank you. You are?" Cam thought she smelled an early-morning cocktail on the woman's breath.

"Camellia Harris. I was a professional acquaintance. It's just so sad."

"Well, yes. I'm more here for my daughter. I'm actually Mrs. Langston now, but I appreciate your sentiments."

"I'm so sad for your daughter. I hear she lost her husband recently, too."

"Yes, well. Good riddance to him."

"Really? Was he so awful?" Cam crossed her fingers that the alcohol the woman had imbibed loosened her tongue.

"She wanted to leave him. Had for years, but her father wouldn't hear of it." She then stopped and narrowed her eyes. "I'm sorry. I really shouldn't be gossiping."

"Oh, no. I quite understand. Sometimes you just need to ease a little of the pressure. We won't say a word. Will we, Rob?"

Rob shook his head dutifully.

"It's just . . ." She leaned in conspiratorially, like she relished the gossip, however inappropriate. Cam decided it was definitely the drink. "He had some gambling problems. It made it impossible for them to get ahead. And then I think he was a bit of a womanizer on the side."

"Then why would Mr. Windermere object to her leaving him?"

"He claimed he was old-fashioned, but I know better. He divorced me, didn't he? And he's been living with that tramp for years. Actually, I think it was the family connections."

Cam tried to act dumb. A son-in-law connected to a former senator and a cop was possibly very appealing to someone with criminal tendencies. She wondered if Derrick had ever taken advantage. She knew what Elle had said, but Elle had perhaps only said what she didn't mind her husband knowing. There might have been a lot more to it.

"Living with . . . so the woman up front wasn't his wife? She seems to have a lot of support," Cam said, thinking gossip on that front might be even more forthcoming.

"Heather? Oh, honey. He never married her. Poor idiot has been biding her time for years and just missed the gravy train."

Cam thought Char-whatever Langston looked particularly smug.

An argument broke out then, at one side of the reception. One man was a police officer in his formal blues and the other was none other than Chad Phillips.

"Oh, dear," Mrs. Langston said. "I'll need to intervene there. I hope you'll forgive me." She rushed off, wobbling on her first few steps.

"Three guesses what that's about," Rob said.

"Why on earth would he show his face here?" Cam asked.

"And how would Vera's mother be the best person to intervene?" Rob asked.

"No clue. You don't think Vera is tied to Phillips, do you?"

The gleam in Rob's eye told Cam that was exactly what he thought and that this story appealed to the journalist in him, even if it was fairly tawdry.

"You do know who that cop is, don't you?" Rob asked.

Cam shook her head.

"*That* is Len Sullivan, our suspicious cop. Looks like he thinks *something* about Chad Phillips being here is inappropriate. Is there anyone else here we need to talk to?" Rob asked.

"Have you noticed who Vera's friends are? I can see it being helpful to talk to one of them."

Rob pointed. There was a quartet of women hovering near one wall. One was turned with her back to them, and Cam could swear it looked like she was spiking her coffee. It was confirmed when she passed something to another woman in the group. The rest of them watched as Mrs. Langston lectured both of the men who'd been arguing. Vera was to the side looking petulant, but she followed her mother as she walked away, looking back over her shoulder sadly as they left. Cam could have sworn the look had nothing to do with the inappropriate behavior at her father's funeral.

"Come on." She took Rob's hand and pulled him toward the women.

They looked at her questioningly as she and Rob arrived, but Cam just dived in.

"It's so sad. Vera could really use that support today."

"Who are you?" one of the women asked.

"Cam Harris. I worked with Mr. Windermere—he talked about Vera all the time. You must be . . . sorority sisters?"

"No, we've been friends longer. Vera's never mentioned you."

"Well, I don't imagine Mr. Windermere mentioned me to her. His secretarial pool would hardly be interesting family conversation."

They seemed to relax a little, except for one who reminded Cam of Kim Kardashian.

"So if you're the secretary, what business is this of yours?"

Cam would have been shocked had she actually had a less sneaky interest, but this seemed to reflect the class of this group. "Mr. Windermere was good to me. I wanted to pay my respects. I just thought . . . well, I don't want to approach Vera directly, so I hoped as her friends, you might pass on my sympathies."

"Don't be a bitch, Aubrey. That's nice of you," one of the other women said. "But what were you talking about . . . use that support?"

"Chad Phillips? I . . . I took it they are close—Vera and Chad."

"Close?"

The woman she was talking to seemed clueless, but the face of one of the others behind her told Cam she'd guessed it.

"Maybe I'm mistaken," Cam said. "It was just an impression I had."

"I'm sure that's it," the knowing one said. "Look, we'll pass on your message."

"Thank you." Cam took Rob's arm and led him off.

"Vera and Chad," Rob said. "Well, well."

"I could see her face—she was sad he was going, and it completely explains why Mike and his brother would both be so mad at the guy—the fight at the poker game when Sully had learned something."

"You think there was an affair?"

"I think it's likely," Cam said.

"Then Jake dropped the ball there. I'll make sure he knows he needs to follow up on that poker game."

"Are you sure? Maybe *we* should look into it?"

"How would we do that?" he asked.

"Maybe we should go play some cards."

Cam couldn't remember later how she convinced Rob to go along with it. She had to get him past his Dylan hang-ups, his hesitation at going behind Jake's back, and his arguments that Cam had no poker face. In the end, she conceded he could play. It was true—*she* certainly couldn't. She called Dylan to find out how to go about it.

"Cam, these are big-stakes games. Nobody can get in for under a grand, ten grand if you want one of the really big ones, which I think you do."

"What?"

"The people you want to talk to—those games are closed, and if a young guy like Rob comes in, they'll smell a rat if he doesn't come with a pedigree. It's not that they care where the money came from, but they don't want cops or investigators buying in. Which you are, by the way."

"But we're looking into the death of one of them."

"And some of them probably think, good riddance. Sully was a teddy bear when he won, but he didn't win much. And when he did win, it usually went up his nose."

"Wait. Not just the gambling? Drugs, too?"

"Look, I never saw it. They try to keep it looking clean. Everyone knows there's an escort or two hanging around, and everyone knows the reason when someone comes back from the john sniffing, but they don't do anything illegal in the main room."

"Other than gambling," Cam said. "So how do I get in there to talk to somebody?"

"I thought your buddy Jake was calling them."

"He's focused on another suspect and I think he dropped this angle prematurely."

"Look, if you want to put on a real-short skirt and help me pour drinks, you can come to one of the games Wednesday. I get half your tips because they'd all be my tips otherwise, but I admit you'll get more than me, so you can keep half."

"Deal!"

She wished Rob was as enthusiastic when she relayed the plan to him. In fact they argued about it and he went home early, but she knew he'd come around. He'd bought in to going to the card game himself. And she was sure he knew he wouldn't make a credible silver-spoon heir coming to the table, not to mention neither of them had ten thousand dollars lying around.

Cam went to work the next morning and found herself inundated with mundane tasks. The Roanoke Garden Society was sponsoring a winter garden that needed coordination with the city, a nearby elementary school, and a neighborhood group, so Cam made a series of calls. She felt like she was playing the telephone game before long and finally just requested a meeting.

When Evangeline arrived, Cam filled her in. "It will be so much easier than having the same conversation with a dozen different people, each wanting to add their own thoughts."

Evangeline thought it was a great idea and started to head to her office.

"Wait! I forgot to ask what you found out from Melvin."

"You mean before that fiasco of a rescue?"

"Yeah. Sorry about that."

"I was brilliant, actually. I told him a mutual friend had told me Elle didn't lose anything. I asked how that was possible. He said Derrick must have known something and passed on the information to his wife or son-in-law."

"Which is what Elle said really happened," Cam said. "Shoot. Looks like another dead end. So what was the 'tied up and helpless' bit about?"

"What Melvin said about his connection who'd gotten him into this. It was why they couldn't move the money—just a metaphor."

Cam sighed. She began trying to schedule the planning meeting, which it turned out only changed her headache from event details to coordinating a dozen schedules during the holiday season. By noon, she was ready to murder several people herself, so she left the building and walked to Sweet Surprise.

"I need chocolate, caffeine, and sugar in the same bite," she said when she walked in. It was what she always said if she was up for a cupcake. The chocolate mocha fudge cupcake was her favorite.

"You'll have to frost it yourself. Somebody bought me out during lunch so I've baked some more, but they're still cooling," Annie said.

"I can play with frosting."

"Rob says you're more of an artist."

"Oh, stop it." Annie's innuendos always made her blush.

"Can we all do the Scooby thing tonight?" Annie said.

"Scooby?"

"Yeah, like on *Buffy*—where we all get together and crime-solve . . . or monster-solve, but whatever. It's been too crazy a week and I need some Scooby time."

Cam laughed. "Okay, Scooby time it is."

"And your price of eating that cupcake is frosting the whole batch."

"Fair enough." Frosting was fairly mindless, and Cam knew she could use the downtime. "It smells great. What's in the oven?"

"Pumpkin! I've got so many Thanksgiving orders! Some for tomorrow and a ton for Wednesday. In fact, come to think of it, we ought to meet here tonight so I can keep going on my pumpkin fest."

"That sounds good."

The break gave Cam the energy she needed to get back to musical schedules. Unfortunately, an afternoon call from her dad unraveled everything.

"Sunshine? We've run into another snag."

"Uh-oh. What is it?"

"Vi had to turn in her cell phone records and . . . I guess there are some questionable calls. She doesn't want to answer me about what they are, but I'm really worried."

"Do you want to meet us at Sweet Surprise tonight— Annie, Rob, Jake, and me?"

"Oh. You kids have plans!"

"No. Seriously. They're crime-solving plans. Annie called us the Scoobies."

"Like from *Buffy*!"

"How did you and Annie watch that and I totally missed it?"

"You were away at college."

"Annie and I went to college together."

"Yeah, but Annie and I liked to talk about *Buffy* sometimes."

"Doesn't that seem like . . . an odd choice for a man your age?"

"I wasn't my age then. This was a dozen years ago. And in case you've forgotten, I've always loved tough little girls."

Cam laughed. She'd never been particularly tough, but her dad had treated her like she could conquer anything. It wasn't true at all physically, but his attitude had contributed to her confidence and drive in other areas. Petunia had taken the challenge in the more physical sense, which annoyed Cam. By the time she was about fifteen and her little sister had caught her in size, it scared her, as Petunia could out-wrestle her on any disagreement.

"So come join the Scoobies," she said.

"I think I will! Maybe I'll bring y'all a pizza."

"Good idea."

When Cam hung up, she tried to envision what sort of people Vivian could have been in contact with that she'd be too embarrassed to admit to her dad. He was a pretty open-minded guy. Surely Vivian knew that. If she really did know Cam's dad, as Cam thought she did, then the things Vivian would be embarrassed about would be vanity related—but then the police wouldn't care about those. They would hardly have called her out over a waxing appointment or a Botox treatment—not that Vivian appeared to be a Botox woman.

Cam finally just created an availability survey online for the meeting she was trying to coordinate for work and sent it to all the people who needed to be there. She would check it in a few days and schedule the meeting on the date the most people could make it and be done with it. She wondered what people had done before the internet made such things possible.

She then justified an hour online perusing winter gardens to see if she could bring some fresh, attractive ideas when they had the meeting. She was relieved to end the day with no more in-person conversations.

"You look exhausted," Evangeline said as she was leaving.

"I've been herding cats since nine this morning."

"I saw your emails. It's a bad season to try to plan meetings. We probably should have thought of this in October, but . . ."

"We were doing this fund-raiser, so it wouldn't have fit," Cam finished.

"That fund-raiser never should have gobbled Roanoke Garden Society time, much less yours."

"It worked out okay for me. I would have helped Annie anyway—she's helped me enough times."

"I envy you girls' friendship. I never had girlfriends like that."

"You're welcome to hang out with us any time."

Evangeline laughed. "You're sweet. You're at a different life stage than I am, so it wouldn't fit. And I love my time with Neil. I think the pageants just created such a phony atmosphere that the women I spent time with never truly bonded. I have several people I'm fond of, but there was never any real trust."

Cam frowned, as something had struck her. The women at the funeral and Vera Windermere . . . there had been something familiar about her.

"Was Vera Windermere a pageant girl?"

"She was! I was actually a junior host when she was in the Little Miss Begonia, and I volunteered the year she did the Miss Dogwood."

"So she would know you?"

"Not well."

"Okay, just tell me to go away if I'm imposing on you, but her father was killed last week and her husband this weekend. Both men were murdered, and . . . I think she's having an affair and I was wondering . . ."

"What, if I could call an almost stranger and probe into her personal life?" Evangeline was teasing, but it was the kind of teasing that showed she was worried Cam might have been that delusional.

"Nothing nearly so intrusive. I wondered . . . if you knew where she hangs out."

"Well, I see her at the country club. Their family membership is lifetime, I believe. I've seen her in the pool there."

"The pool?"

"Yes. She swims."

"I knew what the pool was for," Cam joked. "What I didn't know was if you might get me a few guest passes."

"Do you swim?"

"Not well. Rob swam in high school—well, played water polo, actually. Swimming interfered with baseball. I thought maybe we could pretend he was helping me improve."

"Well, I'm happy to do that. Helping the two of you run into her is no problem at all."

"Perfect! Thank you!"

Cam felt like things were perking up as she made her way back to Sweet Surprise. She stopped at Sumdat Farm Market on the way and bought a couple of bottles of wine and a six-pack of seasonal beer. There were a dozen take-out places near Sweet Surprise for whatever they needed to supplement pizza for dinner, but beer and wine was a decision she could make on her own.

She went into Sweet Surprise through the back door, as the customer door had been locked for the day. Annie was covered in flour, but she looked content. She was in baking Zen. Cam had seen it before.

"Hey there," Cam said as she set down her purchase.

"Hey yourself. Open one of those bad boys."

Cam laughed. "Hey. How did I not know about you and my dad watching *Buffy* together?"

Annie mumbled something akin to "I don't know," then swallowed whatever she had in her mouth. "He let me set up that darkroom in your basement, remember? The lab at school was impossible to get at reasonable hours, and I was doing my best to separate from Daddio. And then Mom said it stank. Your dad was a superstar."

"The details I missed," Cam pondered.

"You were Miss Club Fiend. I think our *Buffy* night was when you and your mom were both at that community gardening club, 'cause she was gone, too."

Cam found the corkscrew and the cups—after the last fiasco, they'd settled on sturdy plastic cups, even for wine. It was easier not to have to stop and sweep and mop in the middle. Besides, the wineglass set was getting thin.

Cam opened the bottle of merlot, Annie's favorite.

"When do Jake and Rob get here?"

"Jake, not until six, but Rob stopped by already and I sent him for food."

"Oh, good work. I'm starving. Though when my dad comes, he's bringing a pizza."

"Pizza goes with everything," Annie said.

"And I could use a little extra," Cam said.

Annie stopped mid-frosting to stare at her. "Since when?"

"Since I learned I need to go swimming tomorrow. That takes a ton of energy."

"Have to? Why don't I ever *have to* do things like that? I love to swim."

Cam had sort of forgotten that. Annie had swum circles around her in the pool as kids. It helped that Annie's house had a pool, but Annie loved the water. Cam didn't dislike it but was more cautious, not to mention modest and worried about sunburn.

"Vera Windermere-Sullivan swims at the country club pool nearly daily, according to Evangeline. Evangeline gave me some passes, so we can watch and then go in when she does."

"You and me?"

"I was thinking me and Rob because of your job. Evangeline thought she'd do it early—like before noon, but thanks."

Annie stuck her pouty lower lip out just as Rob returned with what looked like burgers, though Cam was sure Rob knew Annie would want a garden burger and she would want a chicken sandwich. They'd spent enough time together to know each other's preferences.

"Why is Annie pouting?" he asked.

"She has to work while we go swimming," Cam said.

"I can't swim," Rob said. "I have a new tattoo."

"What?" Cam shouted, her eyes popping.

"Kidding. I just wanted to see that."

Annie snorted loudly. "Nice one! Though you really could use a tattoo. I saw a great steampunk one where you'd look like your skin was peeling and you were a robot underneath . . ."

"Nice!" Rob said.

"Stop it! Both of you!" Cam was squeamish about needles and didn't really like tattoos anyway, but the idea of somebody actively getting one really turned her stomach.

Annie and Rob guffawed.

"You two aren't supposed to gang up on me," Cam said.

"You think this is ganging up? Ganging up is when we both tackle-tickle you," Annie said.

"Which we plan to do later," Rob said.

"Okay, no more bonding time for the two of you!" Cam

shouted, which made them laugh all the harder. Finally Cam couldn't help but join them.

When they stopped, she explained the plan to get near Vera, and her idea that Rob could give Cam swimming pointers.

"Then maybe I could get frustrated and ask for her help instead," Cam said.

"Or I could flirt with her. I'm a whole lot better looking than Chad Phillips."

"Smarter, too," Annie said.

"I think power is her drug," Cam said.

"So I make up a pedigree."

"You really are set on pretending to be one of these silver-spooned playboys, aren't you?" Cam said.

"I might be. I'd love to test whether I can do undercover or not."

The idea finally hit Cam for what it was. It wasn't acting or playing around. He wanted to test himself as a reporter. "That's sort of hot."

"You didn't think it was hot before," he said.

"I didn't understand why you wanted to. It just seemed dangerous. Now it's more like . . . Woodward and Bernstein."

"Only taller," he said.

"That's an illusion created by Dustin Hoffman," Annie said.

Cam laughed. She didn't know if the reporters were tall or short, but the assessment amused her.

"Okay. We fight. You flirt. I storm off. You see what you can find out. But no following through," Cam said.

"Got it."

"And if she's with anyone, we're back to my plan. She won't want to seem like she's flirting when her husband and father both recently passed."

"I forgot about that. Do you think she'll even talk to me?" Rob asked.

"My money is on yes," Annie said. "But go with a Speedo just in case."

Cam glared at Annie.

Jake arrived a little while later. His burger had cooled, but he was happy to disarm and eat and drink. He sat contentedly at the table and looked at the other three.

"So . . . how's it going?" Jake said.

Cam was on her third glass of wine by then, and was a notorious lightweight, so this struck her as funny. She leaned over to Annie and stage-whispered, "Does he know?"

Rob looked annoyed, but Annie didn't miss a stride.

"No. And it won't be a surprise if you tell him." She made it sound like they had been talking about some grand adventure rather than the snooping about Vera they planned to do. Jake was used to Annie and liked surprises, so he just grinned.

"So how's the investigation going?" Rob asked. "You ever follow up with those poker guys?"

"One of them. He said it was personal. The wife—Sullivan's wife—was mentioned, but it's hard to say."

"Does he know about the affair?" Cam whispered.

Jake narrowed his eyes. "What affair?"

Rob shook his head. "Cam can't hold her liquor."

"It's wine," she said.

Annie snorted.

"What affair?" Jake repeated.

"There is an unconfirmed rumor," Rob said, leering at Cam, "that Vera Windermere-Sullivan is having an affair with Chad Phillips—that she wanted to leave her husband, but her father objected."

"And where would this rumor come from?" Jake asked.

"Cam and I attended the funeral—out of respect, of course. Vera's mother—Derrick's ex-wife—might have said something to that effect. There was definitely a scene between Chad Phillips and Len Sullivan."

"Lenny was there?"

"He's sort of family," Annie said. "His brother's father-in-law died—it isn't such a stretch it was expected he would be there. Especially as his own brother also just died."

"Your dad and Elle were there," Rob said to Annie, "probably for the same reason, though they didn't stick around for the reception."

"And the two murders were probably connected," Jake said.

"Makes so much more sense than Vivian Macy as a suspect," Cam said.

Rob pinched her.

On cue, her dad knocked at the back door.

"Well it does!" Cam said as she let her dad in, trying her best to sober herself when she realized who it was.

Jake narrowed his eyes at Cam. "What do you care about Vivian Macy?" he asked.

"She's an old friend of my parents," Cam said.

"And a fine woman," her dad said softly.

"That doesn't mean she didn't have means, motive, and opportunity."

"Though the fact that she didn't actually have opportunity does," Cam said.

She caught Rob smirking and her dad grinning. She was glad he seemed not to care that she was obviously tipsy.

"It's true," Annie said. "Solid alibi for both murders."

"She isn't the kind of person to get her own hands dirty. She was in contact with a suspected hit man," Jake said.

"What?" Cam blurted.

"Brian Fontana. Calls her on a regular basis."

"And he's a hit man?"

Cam's dad was shaking his head.

"Suspected," Jake said.

"But not in jail? Like . . . you don't actually know . . ." Cam said.

"He makes problems go away."

"Like a security guard?" Cam said.

"That's his title, according to Vivian Macy, yes."

"Why on earth would you think he's a hit man?"

"People have a habit of disappearing when they bother one of his clients."

"But nothing can be proven?"

"Not yet," Jake looked annoyed.

"This sounds like we just need to ask him," Annie said.

"I don't know that that's necessary," Cam's dad said. "He and she talk because they're family. He's a nephew. Nothing suspicious in talking to a nephew. And he *is* a security guard, so when she has events, she hires him. But that's not so strange—when you need something done, hire a family member."

Jake stared. He clearly hadn't realized he was in the middle of the Vivian Macy fan club.

"Maybe we just find a couple of these people rumored to have disappeared," Cam said.

"Okay, this little investigation game needs to be over," Jake said.

"Tell you what," Rob said. "Tell us a few more details, and if you can convince us, we'll drop it. Starting with why the other poker buddies haven't been talked to."

"Look. Thanks for the grub, but I don't need this." Jake stood, ready to go.

Annie went to him and put her arms around him, "Please. This is important to Cam's dad, who you know has supported me when no one else would."

It was an exaggeration, but the comment was pointed at Jake. Cam and Rob had believed in Annie when she was accused of murder, but Jake hadn't. It had been Cam's dad who bailed Annie out and helped explain her behavior, which at the time had been strange. With him present, it was a point much harder to ignore.

Jake made a sour face, but he sat back down. "Okay. I'll entertain your theories. I will only answer questions about whether your guesses are on or off. No confidential info, but I can give you some warmer/cooler clues."

Annie kissed him soundly and then fetched him a cupcake.

They all continued talking for another hour or so, Jake confirming the details they'd learned about Vivian and how the two dead men were connected to her. Cam was impressed her dad could refrain from commenting, but then he had a bit of practice. Jake wasn't willing to believe their conspiracy theories, but he promised to look into any connection between Vera and Chad Phillips. And through it all, no mention was made of the undercover mission set for the next day with Vera Windermere-Sullivan.

When they got back to Cam's apartment, Rob opened Cam's computer.

"What are you doing?"

"Hunch," he said.

"About?"

"Brian Fontana. I know that name."

A picture popped up and Rob nodded. "That's what I thought. I didn't recognize him when I was there, but this is the guy from Chad Phillips's office."

"He's working with Chad Phillips? And calling Vivian? That doesn't make any sense."

"None at all, but I'm sure this is the same guy."

"So even if he's a hit man, it may have nothing to do with Vivian."

"I'm more likely to believe she's set her own spy, or

maybe he's taken it on himself . . . help his aunt and all," he said.

"Oh, man."

"No. It's good. It's a sneaky tactic that is not nearly as extreme as murder."

CHAPTER 16

The stakeout started way too early the next morning. Cam felt guilty, on top of it. She'd told Evangeline what she was up to but had called in sick to her boss, Madeline Leclerc. A murder that didn't involve a Roanoke Garden Society member as a suspect was not of interest to Madeline, even if the woman had urged Cam to "solve" the first pair of murders that had brushed past the RGS radar. When Cam thought about it, she was lucky she still had a job with how that one had turned out. Madeline hadn't been at all pleased.

The country club had a huge parking lot and apparently a lot of golfers and early-morning exercisers, so it was easy to pass unnoticed as they sat looking out for Vera Windermere-Sullivan's BMW. At around ten, Rob sent Cam to buy coffee and he hovered in the trees near the entrance, but there was still no sign of their quarry.

Only after eleven did she finally appear. Cam thought she looked the worse for wear—like maybe she'd partied all night and was now here to try to get back some semblance of respectability. They gave her about five minutes and then followed her in with their guest passes.

Once they'd given Evangeline's name and the passes to the front desk, they each headed separately to the locker rooms and planned to meet at the pool.

Cam changed and went out, but there was only a pair of old women swimming laps. She wondered if she'd missed some key piece of information about Vera's workout, and when Rob came out they discussed it, guessing Vera had probably stopped in the sauna. Cam headed back to check and, sure enough, there she was.

"Oh. I'm sorry. I didn't mean to interrupt," Cam said as she entered.

Vera didn't answer. In fact she didn't open her eyes. She was propped against the cedar wall, clutching her towel as if it would leave her of its own accord.

Cam sat a step lower. She knew heat rose and was feeling the dehydrating effects of the wine from the night before. Thankfully, she'd had about three bottles of water while they watched for Vera that morning. She really hated to sweat but tried to fake enjoying it, wishing Annie had taken the early shift.

"Do you come here a lot?" Cam asked.

"Mmmm."

Cam took that for an affirmative, but one not meant to encourage conversation.

"Because my boyfriend and I are thinking about joining. We're checking it out today."

The woman opened an eye, but gave no more encouragement than that.

"Do you like it?"

"It's pretty pedestrian if you've ever spent any time at a club in a city, but it seems to be the best of the very limited selection around here. I've been a member my whole life, but I've been to all the others."

"You have? Would you be willing to tell me about some of them?" Cam hoped the eager-beaver icebreaker would get Vera talking, and apparently the encouragement to talk a little trash was what was needed. Vera rattled on for about ten minutes about the other clubs. Unfortunately, Cam was beginning to feel light-headed.

"I am so sorry. You've been so nice to me, but I'm not used to this sauna. I think I'm going to go swim a few laps," she said.

She almost fell over as she left, so it was a good thing she hadn't stayed longer. She had several drinks from the water cooler and then made her way out to the pool where Rob was already swimming laps.

She stopped on the edge and watched him with pleasure. He played baseball in the summer, but took care to get some exercise year-round and he sure looked good in a swimsuit—sort of a Speedo, but the kind with longer legs. He insisted trunks caused too much resistance, and that was okay. He filled these out well. He stopped at the wall in front of her and looked at her questioningly.

"Just admiring your form," Cam said.

He grinned. "She coming?" he whispered.

"Yes, but we have a minute, or possibly several. I had to get out of there, though. I almost passed out."

"Yeah, I thought you might be heat sensitive. So let's make this look real."

"What do you mean?"

"I'm going to help you work on your stroke—it means I get to put my hands all over you," he teased.

Cam rolled her eyes, but other than an older man in the end lane, they were alone in the pool at present, and the idea didn't sound too bad, so she jumped in beside him, then came up with a squeal.

"That's cold!"

"It's not bad when you're moving. It's a good temperature

for laps, actually. A lot better than some of the silly pools I've been in that are for geriatric water aerobics or something."

"You be nice," Cam said.

"I'm just saying warm is fine if you're standing around, but cool is better to swim."

She liked warm better, but she knew Rob was probably right.

They made a good effort at "Rob helping Cam," at least to the degree she could control how ticklish she was. She tried extra hard when she saw Vera come out in her sleek black suit and dive into the lane next to them. She went down and back ten times before she stopped to talk to them.

"So what are you two doing?" she asked.

"This is my boyfriend, Rob. Rob, this is . . . wait. I didn't get your name," Cam said.

"Vera."

"Vera. Nice to meet you. Anyway, Rob swam in high school and so he's trying to help me swim better."

"I did that," Vera said. "Club team here and then my high school. You from around here?"

Cam thought she was flirting with Rob, which annoyed her, but then that *had* been one of their plans. She just wished it hadn't been so easy to get it going.

"I grew up in Michigan," Rob said. "And it was water polo, actually. At least once I hit high school."

She giggled. "Race you." And then dived under water.

Rob, ever competitive, dived too, without even giving it a thought. Cam moved over a lane. She thought about swimming a lap, and then debated the importance of being there when they got back. Finally, she let the mission win. Rob would get more out of Vera if they could bond as swimmers. He knew the cover story and he was a reporter. She pushed herself off the wall and made an attempt at a real lap.

Rob and Vera were laughing and in conversation when

she reached the original side again. She thought she might be getting a stitch and scolded herself for getting out of shape, even though she rode her bicycle regularly. She took a breath and pushed herself to do another lap to give Rob time to work Vera.

When she finally arrived back a second time, Rob thankfully stopped her.

"Cam, Vera is the daughter of the man from the funeral we went to Monday—Derrick Windermere's daughter."

Cam gave her best surprised face. "I didn't recognize you with no clothes and your hair up. I'm so sorry about your dad."

"Yes, well . . . I appreciate that. And I'm sad, of course. But there is a part of me relieved to not have my life meddled in anymore."

"Oh! I guess I can see that. He was very powerful. My best friend is Senator Schulz's daughter, so I know powerful men can be fairly opinionated."

She didn't share that strong people didn't let that stop them. Not everybody could be Annie. Probably if everybody were, chaos would reign, but Cam knew which kind of person she preferred as a best friend.

"I think I've met that friend of yours—Annie. Mike, my husband, was the brother of the Senator's wife, Elle. We were at their wedding."

"*Was* her brother?" Cam said, hoping she wasn't overdoing her acting.

"Mike was killed this week, too. It's been a horrible week."

Vera seemed to take heart in the sympathy Cam and Rob offered her, so maybe it wasn't overly contrived. They swam some more, or rather Rob and Vera did, Cam moving to the Jacuzzi spa, and then Vera offered to treat them to lunch in the bar.

"It's the same menu as the clubhouse, but with a much better choice of cocktails," she said.

Cam fought the impulse to seek out the clock. She could tell something had transpired conversationally between Rob and Vera. Vera kept saying it was so nice to talk to someone who wasn't giving her advice or judging her, so somewhere they'd shared something. She tried to squash the fact that it bothered her. And she couldn't be sure whether she was jealous that Vera was flirting with her boyfriend, or jealous her boyfriend was the one making progress on the investigation. Either reason was silly. This was the plan. But it didn't stop her from ordering a salad with fresh crab on it for lunch. If Vera was paying, a small part of her wanted to take advantage.

Rob ordered a Cobb salad and a beer, and Vera a cup of soup with a roll and a glass of wine. By the time their food arrived, Vera was ready for a second glass, but Cam wasn't going to complain. Her sweet tea was just fine and it would give her and Rob a conversational advantage.

"I am so sorry you have to deal with all of this tragedy. Do they know anything about who might have killed your dad yet?" Rob said.

"Mike was murdered, too."

"That's horrible," Cam gasped.

"Were the deaths related then?" Rob asked.

"I can't see how. They ran in entirely different circles."

"So what did Mike do?" Cam asked.

Vera sighed. "He worked for Windermere, which I know sounds like I'm contradicting myself. But seriously. He was a nobody in the company. It was just Daddy being charitable."

"Speaking of Windermere," Rob said, "I hope this isn't too personal . . . was there some sort of lawsuit trying to get your dad out of Chrysanthemum Holdings?"

"Wouldn't surprise me at all. Dozens of people would have liked him out of their way. Possibly even Heather, claiming in his right mind he would have married her, though the reality is, he couldn't. Mother was blackmailing him on that front. She claims she was protecting my interests, but I think she just never wanted a second Mrs. Windermere."

"Heather. That's his . . ."

"Heather Saunders. Girlfriend. For ages."

"And your mother kept them from marrying?"

"Believe me. She has piles of dirt on my dad. She wouldn't use it, of course. It would mess with her alimony. But she threatened to where Heather was concerned."

"Do you know anything else about Chrysanthemum Holdings?"

"Only that that Melvin Entwhistle is a piece of work. My father never should have trusted that weasel."

"Melvin? Really. Weasel how?"

"Oh, it's nothing, I'm sure. He just gives me the creeps."

That seemed to have turned Vera off from official conversation. Instead she wanted to know about what part of Michigan Rob was from, how he'd ended up in Roanoke, and how he and Cam had met. Cam felt like a third wheel, but they'd gotten a lot of valuable information, so she tried not to pout about it as Vera talked through a third glass of wine and a single bite of her berry sherbet.

CHAPTER 17

When Rob dropped Cam off at her place, she had to lie down for a while. She'd forgotten how much energy swimming took. Finally she dragged herself to the shower, as this was the night she was scheduled to bartend with Dylan. She had a new appreciation now for Rob's feelings on the matter. She'd acted far less jealous than Rob had, but then again, the ruse with Vera had been agreed upon beforehand.

Hopefully, because Rob knew what she was doing with the bartending gig, he wouldn't be upset this time. That reminded her of the very steamy, if slightly medicated, kiss she'd once shared with Dylan. A secret she intended to take to her grave.

Cam chose a shortish black skirt and white cotton blouse for the night. She figured she looked like a waitress in it. Overly traditional would be the only criticism, and probably not a lot of that, as she was showing some leg.

Annie let herself in while Cam was dressing and lectured Cam on safety, hanging a thin rope around her neck with a small container of mace at the end before she left again. Cam wondered when Annie had become the paranoid one, but then remembered that their past investigations had gone a lot worse for Annie than Cam, and it couldn't hurt to have this just in case.

Dylan had agreed to pick her up to go to the "casino," which wasn't a casino at all, but a lush game room in one of the fancier homes west of Roanoke. At seven, he arrived and they drove to Copperbrook to set up. It was a strange name for a manor, but Cam was willing to bet that money from copper mining had paid for the place.

A maid let them in and led them through to the back of the house. The room was decorated in dark wood with thick-cushioned, tapestry-covered furniture. It was semicircular and had windows with a view of the Blue Mountains on the south side, though it was only a silhouette, as the sun had set just before they arrived. More impressive to Cam was the view to the east of a large greenhouse filled with a variety of flowers and vegetables. Drawn, she moved toward it and peered through the glass. Though the light of the day was fading, she saw one corner with tropical flowers— African violets and bird of paradise—that were still under lights. Nearer to her were orchids and hibiscus on one wall and tomatoes on the other. Someone loved both flowers and fresh food.

"Ahem!"

Cam started and turned back around to find Dylan, ready to instruct her.

The bar was an old-fashioned one, pretty big for somebody's home. There was room for half a dozen tables, but at the moment, there was clearly only one table that mattered. A large round table with a felt top trimmed in wood sat at the center of the room, all others pushed to the periphery. She wondered if it had come from Atlantic City or something. It had an air of being expensive and seedy at the same time.

"You ever tend bar before?" Dylan asked.

"No."

"Well-drinks . . . you know what those are, right?"

"One liquor, one mixer."

"Right. You can probably do those. One third alcohol, two thirds mixer for most—half and half at the main table. High-end booze allows us to charge more, so use it for everyone, unless they give you a brand. Then do what they want. Beer and wine are easy. You get any mixed-drink orders, otherwise tell me."

"Got it."

"Don't ask any questions. That going to screw you up?"

"I was actually just hoping to observe."

"Yeah. That's better. But try not to be too obvious about it. It's not like these people want their business in the tabloids, so they're paying attention to who's paying attention, if you know what I mean."

That worried Cam. She'd sort of thought, as a waitress, she would fly under the radar.

"So how many people are usually here?" she asked.

"Five or six players at the main table. Anywhere between nobody and a dozen watching. If the main game isn't too big a deal, sometimes there's another game or two at the other tables."

"And are they going to be okay with two bartenders?"

"I expect the higher-end turnout tonight. Sully's death will bring some more people out of respect, so they'll be glad I anticipated and they don't have to wait for drinks."

"So they're gambling? With a dead friend?"

"Well, sure. It's what they did with him. How better to pay their respects? Probably more girls, too."

"But playing, it's all men?"

"All but one time that I ever saw. That Ellie was a firecracker."

"Ellie? Elle Chamberlain Schulz?"

Dylan shrugged.

"Was she Sully's sister?"

Cam could see recognition cross his face. "Yeah. I think she was."

"That's Annie's stepmother."

He stared at her like she'd just grown a third eye.

"How often has she been here?" Cam asked.

"Only once that I was, but everybody knew her so I figured she'd been here a couple times before."

"You don't think she'll be here tonight, do you?"

"I have no idea."

Cam thought about Elle and her very recent reconciliation with her husband and doubted it. Elle had bigger things to manage, even if she was grieving for her brother.

They were set up early, as Dylan was used to working alone, so Cam took a soft rag and began to wipe the brass rail that ran around the base of the bar. She had just finished when the first players began arriving.

Cam listened and let Dylan greet people. She poured several drinks as they ordered, so Dylan could just grab them and deliver them immediately. She was surprised how well they worked together, considering she'd never waitressed before. She had managed a lot of parties, though, and the size of this crowd was far more comparable to that than a real restaurant.

Cam recognized several faces as they came in, including the gambling trio Rob had pointed out at the funeral. The lawyer had a young man trailing him who came over to get their drinks, and she thought he looked a little familiar but couldn't place him. The only face that gave her pause was Melvin Entwhistle. She hadn't expected to see him in this environment. He looked at her closely, but must have decided he only recognized her from a similar job, as his face didn't change expression.

People continued to mill for a long while, renewing drinks and talking and laughing. Then, at a little before nine, a whale of a man with silver hair, black pants, and a pin-striped vest entered the room. He had a cigar, which would have been illegal had this not been a private residence. He lumbered to the far side of the main table and sat. The four men who were meant to play poker with him sat around him immediately as a hush fell over the room.

"Who's that?" Cam asked, as Dylan poured a bourbon on the rocks.

"Harry Taggert. This is his house."

Cam's knees nearly buckled. He was rumored to be a mobster, though he managed to never get caught at anything. Cam thought the pictures the newspaper had of him must have been fifteen years old. He was significantly heavier and grayer now, though she supposed the expression was familiar. She was pondering what a strange world this was that a known mobster would be a gardening buff when she heard her name.

"Cam?"

Cam was startled out of her observation and turned to see Elle standing at the bar.

"Elle! How nice to see you."

"What are you doing here?" Her voice held suspicion, but it was quiet.

"I'll bring a drink right over to you, what would you like?"

"Chardonnay, if you've got a good one."

She went and stood off from the crowd. Annie complained Elle was a bimbo, but she'd clearly gotten Cam's hint that she would answer her question if they could have just a little privacy. She opened a new bottle of chardonnay and poured a glass, taking it to Elle.

"Here you are," Cam said in a normal voice, and then she lowered it to a whisper. "I'm trying to help figure out who killed your brother and why. My boyfriend is a reporter, but I was the one who had a way in here."

"Oh?"

"I'm friends with the bartender. He said I could help."

Elle turned to stare at Dylan. "Interesting. Well, I'm all for your quest, so I certainly won't say anything. I may not be the only familiar face here tonight, though. They're donating half the winnings to a charity Mikey chose. Homeless kids. He wanted to build them a rec room—give them something to do off the street."

"That was nice of him," Cam said.

"It was. I'm in the game second round."

"Well good luck!"

At that, a circle of women called Cam over and she took drink orders, though she had to ask Dylan to make them, as she had never made a dirty martini—in fact she wasn't sure what one was.

"It's just extra olive-y," he explained as he made it.

Cam frowned as she watched. This had less appeal to her than, say, an appletini—something she had actually bothered to try. She had to stick to her "can't handle the alcohol" policy too often to try many things like that. Mostly she just drank wine.

She delivered the drinks and spotted something that hadn't even occurred to her, though it should have when she learned the proceeds were going to Mike's charity. Vera Windermere-Sullivan had just entered. Fortunately, she was shoving her fur coat at someone and so not looking in Cam's direction.

Cam put the last drink down and scrambled back behind the bar.

"Shoot," she whispered.

"What?"

"She knows who I am. Rob and I met her earlier today."

"Who is she?" Dylan asked.

"She hasn't been here before?"

"Why would she be?"

"She's Sully's wife."

Dylan understood the ramifications immediately and bolted over to Vera to see what she wanted to drink and make sure she never had to look to the bar. Cam tried to think of a way she could change her appearance, but her shoulder-length hair was only so flexible, and Cam had had it down both when they were in the sauna and back when they'd swum together.

She looked to the other side of the room, hoping she could keep it happy and Dylan could run the side Vera was on, along with the table that was the center of attention.

She saw Melvin Entwhistle called over to consult with a man at the table, the one Rob had said at the funeral was Big Al, though he looked fairly svelte next to Harry Taggert. Melvin nodded a lot and then patted his breast pocket. Cam wondered what planet they were on that this was somehow considered investing, but it wasn't really her business. She realized that another familiar face was also on the other side of the room—Heather Saunders, Derrick Windermere's girlfriend. She was leering at Vera. Cam hoped Heather's evil eye would keep Vera from looking toward her, and she hustled back to fill the drink orders she had just taken.

"You realize this place is a time bomb," she whispered to Dylan.

"I'm getting that sense, yes." He was grinning. She didn't have time to ask what was so amusing, though. She thought they would both draw far less attention if they were completely efficient, so she hurried to keep up with the increased flow of alcohol.

Her plan worked, right until the change in table participants. Harry Taggart stood and went through the door to the greenhouse, breathing in what Cam knew would be warm, humid air. She wondered why a man who liked that so much would also enjoy cigars. The two were opposite. The other players and observers took Harry's hint and all got up to mingle. Suddenly everyone's attention focused on a broader scope, and Vera spotted Cam. She started to make her way over to question Cam, but was intercepted. Time slowed to a crawl.

Heather grabbed Vera's shoulder and spun her. "What are you doing here?" Her volume was low, but the tone of it carried.

Cam made her way over to Elle, who was casually seating herself at the poker table.

"Do you know what this is about?"

"Money. Vera is inheriting it, and Heather thinks it should be her. Probably she's right. They lived together nine years, but Derrick treated her like a dog. Until Mikey died, though, I wanted Vera to have it because then Mikey would be set."

"Have they always fought like this?"

"Not outwardly. They usually avoid each other. But Vera grumbled a lot. I'd bet Heather grumbled more, but she avoided me, too—knew I was Vera's family."

At that point, though, Vera slapped Heather, and chaos ensued as several people tried to pull the women apart. Elle stood and gave a whistle that shocked Cam.

"Heather, I know you're upset about your loss. We're sad for you, sweetheart. But tonight is about Mikey, so if you can't leave his poor widow in peace, you probably shouldn't be here." She sat down and took a sip of her drink. The majority of the other people in the room silently went back to what they were doing, but Cam saw two large men take Heather by the arms and escort her out.

Vera finally made her way to Cam.

"Are you following me?"

"No! I had no idea you'd be here! I didn't know this game was raising money for Mr. Sullivan until I got here. I'm just moonlighting. I swear."

"And how do you know my sister-in-law?"

"We talked about Senator Schulz earlier. Remember?"

Vera frowned and seemed to remember. "You're sure this has nothing to do with me?"

"What would it? I only just met you today."

"Could I get a dirty martini?" she asked.

Cam nodded and rushed off. She thought she'd figured it out, so she just made the drink and rushed back with it. The woman needed to relax, and Cam thought she might benefit if Vera's inhibitions were toned down.

"Here you go," Cam said, handing it to her.

"I'm sorry I went off on you," Vera said. "I just get paranoid. A woman with money has to be so careful."

"I imagine that's true," Cam said.

"Do you come from money?"

"Not particularly. We weren't poor, but my dad was just a carpenter. I guess in those days it was decent, but not fancy."

"You're lucky. You know who your friends are."

"You know, I've had a best friend for a very long time with the same issues, so I really do know what you're talking about. Annie always handled it by being a little outrageous. If she was sort of out there, then the people concerned about appearances shied away. I guess in her family, it was more about power than money."

"She's lucky she had the courage to do it that way. I really just relied on being a rebellious bad girl, but that got me about what I deserved."

"I don't think anyone deserves to be taken advantage of, if that's what you mean."

"No. I just married my bad boy, and . . ."

She trailed off and Cam debated whether to probe.

"Did he get mixed up with the wrong people or some-thing then?" Cam said.

"Oh, which set?" Vera said quietly.

"There were lots of wrong people?" Cam asked, not sure she'd understood.

"The loan sharks, the drug dealers, the money launder-ers. You can find all three right here."

Cam feigned shock but didn't want to overdo it. "But they all seem to really have liked him."

"Sure. When he was paid up."

"I'm . . . um . . . sorry about that. I'm sure it was hard. Why didn't you leave him?"

She laughed bitterly then and handed Cam her empty glass. It had been too quick for as much alcohol as was in it, but Cam knew it worked in her favor, so she rushed back to make another one, ignoring an annoyed look from Dylan that she wasn't pulling her weight with the other guests. She would catch up in a minute and help him out.

"Here you go," Cam said, handing her the drink.

"Thank you. It's just . . . leaving was never an option. Not for a shallow girl like me. Dad said he'd marry what's-her-name if I didn't stay married to Mike. That meant half or more of his fortune, which isn't nearly so enormous as he pretended, would go to her. If he really was enormously rich, that would have been one thing, but I'm used to a cer-tain lifestyle. I just couldn't take that chance."

Cam doubted it would have left Vera clipping coupons. His fortune couldn't be *that* small in reality, but she had some idea what wealthier people worked with. Derrick Win-dermere certainly had lived like a very wealthy man, so his daughter was used to that, too.

"How did he do everything he did if he didn't have . . ."

"Oh, he wrote it all off! Wining and dining clients, travel, club memberships. All part of doing business with the peo-ple he did business with."

Cam wondered what job she could do that would require her to go for massages and get her nails done. She knew in spite of liking that kind of luxury, she actually had too strong a work ethic.

"I should probably get back to helping out," Cam said. More glares were coming her way than just Dylan's, so she rushed to take care of several clusters of people. Now that she was in a hurry, she didn't feel nearly as efficient at the task. In fact, she was beginning to feel a lot more sympathy for waitresses than she ever had before. It wasn't that she'd thought they were lazy or anything, but it seemed a job anybody ought to be able to do. She found that being in a hurry, trying to remember too many things, and being constantly interrupted by people made for great difficulties in getting the right drinks to the right people.

When shouting arose at the poker table, everyone seemed to forget they were still missing drinks. One of the men had stood and stormed to the door. He had Chad Phillips, who'd been trying to enter, by the collar, but the bigger news was an accusation at the table that one of the other players had stolen the man's chips when he walked away. The man who'd walked away was Big Al, and Cam watched as Melvin pulled the man's chair over backward and began hitting the man next to him in the face.

Finally, the whale man, Harry Taggert, stood and shouted. "This is supposed to be a civilized game in memory of Sully! Sully was the best of us and we should be respectful!" He picked up Elle's hand then and kissed it.

Cam wondered if she should just get as far out of the way as possible or if people would remember they were thirsty any minute and start clamoring for their drinks again. She decided to err on the side of delivery. She thought she could watch for flying bodies, and hoped that Harry had actually just halted any other bad behavior, so she rushed to pour several drinks and get them to the next table on her list.

Unfortunately, that was when Melvin spotted her, or rather, finally seemed to recognize her. He came toward Cam with unusual speed and grabbed her arm.

"Well, don't you seem to be everywhere?"

"I beg your pardon?" Cam said.

"You planned that little shindig where Windermere got offed, didn't you?"

Chad came over and the two had a whispered conversation, Melvin never letting go of Cam's arm.

Vera stood and stared at Cam. She hadn't known that detail.

"I helped with it, yes."

"And then what are you doing *here*?"

"Chad?" Vera said. "This isn't the place. You really shouldn't be here," she said. "And . . ." She gestured to Melvin, and Chad pulled at his arm so he finally let go of Cam.

Chad made an ugly face and then turned to leave. Everybody backed away a step to let him pass like he was contagious. Cam thought it was over, but Vera rounded on her.

"You were there when my dad died?"

"Yes. I was working. I told you . . ."

"So you really have been following me around?"

Another woman neared them whom Cam only now recognized from the funeral. Cam tried to remember what her story that day had been. Something about working with Windermere, but she knew she was busted. What she didn't know was how to spin this so it sounded perfectly reasonable. It was something she did well, but not on the fly. She had never been able to improvise well. She closed her eyes and tried to conjure Annie. Annie would have the perfect cover story.

"Look, I know it all seems odd, but I swear. I was at both events because I am best friends with Annie Schulz. She asked me to help with the other, and Elle alerted me they might need help here. I just bought a new car and my savings is depleted, so they were both doing me a favor."

"The club?"

"Complete coincidence."

"But you're not thinking of joining?"

"No. I thought we'd be treated better if we said that. Evangeline Patrick is a friend of mine, and I did her a favor recently, so she gave us a few guest passes. That's all."

"You're sure?"

"Positive. What was that all about?" Cam pointed to where Chad had just left.

"You know who that is, don't you?"

"He's a politician. I recognize his face, but don't know him by name." Cam hoped she could pull off this lie.

"Well, I apologize for his paranoia, and more so for his friend's." She glared at Melvin. "I suspect he thinks you're an enemy spy working to undermine his campaign." She laughed then, which relieved Cam. Whatever relationship Vera had with Chad, she at least seemed to have a read on what he saw as important—him.

All in all, Cam was glad when the night was finally over. Her feet ached, her brain was numb, and she felt like the stickiness from the soda dispenser would never come off. More than nineteen thousand dollars was collected for Mike Sullivan's charity, something that amazed Cam, though she'd seen the guy there giving charity receipts to people, winners and losers alike, so there was a tax benefit. It was strange to imagine these thug do-gooders. It all seemed so contrary.

She and Dylan took more than an hour to clean up after the place had cleared out.

"Didn't know you'd be bringing your own excitement," he said.

"Not on purpose! I had no clue those people would be here."

"I probably wouldn't have guessed it, either, so don't worry too much. Couple of fights, though? Especially that catfight. I was hoping . . ."

"Yes, yes. That they'd get to hair pulling and wrestling and then they'd kiss," Cam said.

"No. I've just never seen a chick haul off and deck another chick before. Like a punch. I was hoping for blood."

Cam rolled her eyes.

"Only because I sort of know this crowd. I wouldn't want to see *you* in a fight like that or anything."

"That's good, because I'm a major wimp."

"You are not. Are you forgetting you rescued me once?"

Cam laughed. It was true. She, Annie, and Benny had rescued Dylan, but it had nearly been a fiasco.

She was glad when they finally finished cleaning up and she could just sit in the passenger seat of his pickup with the window cracked.

R ob was waiting for her when she got home. She was surprised to see it was barely past midnight. She kicked off her shoes and flopped onto her futon.

Rob gave a bemused look. "So . . . rough night?"

"Why did nobody tell me how hard waitressing is?"

"It is?"

"Yes. We should tip like thirty percent from now on."

"Thirty!"

She turned and threw her feet across his lap.

"That bad, huh?"

She propped herself on a couple of pillows and lay back while he massaged her feet.

"Ouch! Gentle! I think the bottoms are bruised."

"You get hazard pay?"

"No, but I made seventy-two dollars, and that was with

Dylan penalizing me for the half hour I spent talking to our friend Vera."

"Vera was there?"

"She thought I was following her. That I was some tabloid reporter or something."

"Imagine what she'd do if she knew I *really* was a reporter."

"And Elle had to protect me . . ."

"Say what?"

"I told her I was looking into her brother's death—with you, for your job. Which I sort of am, right?" Cam asked.

Rob scoffed. "If you say so."

"I figured it would keep her on my side. It's something she wants solved. And if we solve the murders, then it works for everyone, right?"

"You're a spin queen. You do know that?"

Cam sighed. "Part of the job."

"But yes. If we do what we're trying to do for your dad, we also figure out who the killer is, and that will make Elle happy, so there's no harm in it." Rob said. "Say, speaking of Vivian . . ."

Cam had been about to drift off, but that brought her around again, especially as they *hadn't* been speaking of Vivian. "Yeah?"

"I've got a lot better grasp now on why the police have been so focused on her. If we look into the stuff, we . . . well, we either help them prove it was her, or we prove it couldn't have been. Do you want to pursue it?"

"Yes! I mean, I don't want it to be her, but I'd want my dad to be with a murderer even less, so either way we should definitely do it! What do you have?"

CHAPTER 18

As it turned out, Derrick Windermere's history with Vivian Macy was not strictly political animosity. Rob told Cam he'd turned on her because of something that had started romantically and then gone sour. Friends of Vivian's had admitted to police that they'd dated briefly, and when Vivian found out the kind of ethics he had in business, she'd ended it. He hadn't taken it well.

"How did you learn this?" Cam asked.

"Annie. Jake keeps a notebook and she keeps reading little bits. This was the first real surprise in a while."

Cam wondered if it was time to go talk to Vivian again. She thought the woman herself would have the best chance of clearing things up, even if the conversation would be awkward. She was a little worried, though, and felt maybe she should gather additional information before she pursued it directly. She considered going to her father, but he might be defensive or sensitive, and she imagined that if this really was headed in a romantic direction, Vivian might not have

revealed her past love-related fiascoes to him. She scanned
her brain for who else she knew who would know Vivian
well, and came to a very strange conclusion. Neil Patrick.

She'd never approached Mr. Patrick directly in a murder
investigation. She found his wife, Evangeline, significantly
more approachable. But Evangeline was too young to have
been a part of the social circle before Vivian left town to
make her name, returning only to take her place in local
politics. Cam thought Mr. Patrick had been at college with
her mom and Vivian, even if he was a little older. Besides
that, he'd been on every who's who list Roanoke had ever
produced, so he knew everyone involved, yet he hadn't been
one of the people pushing a specific political agenda. She
thought his neutrality would be good for getting at the truth,
unlike Samantha Hollister, who clearly didn't care for Vivian.

Then again, understanding *that* might be helpful, too.
She had a hard time thinking of a reason somebody wouldn't
like Vivian, unless their politics clashed, which they probably did. But Samantha's agenda seemed more personal.

As Cam sat at her desk trying to work, she debated whom
to talk to. As she went back and forth, Neil Patrick
returned from a meeting, so she decided to just bite the
bullet.

"Mr. Patrick? Do you have a minute?"

"Of course I do, Cammi! What can I do for you?"

She went into his office and shut the door, something that
caused an alarmed expression to cross his kindly face.

"I trust Evangeline. In fact if you'd like, she can come
in. It's just that we never know who *else* might come in,"
Cam said.

"I see." He didn't look particularly calmed by that.

"It's . . . the murder at the fund-raiser the other night . . .
and the one that followed in Newport News . . ."

Mr. Patrick looked confused, so Cam explained.

"Mike Sullivan, Derrick Windermere's son-in-law, was killed just a few days later."

Mr. Patrick's face fell. "This doesn't have to do with the Roanoke Garden Society, does it?"

"Not in any way I can think of. Actually, I'm helping my dad out. His lady friend, Vivian Macy, has been connected to both victims. And my dad asked me to help him show she didn't do it, and I don't think she did. But I'm also a little worried he's looking at this through . . . a filter . . . because he likes her. I just wanted to talk to somebody who knew all the parties, who'd been around Roanoke and politics for a long time. I mean, I like Vivian, but if she *is* a killer, I'd rather know and warn my dad. Do you . . . know her?"

"Of course I do. I've known her for years."

"Do you know anything about a romantic history with Derrick Windermere?"

His eyes popped and his jaw dropped. "Oh, I don't think so! I wouldn't imagine they'd get along. Derrick was always . . ."

"A little shady?" Cam finished.

"Well . . . yes."

"Evangeline said you didn't trust him."

"Not even a little. And that was before that deal Melvin talked me into where I lost my britches, so to speak."

"Why do you think Vivian might have been convinced to go out with him?"

"I can't think of anything except a mutual friend trying to set them up."

"Set them up? Like a joke?"

Mr. Patrick looked startled. "Well, no. That wasn't how I meant it; it seems like a rotten thing to do. But I suppose that could be true, too. I meant someone who . . . either didn't know one or the other of them very well. Just a date.

Attractive people, both divorced. There was a time divorce was sort of a mark of shame."

Cam knew in some upper circles, it still was, but Mr. Patrick, a widower, was too kind to say so.

"I suppose someone might be intentionally putting them in each other's path for other reasons," he continued.

"And why might they do that?"

He stroked his mustache and looked confused for a minute, and then narrowed his eyes. "Because they didn't have the power to get Derrick to stop his shenanigans, but wanted him to?"

"Somebody trying to scare him straight?"

"Yes. Like that."

"Might somebody trying to scare him straight have gotten angry if it didn't work?"

"Maybe. But I can't imagine a person who tried to help him do the right thing then committing murder if it didn't pan out."

That was true. The moralities didn't match.

"Did you know Mike Sullivan at all?"

"I can't say I did."

"He worked on Vivian's campaign for a while . . . stole some money."

Mr. Patrick shook his head, so Cam thought that was as far as she was going to get with him. It was an intriguing thought, though, somebody setting up Vivian Macy and Derrick Windermere—for whatever reason.

Cam worked for a few more hours, then decided to make an afternoon visit to Samantha's house. She was ready for the "anti" argument where Vivian Macy was concerned. She didn't think she could be convinced, but she thought she needed to hear it.

She called ahead. She'd dropped in on Samantha a number of times without calling, but sometimes the surprises she found there were too unsettling. Besides, she didn't want to solidify a reputation as being rude. Thankfully, Samantha was happy to talk to her and invited her out to her house.

"Camellia, darling! Come in!"

Cam was a little wrong-footed with the over-the-top hospitality and she felt a strange sense of déjà vu. She'd been here once before claiming to be worried about a loved one's romantic endeavors. It couldn't be helped, though. This really was an important angle, and since she had a precedent, convincing Samantha that was the total reason didn't seem improbable.

"Thank you so much for seeing me, Samantha. I know how busy you are."

"Nonsense. Now that that fund-raiser is over, I'm shopping at my leisure for the holidays. I'll have Thanksgiving at the country club. Margot is joining me, but you know my family history. Nobody else I really care to see."

Margot was Samantha's niece, and Margot's brother, an undeniable scoundrel, had been killed about six months earlier—the first murder Cam had solved. In fact, she didn't like to think about it, as it seemed to have set off a really bad string of luck where dead bodies were concerned.

"That sounds nice," Cam said. Nick was cooking her own family's Thanksgiving dinner. It was sure to be divine, as he was a great cook. Cam and Annie were on pie, roll, and eggnog duty. "I'm glad you're getting a break then."

"Gin and tonic?" Samantha asked.

"Yes please: weak, if you don't mind."

"Of course."

Samantha poured and chattered about how much money had been made for Jared Koontz at the fund-raiser.

"So how do you know Jared?" Cam asked.

Samantha paused and seemed to be thinking. "I'm pretty

sure I met him when he was working as a staff person for Alden."

"Was that before your falling out with Alden?"

Samantha narrowed an eye. "Now I wouldn't call it a falling out, exactly. Alden and I run in the same circles and have known each other a very long time. We get along for the most part. We've just had a few ugly disagreements over the years."

That hadn't been how Cam understood the relationship at all, especially as Samantha had recently suggested Alden murdered somebody. "Why did you think he would have killed Derrick Windermere?" she asked.

"Oh, that was silly impulse. Now those two I know didn't get along, but Derrick could rub people the wrong way. It's too bad, really. He was so charming."

Of all the adjectives she'd heard about Derrick Windermere, this was certainly the most surprising. It wasn't the first nice one. She'd heard "generous," or "smart," or "ambitious." But the man didn't seem very well liked. Charming went with likability in her mind.

"Listen, this is strange. My dad has asked me—he has been seeing Vivian Macy—I'm sure you noticed. And . . . well Vivian has been connected to Derrick. Dad wanted me to learn what I could to . . . cast doubt?"

"Oh, Cam, I don't know if that's such a good idea."

"Well, I'm not either. If Vivian did this, I certainly don't want a murderer dating my father! But . . . people seem to like her . . . except for you. So I thought maybe I should ask you to give me the other side of the story."

Samantha looked surprised, and Cam took a sip of her drink to try to appear relaxed. She hoped Samantha could calm down, too, and treat this like a normal conversation.

"She and I were friends once upon a time," Samantha said. "From years ago—elementary school, maybe. We always got along just fine. She changed though."

Cam tried not to cast any judgment about that. Change could be good or bad. It sort of depended on the direction. And Samantha was definitely a person Cam saw both good and bad in, so really, it wasn't fair to assume Vivian had improved and Samantha had stayed the same materialistic, vain person she'd been when she was younger.

"Somebody said Vivian and Derrick had dated. But . . . they seem ill suited. Do you know how that happened?"

"That was my own stupidity! Vivian was moving back to town after spending several years in Richmond, and I knew Derrick was just getting over his divorce. I thought they'd have fun together."

"*You* set them up?"

"I was trying to do a good deed! It was before I realized how much Vivian had changed."

"I see." And she did. Samantha was unlikely to try to make Derrick learn the importance of integrity—Samantha didn't seem all that concerned about alternative ethics. She didn't say it, but the thing that was still possible in Cam's mind was that Samantha really did know Vivian had changed for the better and maybe wanted to tarnish her reputation a little.

"So you don't think Vivian would . . . murder someone, do you?"

"Well, I never would expect that of anyone. In Vivian's case, part of it is that I don't think she'd get her hands dirty. But I wouldn't put it past her to . . . play victim and inspire somebody else to do it."

That didn't sound even remotely right to Cam. She wondered what exactly had happened between Samantha and Vivian that had soured their friendship so badly.

"So you think I really need to be cautious about Vivian. Should I worry about my dad?"

"Well, only if he gets in her way. I think she can be ruthless in her ambition."

"Would Derrick have gotten in her way?"

"I can't say. I think maybe he could have. He had great resources."

"So this would have been politically motivated? If she did it, I mean."

"Honey, ambition is all that woman has. Everything with her is politically motivated."

Cam finished her drink and thanked Samantha for her time. She left the conversation feeling more negatively about Samantha, rather than Vivian, but she knew she should try to maintain some objectivity. At least she had a good solid set of questions to ask Vivian.

Cam didn't want to go through her dad to set up a meeting with Vivian. She didn't believe, yet, that Vivian was dangerous, but at the same time, there had been enough doubt thrown out that she preferred to leave him out of it in case things didn't go well.

The trouble was, finding access to Vivian without going through her dad meant going back to her office to look at the official roster from the fund-raiser. She had never contacted Vivian directly except by email, and she couldn't think of another route to find the woman's personal contact information.

When she entered the Patrick Henry, it was evening; eerie piano was playing even though no sound system existed and the piano sat unattended. It was the haunted hotel stuff Annie loved to tease her with, but Cam had spent enough time there that she was starting to be fond of certain aspects of the haunting. Though as she came out of the elevator on the second floor, she had to amend that—not all of it pleased her. The smoky smell hovered from the man who'd been killed there in the twenties—the same man they'd based their murder mystery dinner on.

Through the glass doors she thought she saw a light from the door of Evangeline's office, but when she got inside, she realized she was mistaken. It must have been a reflection from the security lighting in the hallway. She locked the front door again behind her. She doubted anybody else would come into their private suite, but a woman alone at night couldn't be too careful. She went into her office and turned on the computer.

Cam logged on and accessed the shared folder with the contact information. Vivian's list was longer than most, so she hit "Print" to take the list with her. When she went out to the central office to retrieve it, she was grabbed from behind.

The man was strong, not particularly tall, but stocky, and he had gloves on. He pulled her back into Evangeline's office, where he had a chair and telephone cord waiting.

"Scream and I'll make this hurt," he said.

Cam nodded agreement but he strong-armed her anyway, slapping her. It wasn't so hard she blacked out, but it disoriented her and made it more difficult to fight him off. He wrestled her into the chair and tied her to it with the phone cord, shoving some sort of fabric in her mouth; then he came close to her face, a ski mask covering most of his. His eyes looked dark, but maybe only because it was dark in the room. All she could really see was the glistening intensity.

"You leave this alone! You are not ready for the answers you are going to find."

He left then. She heard the lock as he opened the door, followed by the elevator ping as it arrived to pick him up. When she finally believed he was gone and all she could hear was her own heart pounding in her chest, it was time to find a way out. She breathed in deeply, trying to focus. She imagined he had removed the mask and was nothing more now than a nondescript man in a dark suit.

Concentrate. She worked her tongue to force the

cloth—she'd identified it as a glove after having it against her tongue for a while—out of her mouth. It tasted disgusting, but she tried not to think about it. She managed to get the glove out, after a time, but didn't think screaming would help. Thankfully, the man had tied her to a wheeled chair. She used her legs to push to the desk, then threw one up to knock the phone on the ground. She had to use her feet to flip it over again and remove her sock to be able to push the buttons. She had to start over twice because she didn't have the dexterity in her toes. Finally, she managed to call Annie. Annie was physically closer, but more important, Annie's phone number could be pushed without having to go to the center of the grid of numbers, making it easier to dial. She hoped Annie had her phone on. The next obstacle was that she couldn't hear when it was answered, so she just began the mantra, "Tied in my office, come help me. Tied in my office, come help me."

Rob arrived first. She heard him shout as he came in and she responded with her own crazy screaming.

"Annie called. She was stuck on the other side of town, but she called me. What the heck happened?" Rob said as he worked the cord. "And why didn't you call 9-1-1?"

"I don't know—I think I panicked. Somebody thinks we're too close, but I have no idea who. We've been all over the board looking." She rubbed her wrists as Rob hugged her.

"I sure wish you'd stay out of these things," he said.

"I didn't really mean to end up gagged and tied to a chair. I was just here for a phone number, and we've *all* been asking questions."

"Obviously the right ones."

"Yeah. If we could just figure out *which* of the questions made someone nervous enough to try to scare me off," Cam said.

Rob helped her up. "Are you done for the night?"

"Hardly. I came here because I needed Vivian Macy's

contact information. Plus, we need to report what happened. They'll never catch this guy if we don't."

"*Now* you want to report it." Rob shook his head.

They called the security office from where they were, and while they waited for the man to come up from the basement, Cam dialed Annie to reassure her she was okay. Annie called her a whole slew of names, but Cam had to hang up when the security man arrived to get a statement. He assured Cam the police needed to be alerted, but agreed Cam could talk to them the next day. Then he left.

Rob frowned. "I guess that's that. Does that seem strange to you? Just letting you go without talking to the police tonight?"

Cam agreed it was, but was more relieved than anything. She felt like she wanted to get on with their business.

"Can we call Vivian together?" Rob said. "Ask her to meet us for a glass of wine or something?"

"Sure."

"Because that's my requirement from now on. Enough solo investigating for you."

"My *solo* stuff was with Mr. Patrick and Samantha. I am alone with them all the time anyway."

"Well, you spooked somebody."

"Maybe *we* did—or maybe it was about the poker game."

Rob sighed. He knew she was right. It was far more logical somebody from the night before had come after her than her employers.

"But how did they get in?" Rob asked.

"They had to already be here," Cam admitted. "Unless they got a key somehow, but I would have heard that."

"Exactly. Buddy system until we get this thing figured out."

Cam rubbed the side of her face. It was the first time

she'd been hit, at least since Petunia reached her teens. Somehow, after that, the buddy system didn't sound so bad. She agreed and then dialed Vivian, asking her to meet her and Rob at Arzu for a glass of wine.

Vivian sounded confused at first. She asked if she should bring Nelson, Cam's dad. But Cam explained she wasn't sure how comfortable Vivian would be because some of the questions had to do with old flames.

"Oh! Well aren't you mysterious? I'll see you in about forty minutes," she said.

Cam had Rob run her home to change, and then they went to Arzu to wait.

"This is going to be awkward, isn't it?" Rob said as they ordered a bottle of wine.

"Probably." She filled Rob in on what she'd learned so if she got tongue-tied, he could jump in. He was much better at these uncomfortable conversations than she was. When she reached the part about Samantha being the link, Vivian arrived, so Cam quit her tale midsentence.

Rob poured while Cam stood up to greet Vivian.

"Oh, this is so nice. I haven't been here for ages. It's one of my favorite restaurants."

Cam knew it was one of her dad's favorites, too, and wondered how they hadn't ended up here before. They ordered an appetizer and began with small talk, but Cam knew Vivian didn't have all night to devote to them, so she finally convinced herself to begin questioning her

"This is really awkward. But I know you know my dad wanted us to look into this. And I've just learned a couple of things that I felt like only you could explain."

"I have a habit of protecting my privacy, Cam. It's hard to come by when you live in the public eye. And if it will help you clear me from police suspicion, I do have a theory. Though I already shared it with the police and they aren't giving it any merit."

"Somehow that doesn't surprise me," Cam said. "Law enforcement in this town can have tunnel vision. What is it?"

"I was on my way into the courthouse to answer some questions about my telephone calls the day before yesterday and I passed Melvin Entwhistle on the street. He was being read the riot act by, I believe, Derrick Windermere's daughter."

"Vera? What did she say?"

"The little bit I heard was, 'well, I could do a lot more damage than that,' or something."

"Interesting. We'll have to think about what that might mean. But the reason we called . . . one of the things the police are looking at is a romance that went sour between you and Derrick Windermere."

"I'd hardly call it a romance. We were set up on a blind date by a mutual friend who thought we might get along. I didn't know anything about him at the time, and he was relatively charming. But by the third date, I'd learned something about his ethics and practices, and I told him it wouldn't work."

"But he couldn't take no for an answer?"

"He seemed fine with it. He understood. In fact, I think he didn't care for my ethics, either."

"Then why did he start to threaten you?"

"Because I had threatened him, but that came about years later and had nothing to do with those few dates. I learned some of the loopholes he used and planned to close them when I got into office. I told him so, as a courtesy, so he could clean things up. But he took it as a threat and started threatening back. The trouble is, his kind of politics don't really influence my kind of voters, so his threats were hollow."

"Why would your friends talk about a sour relationship as the reason for the animosity then?" Rob asked.

"I'd have to know which friends to know that. It doesn't

make any sense to me, as I really never talked to anyone about it. I just chalked it up to a lesson learned. No more blind dates."

That was curious, Cam thought. Somebody *did* want to frame Vivian, unless she was being less than forthcoming.

"Samantha admitted she was the one who set you up," Cam said.

Vivian sighed. "And to this day, I don't know if she was being stupid or trying to strap me with baggage my political career couldn't handle."

Cam laughed. She'd wondered exactly the same thing and admitted it.

"Do you think all of this—framing you—is just about hurting your career?"

"I doubt the murders were about that at all. But pointing to me after the fact? I think choosing me to frame could very easily be motivated by ruining my chances at a House seat."

CHAPTER 19

"Interesting about Vera and Melvin," Cam said after Vivian had left.

"She *did* say she despised him."

"I wonder how she could ruin him, though."

"It was probably just talk," Rob said.

Cam didn't want to argue, though she was a little annoyed that Rob seemed to keep defending Vera. But she went on to her next point. "So the person we're looking for is a person who had it out for Derrick and Sully, and who also had it out for Vivian."

"Yeah, if it were only that easy," Rob said.

"It should be easy, shouldn't it?" Cam said.

"Probably, but I don't know if in politics it is. And do we believe Vivian?"

"I do."

"So then, what we need is the source of those friend comments."

"Which we could get from Jake," Cam said.

"If Jake were interested in sharing that kind of thing with us. Annie said the notes didn't have names."

It was a fair point. Jake wasn't always forthcoming, and definitely wouldn't be about a witness whom they might then harass. Especially one who had been discovered by their sneaking around.

"But let's think about this logically. How would the police have identified Vivian's friends?" Cam asked. "I mean . . . they don't know who she socializes and spends time with, do they?"

"It would be people she's seen with regularly, like lunch dates, colleagues, or volunteers."

"*Supposed* friends who just come forward with details," Cam said.

"Well, that class of people we can probably convince Jake to look at with a grain of salt."

Cam swallowed wrong and had to cough. Rob using a cliché was fairly unheard of. "True," she said as she recovered. "People who volunteer information we can discredit as potentially having an agenda. So, Mr. Hotshot-Reporter, how do we figure out who she was seen with last week?"

"She's a busy lady. Let's look at her appointment book."

"Right!"

Cam called Vivian back, and fortunately, Vivian and her dad were having dinner in the very next room. Cam wondered how that had happened. Probably Vivian had called him and when she told him where she was, he'd just told her to stay put. It was his favorite restaurant, after all. Cam and Rob finished their dinner and then made their way into the next room.

Vivian helped Rob access the archived calendar and they went over names, Rob taking note of the few who were social instead of professional. Vivian then sent the week's worth of appointments to him by email so he and Cam could peruse it more slowly.

They thanked her and left, heading to Cam's house.

"You really think the killer is one of these appointments?" Cam asked.

"Not really. But I think one of these appointments is either friends with the killer or is gullible enough to be fed news."

Cam poured them each a glass of wine as Rob pulled the list up on the computer so it was large enough so they both could see.

"There are a couple of familiar names here. That's for sure," Rob said as Cam sat back down.

"Who?"

"Vera Windermere-Sullivan, for starters."

"What? What would she have to do with Vivian Macy? Vivian told us the story about her and referred to her as Derrick's daughter—it sounded then like she barely knew who she was."

"I think we'd need to ask Vera, though maybe we should ask Vivian first. It's possible she just didn't think *we'd* know who she was. Vera seems unlikely to be considered by the police as a friend, though. She's the wrong age, and she's connected to not only both victims, but a political rival, too," Rob said.

"I don't know when logic has ever guided the police in this town," Cam said.

"That's not fair. Granted, they've snuffed up a couple murder investigations. But for the most part, it's a good, reliable squad. They just aren't . . . very creative."

"They want easy answers," Cam argued.

"Don't you think that's understandable? And maybe because murder isn't so common around here, they've been able to solve them more easily before this . . . spree we've had."

Cam had to agree that might be the case. "Anybody with a more logical friend connection?" she asked.

"The other familiar name is Melvin Entwhistle, but he

hardly seems the sort to gossip, and certainly not about a romance."

Cam scanned the list. There were about two dozen people in appointment slots in the week leading up to the fundraiser, but Cam didn't know most of the names.

"Wait. This woman . . . Vivian said she's a constituent, but didn't you mention her name when you tried to talk to Chad Phillips?"

"Lorraine Patterson? That sounds right. I'd need to check."

Cam dialed her cell phone and asked Annie to come downstairs. "Bring your laptop."

"Can Jake come?" Annie asked.

"Sure. Bring him, too." She wasn't thrilled to have Jake in on things at this stage, but maybe it was best they start raising doubts about some of these supposed friends of Vivian's.

"Wait a minute," Rob said. "Lorraine Patterson . . . Brian Fontana! I knew that name was bugging me!" He typed a search into his computer. "There!"

"What?" Cam said.

"Brian Fontana was working in Chad Phillips's office when I tried to visit."

"You said that earlier, but it doesn't make any sense," she said.

"And he and Lorraine Patterson had their heads together," Rob went on.

Annie entered in pajamas and Jake followed behind her looking sheepish. Rob shot a look at Jake and Jake blushed, embarrassed to have been called when they were apparently settled in for the night, but Annie seemed to figure they were all family. She plunked her laptop across the table from Cam's, then came around to Cam's side.

"What are we looking for?" she said and half shoved Cam off her chair to get in next to her.

"We have a Lorraine Patterson here—two of them

actually. Rob says one of them was the gatekeeper when he tried to talk to Chad Phillips. We need to figure out if it's the same one who met with Vivian. Vivian said she was a neighbor and constituent—that she had some concerns, but if that neighbor worked for Chad . . ."

"Wait! Where did you get that name?" Jake asked.

"Vivian Macy's planner," Cam said.

"And why do you have Vivian Macy's planner?"

"She gave it to us," Rob said.

"Nice!" Annie said.

"No! This is not nice. You're interfering with a murder investigation again!"

Rob got up and fetched Jake a beer.

"We talked to Vivian Macy tonight," Rob explained. "She told us there was no ugly breakup, just a couple of dates and a decision not to see each other anymore because they weren't compatible. The bad blood came because of a loophole he was exploiting that she planned to close—something she warned him about, as a friend, so he could clean up his act first. Now, she might be lying, but we thought we should also try to figure out who these supposed friends were who left the potentially faulty information. And since we doubted we'd get the information from you, we figured the most likely people the police would look at were appointments and volunteers. So she gave us the appointments to get us started."

Jake sputtered for a minute. He didn't look happy. Then finally he asked, "So what about Lorraine Patterson again?"

"She was a gatekeeper I had trouble getting past when I wanted to talk to Chad Phillips about the election. Along with Brian Fontana, the supposed hit man, I should mention, but we haven't figured out how that fits yet. Vivian met with Lorraine as a delegate—as a courtesy. But she's connected to Chad, who loops back into this case from a few directions," Rob said.

"And how does he do that?"

"We're pretty sure he's sleeping with Vera Windermere-Sullivan—daughter of one victim, wife of the other."

Jake ran his fingers through his hair. "You people will be the death of my career one day, I am sure of it."

"That's not our goal. We just don't think Vivian did it, and Chad looks like a pretty darned good pick. Is he even on your list?" Cam said.

"Yes, but as yet, it's a pretty long list and he's not near the top."

"We've noticed there's been no rash arrest this time," Cam said. "That's a nice change of pace."

Annie elbowed her.

"What? You were one of those rash arrests, if you'll remember," Cam said.

Rob pinched her then, and since she was sitting between Annie and him with only two chairs for the three of them, she decided it was probably time to shut her mouth.

Thankfully, Rob picked up one of the strands of interest. "How many of Vivian's supposed friends volunteered information?"

Jake looked at the three of them sitting there studiously, Annie in her sheep pajamas. "Just one, but she did suggest a few other names."

"And?" Rob asked.

"And we talked to everybody, but you're right. Volunteers sometimes have an agenda that should be examined."

"And?"

"And Lorraine Patterson was one of the names on her list. So even though we hadn't gone through all Vivian's appointments, we had talked to Lorraine," Jake admitted.

Annie got up and went around to her own computer. She typed in a few things, wearing a look of concentration.

"There!" Annie said.

"What?" Cam made her way around and looked at the computer screen. Annie had just pulled up a picture.

"Rob, is this her?" Cam asked.

Rob followed and nodded.

"The bigger mystery, since I found this by searching for Lorraine Patterson and Chad Phillips, is whether this is the Lorraine Jake talked to," Annie said.

Jake sighed and stepped closer. "Yeah. Same woman."

Annie entered a few more keystrokes and up popped a map showing that Lorraine Patterson lived near Vivian. They weren't quite neighbors, but near enough that they might know each other for neighborly reasons . . . certainly near enough that Lorraine might have made an appointment as a constituent.

"Very curious indeed," Annie said. "Did she claim to be a friend then?"

"She'd already been identified as a friend, so we didn't ask."

"Who identified her?" Cam asked.

"Ramona Pemberly."

Cam covered her face. "Do you know how easy it is to lead that woman down any gossip trail?"

"You know her?" Jake asked.

"She's part of the Roanoke Garden Society, but more important, an incorrigible gossip. If anyone wanted to lead someone to a specific piece of information, letting it slip to *her* is a great way."

"I'll be sure to let the team know," Jake said. He didn't look pleased.

"Certainly worth asking Vivian what the meeting was about," Cam added.

"Now you two just hold on," Jake said. Annie looked pointedly at Rob, obviously curious why he wasn't being scolded, but Jake ignored her. "You should not be following up on murder investigation questioning, but I see your point. We'll look into her further and I'll double-check where all the names came from. But you . . . three . . . are not the police. Do you remember how these things typically end?"

"We solve the murder?" Cam offered.

Annie kicked Cam under the table, and Cam pulled her legs up, tucking them under her.

"Somebody gets captured or threatened," Jake said.

"Covered," Cam said. "Somebody tied me to a chair in my office today."

"Oh . . . I forgot to tell you that," Annie said. "How'd that go anyway?"

Cam snorted, but Jake looked mad.

"And you didn't report it?"

"Yes, we reported it. To building security, who were reviewing footage and said they would call the police. Nobody's here yet, so I guess it's going slowly."

"That's not protocol. You should have been asked to stay. What did he look like?" Jake pulled out a notepad.

"The security guard or the intruder?"

"We'll get to the security guard, because he clearly hasn't been trained well enough, but for now, let's talk about the intruder."

"Dark clothes, ski mask. The lights were off, so I couldn't tell much. I'm pretty sure he was white or nearly, and he wasn't particularly tall, but broad, very strong. If I saw his eyes again, I might recognize them by shape, but it was dark, so I don't have a color or anything."

"Bigger than Rob and me?" Jake asked.

"Rob's height, maybe, but broader. If he was taller, it wasn't noticeably."

"And did he say anything?"

"To stay out of it. Hey . . . maybe it was *you*!"

"Very funny. I guess you're not too shaken up if you can laugh about it."

"Rob rescued me. I dialed Annie with my toes, but she was too far away," Cam said.

"At least you're resourceful."

"So we'll try to stay out of it, if you promise not to drop

this piece—that the people feeding info to the police about Vivian have an agenda, and most likely it's a double one: to hide who really did the crime while smearing her at the same time."

"I promise not to drop it and I'll take your opinion about people offering info under advisement."

Cam nodded and Annie took it as a hint to leave. Annie felt compelled to play peacemaker between her best friend and boyfriend, though Cam knew Annie more often agreed with her. She just worked on Jake in different ways, unlike Cam's direct style. But it could be a tiring task to keep the peace, and Annie looked like she'd had enough for now.

When they were gone, Rob looked at her. "We aren't really dropping this, are we?"

"Heck no!"

CHAPTER 20

Rob called Cam the next morning when she was at work. He sounded elated.

"Cam, I just found some stuff you might be interested in. Are you free?"

Unfortunately, she wasn't. The police had finally arrived to get her formal report from the night before, and she had an appointment with them in the security office in twenty minutes. She was supposed to identify who might or might not be the person who'd attacked her.

"Well then, let's meet for lunch," he said.

"Perfect, but let me call you. I don't know how long this might take."

She spent the next twenty minutes completely distracted. Rob had sounded excited about something he'd discovered, and she was annoyed she couldn't go find out what it was right away. She was also eager to find out who had attacked her. Putting a name to the face . . . or even a face to the face . . . would help her figure out who was so worried about her finding the real answers. It could be the cornerstone to solving the murders.

The security office was in the basement of the building, and Cam almost asked them to come up and escort her. She felt jumpy and worried that someone might see this as the perfect opportunity to shut her up. She made her way down anyway, and felt safer when she saw a policeman standing just outside the elevator waiting for her and a second one in the tiny office with the security man.

"Thank you for coming down, Miss Harris. We want to get your memory of the person and everything that happened first. Security should have had you stay last night. We've asked, and apparently, it was a new man?" The officer looked to the security guard currently seated in the booth for confirmation. "So training will be more thorough in the future. Anyway, let's go over some footage from around the time of the event. Does that sound okay?"

She agreed and recapped everything as well as she could remember it.

"So you think they had access to the office?"

"Maybe, but when someone is there working, the doors are often unlocked. I mean . . . I locked them—I do when I'm there alone. But I don't think Mr. Patrick does. So someone could have snuck in earlier in the day and just hidden."

"And how would they have known you were coming back?"

"Maybe they didn't. Maybe they planned to take something."

"Like what?"

"Well, with what they said, I thought their interest was in that fund-raiser where Derrick Windermere was killed and the money was raised for Jared Koontz. They warned me to stay out of it, and that's the only thing I can think of that I've been *in*, so my guess is some file related to that."

"But nothing was taken?"

"Not that I know of. Maybe I surprised him."

"How long before you arrived had it been since the door was unlocked?"

"I have no idea. You'd need to check with the Patricks to see when they left. It was only six thirty when I came in, so maybe not that long—and even if Mr. Patrick left earlier, if Evangeline was still here, the guy couldn't have done anything until she left."

"You hear that, Len?" the officer said to the one in the hall.

Len. Cam looked at him more closely. There could only be so many Roanoke police officers called Len. This had to be Elle's brother. The same brother Jake thought had removed phone records and that they knew had only pretended to investigate a kidnapping. Though that was because he knew Senator Schulz was safely with his siblings.

"Len" went out to make a few phone calls. Cam leaned in to the other officer.

"Are you sure he should be investigating this? His brother's murder is related."

"And how would you know that?"

"I was with the people who found Mike Sullivan's body. Please—talk to Jake Moreno about all this."

The police officer eyed her very skeptically but then gave the smallest hint of a nod. Lenny Sullivan was probably a perfectly good cop, but he was also possibly too close to this case to do what needed to be done. Cam wondered how he had ended up here in the first place, but then security had only thought this was breaking and entering. They wouldn't have connected it to the murder investigation.

Whatever the case, Cam didn't plan to spill any more information with Officer Sullivan here. Who knew what he might do with it?

"He left five thirty, she left six fifteen," Officer Sullivan said when he returned.

"Listen, can I come look at footage later?" Cam said. "I

feel a migraine coming on and I don't think I can look at that screen."

The police officer seemed to understand her hesitation, and so agreed. "You just come back down and go over it when you can, preferably today."

"I understand. As soon as I feel better. Thank you."

W hen Cam got back up to her office, her skin seemed to crawl with discomfort about what was happening. She couldn't shake the feeling that the involvement of the police officer who had been suspected of hiding evidence earlier in the case was ominous. She wasn't sure whom to trust, so she went to Evangeline.

"Yes of course, someone just called," she said.

Relief washed over Cam until Evangeline went on.

"And I had wondered why my computer was on when I got here today."

"On? I was . . . tied up in here. Wouldn't I have seen?"

"Well, no. The monitor was off. That was what was so strange."

Cam remembered the flicker she'd seen as she unlocked the door. He must have known she'd hear if he actually shut it down, so had only turned off the visible part.

Cam's stomach dropped. "And what time did you tell the officer you left?"

"Neil and I left at five thirty—we had a board meeting for our charity—a dinner that started at seven. I wanted to shower and change before we went."

Cam dialed her phone, and Jake, for a change, didn't sound annoyed with her.

"Lester just called me with your concerns. I'm glad you . . ."

"There's more, Jake. I just talked to Evangeline and have

proof Sullivan—the cop, Sullivan—lied to . . . you said Lester?"

"Officer Simon Lester," he clarified. "What do you mean proof he lied?"

"He told us downstairs Neil left at five thirty, which was true. But he said Evangeline left at six fifteen. She told *me* that she told *him* they left together at five thirty. And she told him her computer was on, which he never mentioned."

"And if they were there together, chances are nobody snuck in while they were there," Jake said.

Cam hadn't thought of it, but it did seem risky.

"You always lock up when you leave, don't you?" he asked.

"Of course." But then Cam double-checked with Evangeline. She was always careful, but it was worth the question. Evangeline affirmed it and she passed that to Jake.

"Which means he may have had help from somebody with building access," he finished.

Cam shivered. "So it was good I didn't go over those tapes down there?"

"Well, yes and no. Lester is a good guy. And now Len has a chance to erase them, though probably if it's a security guy he's working with, it was erased before anybody got there today."

"Rob and I are meeting for lunch. Will you meet us?"

"I think I can do that."

Cam gave him the restaurant name and hung up, passing on the warning to Evangeline that somebody in the building might be involved.

"We have our own security, you know," Evangeline said.

"What?"

"A private system. It's just a camera on the front door, but . . . it might help."

Cam ran over and hugged Evangeline. "I'll bring Jake and Rob back with me after lunch."

"You do that. It's on the computer at reception and I think holds a week at a time—all motion detection, so not bad to watch. Plus, that would be the last computer a thief would sit at, since they'd be seen from the hallway if anybody came—too exposed."

Cam had to carefully hide her grin as she walked out of the building. She didn't want some thug for hire who happened to be loitering or watching on a security camera to see that she was secretly pleased. But she was eager to share this news with Rob and Jake.

When she got to the restaurant, Rob and Jake were already sitting there. Rob raised a questioning look to her, as the lunch date had been made to discuss topics Jake wasn't in on, but when Cam launched into what she'd learned about Officer Sullivan and the probable inclusion of building security, he understood. They ate a pleasant lunch discussing other topics, and then the pair of them accompanied Cam back to her office.

Cam tried not to look at the security guard as they entered the building. She knew he'd see she wore an accusatory expression, and he might not even be the person involved. Still, entering with a police officer always caught extra attention. The man nodded and said, "Hello, Officer," as Jake entered.

Jake waved back and followed Cam and Rob to the elevators. He looked around a lot more than he usually did, and Cam wondered if that police attitude had an on-off switch or if the fact that they usually entered the building when it was relatively quiet made a difference. At the moment, the restaurant and shops on the main floor were hopping with business.

When they entered the office, Evangeline poked her head out and waved. Jake went back to verify with her what Cam had said earlier. It gave Cam time to boot up the computer that sat at reception, where there was currently no actual receptionist.

"Evangeline!" Cam called. "What program is this?"

Evangeline and Jake came out together, and Evangeline showed Cam the folder with the files. They were labeled "Archive," which Cam thought was clever if anyone was snooping around. That was the last place a person would look for something recent.

"There. There's yesterday," Evangeline said.

They opened the file and watched a jumpy set of images. Each time a figure would leave the frame, the time stamp would jump, apparently to the next person entering the frame. The camera caught the full hallway just outside the door of the office, and Cam saw Evangeline and then Mr. Patrick arrive the day before. She saw herself arrive, several appointments come and go, herself leave, the Patricks leave, and finally at six twenty, a man in a mask arrived with a security guard who was intentionally keeping his head in shadow. He opened the door, let the man in, then closed the door again and left. Cam saw herself arrive twenty minutes later.

"Well, I think we have enough for that security guard to lose his job," Jake said. "Evangeline, do you want to call the building manager? When we aren't sure who in security is secure, he is probably the person we want to talk to to identify this man."

It took about fifteen minutes for the man to arrive. He was a classic sycophant and irritated Cam from the minute he stepped into the office, but he was the person they had to work with, so she tried to hold her tongue.

"He doesn't work for *us*. I've never seen him before."

"He has the uniform and keys, so somebody in the security office had to have given him both things. If we could get a list of who was working last night?"

"Oh, of course! I'll get that right away."

"Without letting them know why it's needed?"

"Oh, well . . . of course. I'll do my best."

"Aren't you in charge?" Cam asked. She couldn't help herself and Rob couldn't keep from giving a small chuckle.

"Maybe it would help if I came, too," Jake said.

"I'm sure that's not necessary."

"In fact, Cam, aren't you supposed to be looking at tapes down there? Maybe we should all go."

Cam had to admit it, she liked when Jake was in this mode if she wasn't on the receiving end of it.

They made their way together to the security office, and the building manager asked for the schedule.

"Get the payroll version so you make sure not to miss anything," Jake said.

The man in the little room looked alarmed, but complied. "Did something happen?"

"Yes. You'll hear about it soon enough," the manager said.

Jake stepped forward, though, and said, "Do you recognize this man?"

He had printed a screen shot of the security person who undid the door. It wasn't a clear enough shot for someone who didn't know the man to identify, but it seemed like a coworker ought to be able to.

The man squinted and said, "Might be the new guy. Herald, Harrell . . . something like that.

The manager scanned the list. "Harlon?"

"Yeah, maybe. I mean, I can't say for sure."

"How long has he worked here?"

"Just a couple weeks. We were looking for somebody, and I guess he had a referral from one of the penthouse tenants."

"Is there a file of employees with their identification, including pictures?"

"Sure. We all have a picture ID."

The man pulled up a screen for Richard Harlon and they moved in closer.

"That rat!" Cam said.

"Why?" Jake asked. "Other than breaking and entering, I mean."

"That was the man who came up to take our statement last night."

"Which explains why this wasn't actually reported until I filed it after talking to you later," Jake said.

"No, but I know him," Cam said.

"From where?"

"I moonlighted at a . . . fund-raiser . . . the other night for a little extra money," she said.

Jake looked at her skeptically, but she pressed on.

"And he was following Dave Barrett around."

Jake turned to fully face Cam, then looked up, praying for patience. "And how do you know Dave Barrett?"

"He's the mob lawyer who borrowed Joel Jaimeson's phone at the fund-raiser for Jared Koontz. He told Joel it was for Alden Schulz."

"He's not just a mob lawyer. He's a corporate lawyer. And he's the man who filed the papers requesting that Derrick Windermere be declared incompetent," Jake said.

"Oh, boy," Cam said. Things were pulling together, but rather than a clearer picture, she thought they just kept getting murkier.

"When is your supervisor in?" Jake asked the security guard.

"He's not here very often. He supervises like eight buildings. But I can call him if you need me to."

"Yes. Please do that."

The man did as asked and then Jake directed the security guard to guide Cam through the footage from the day before.

Nobody except the security guard was shocked to learn that the video footage had been stopped during the incident with nothing recorded.

Cam and Rob left at that point, walking to a coffee shop for a latte. Jake had stayed to get things sorted, and had called in Officer Lester to help him out. He'd said there was nothing more Cam or Rob could do, and they'd gladly escaped, as they still hadn't had a chance to have the conversation they'd intended to have that morning.

"That makes me nervous somebody in your building was in on this," Rob said. "Someone with mob connections."

"Sounds like he was planted in the building specifically for this—maybe even to check out the party plans so they'd know who would be where and when."

Rob's face opened up. "That's brilliant! I bet it's true!"

Cam blushed. She didn't like to admit how much she really enjoyed being good at this investigating stuff. It made her feel smart.

"We should see if your footage is still there from then."

"Good idea."

"But I also have the news I wanted to get to you this morning," Rob said.

"And?"

"I thought maybe I would do a little following the money—Derrick Windermere's deal that lost so many people so much. I wanted to look at the source."

"And?"

"Chrysanthemum Holdings, which shouldn't surprise any of us, specializes in building rejuvenation and restoration—buildings that are then leased or sold for a lot."

"Like my building," Cam said.

"A lot like that, but . . . only on paper. I looked several of them up, and the claims to their rejuvenation have been grossly overstated. Somebody has made an art of finding architecturally similar buildings that have been redone and making claims as they look for investors."

"Real estate fraud?"

"Looks like it. What I can't tell is if this firm was the victim or perpetrator of the crime, but two firms own it."

"Right. Windermere and Treemore."

"But what we couldn't find until we—and by we, I mean the police—subpoenaed company papers was that the CEO of Treemore is Melvin Entwhistle."

"So you think maybe one partner was taking the other?"

"Possible. So is the possibility that Derrick sold them a bill of goods and investors got mad, or that Derrick found out about a scheme and planned to stop it. Whatever the direction of the fraud, though, those names pop to the top of my list."

"Wonderful! If we can figure out which of them would want to frame Vivian, I bet we have our man!"

"Trouble is, I bet they all would."

Back at the office, Cam couldn't get comfortable. Ghost or no ghost, the Patrick Henry, and, specifically, her locked office, had always felt like a safe place, but after learning about the phony security guard, she was feeling a little paranoid. Since she couldn't concentrate on work, she sat at the front computer and went back further in the archives to see if she could find any other people who weren't supposed to be at the office. What she found shocked and surprised her. The same little security guard let him in, but this person who came to look in their offices at night was none other than Mike Sullivan.

CHAPTER 21

"It's who?" Rob asked when she told him.

"Mike Sullivan was let in here two nights before the fund-raiser by that slimy little security guard who works for Dave Barrett."

"But then he ended up dead. So . . ."

"Yeah, I don't know either. But it makes it look to me like maybe Sully was killed because he knew too much," Cam said.

"Which makes sense. But he was involved, too."

"Yeah. I don't know how it works. I'm thinking maybe we need more info on that security guard, and we need to follow up about Chrysanthemum Holdings. I think there's something organized going on here."

"I looked up Harlon. He's a lawyer, too. He just passed the bar a year ago. But Cam, if this is organized—like mob stuff—we don't have any business messing with it."

"Don't you see how close we are, though? And Jake can't do what we could—sneaking around and listening in."

"Well I'm happy to do some more troubleshooting on the

internet. But we aren't going chasing after criminals again. It's just too dangerous."

Cam sighed. She knew he was right, but the adrenaline could be addictive. "Okay, meet me at my place after work."

"A little after that. Jake got Harlon. He's in custody. I'm going to the station now to see what we can find out."

"Not without me you're not!"

She hung up and sprinted out of the office. It was walking distance, at least for someone who walked as much as Cam did, so she actually beat Rob to the station. Getting to someone who could help her find Jake was another matter. She got the runaround since Jake was busy processing Harlon.

"That's it. That is exactly why I need to find him," Cam complained.

"I'm sorry, miss."

Thankfully, that was when Rob arrived, whose name was on a list Jake had left. The clerk looked annoyed to let Cam through with him but allowed it, as Rob put an arm over her shoulder and took her along without comment.

When they reached Jake, he was standing outside an interview room. Cam blurted out the things she'd found about Mike Sullivan and the suspicion that there was something organized behind all of this.

Jake looked ready to argue, but Rob backed her up.

"So you saw this guy let Mike Sullivan into your place of work?" Jake asked, pointing to the room where Harlon was being held.

"I did. Two days before the party. It had to be related to planning something. Now we know Sully was in on the kidnapping, but we think maybe he just saw *that* opportunity on the side and decided to do his sister a favor, when the real job had to do with Windermere. We know it was Mike who called Elle to come back from Finland or Italy or wherever she was, and the timing is about right, so maybe *that* happened when he saw the party plan."

"But Sully's dead now," Jake said.

"Maybe it didn't go the way he thought and he threatened to tell. Or maybe he was sloppy, so they were trying to squash the trail. I don't know. I think the kidnapping and murder and all are connected, only maybe it's because Sully made the piggyback plan. These guys don't seem like the type to be very tolerant of somebody adding to their own agenda," Cam said.

"I agree. Sully probably wasn't supposed to do the side project. Maybe somebody got mad about it," Rob said. "Because it made the rest too easy to trace."

Jake looked back and forth between them. Cam was glad he seemed to be at least taking the theory seriously.

"So do we get to watch the questioning?" Cam said.

Jake made a face, but then he nodded. "Since it was your office he was helping people break into, I think that's fair. Just remember you can't do anything to make yourself known or you'll be escorted out."

Cam nodded, but she had underestimated how hard it would be to sit quietly while somebody was asking someone questions that weren't the ones she would have asked. Rob shushed her three times because she kept saying what she wanted Jake to ask, and she almost had to leave to keep herself from pounding on the glass.

Harlon was not very forthcoming. In fact he wouldn't talk at all. Rob whispered that that was why Jake wasn't being more specific—that he didn't want to tip their hand about how much they knew and that a lawyer would really understand his right to not incriminate himself anyway—but Cam thought if he knew what was known, maybe he'd volunteer more to help himself look better. He would understand the benefit of a plea.

"They have him on this. He can't get out of it," Rob said, "but he won't want to give away any more."

"Isn't the whole idea of plea bargaining to give important

information in exchange for a lesser charge on something they have you on?" Cam asked.

Rob made a face, but she knew she was right.

Finally Jake came out. "Sorry about that, guys. We're keeping him at least overnight, but it doesn't look like he's talking."

"No lawyer? I mean isn't he one?" Rob asked.

"They may be throwing him under the bus," Cam suggested. "I mean, he's the peon. He might be being nicely compensated and they will make sure it's nothing permanent while they stall."

Jake narrowed his eyes but didn't comment.

"Can people come visit him?"

"Like who?"

"I was thinking Annie, because her dad got kidnapped. But maybe even Elle, because it was her brother who was killed."

"I think that's a really bad idea," Jake said.

"What about if somebody was in the cell next to him?" Rob asked.

"Oh, no. You're not getting arrested just to get in there with him. And if you did get arrested, I have no control over how near your cell is to his. But if you're right about this being part of something organized, then the walls have ears down there. You put yourself in much greater danger just by being there."

"Good try, though, Tiny," Cam said.

Rob grinned at her.

Annie joined them at Cam's apartment after that, and Jake promised to stop by soon.

"Mob? Are you freaking kidding me?"

"I don't know that I'd say 'mob,'" Rob said.

"I would," Cam added.

"And no rescues needed," Rob said.

"Oh, admit it. It was hot to be rescued," Annie teased.

"Hey, you've needed a rescue, too," he said.

"And that was hot, too. Once it was over, I mean."

"You have a weird view on hot," Rob said.

Annie's phone buzzed then, making them all jump. Cam hadn't realized how tense they were. When she hung up, she turned to them. "No Jake tonight. Apparently they're going to search Sully's house and apartment."

"Didn't they do that already?"

"They did, but they didn't know to look for whatever file or thing he took from your office."

"Didn't look like much in the footage," Cam said. "File is probably right. Or maybe he just took pictures of something. That's . . ." she halted.

". . . what we do," Annie finished. "Rob knows, but we hide this from Jake, so it isn't how he thinks. Might even be a thumb drive they want."

Cam looked at her boyfriend guiltily. She and Annie had just been sort of secretive about these things sometimes.

"Speaking of . . . erm . . ." Annie looked uncomfortable and Cam was surprised. It took a lot to do that to her friend. "Um . . . could . . . is there any way . . . Could Daddy and Elle come to Thanksgiving?"

"Well, of course they can." That had been the last thing she'd expected.

"It's just, I heard them talking and it sounded like they were going to be alone, and . . . after all that's happened . . ."

"I'll need to tell Nick and Dad, but it won't be a problem, I'm sure. But . . . what does that have to do with sneaking around?"

"Annie logic," she said. "It's just . . . Jake is stuck working that day. Jake had to do with sneaking, but then also Thanksgiving, which led me to Dad and Elle . . ."

"That stinks that Jake has to work." Cam knew they'd

only expected him to stop by for dessert, but thought it had been a family obligation until now.

"I know. His mom is mad. She threatened to call the station."

"I can't wait to meet his mother," Cam laughed.

"She's a little intimidating," Annie admitted.

"To you? Uh-oh."

"Well, I think it's about being her son's girlfriend. He's the only boy, so I think no girl could measure up. She likes that I bake, though, so that's something . . . keep her Joaquin healthy!"

"It's still strange to think of Jake as Joaquin."

"I think it's sexy," Annie said.

Rob wandered off. He didn't want to hear any more details. Jake was *his* friend, after all, and most men seemed squeamish hearing about the love lives of their friends.

"Well, if Jake isn't coming with more information, is there anything else we can do tonight?"

"Besides look into Chrysanthemum Holdings?" Annie said.

"Oh, right. Rob!" Cam called him back over. "How do we dig here?"

They spent the next few hours tracking down the holdings, using Google Earth to physically look at them, then tracking the sales history. They were all surprised to realize it looked like Derrick Windermere had been the one duped, and not the crook behind the scam.

"Well, I'll be . . ." Rob said.

"How do we find out who owns this Chrysanthemum Land Trust?"

"It looks offshore, so I guess we try to figure it out in the morning. I'm bushed," Rob said.

Cam had to admit she was, too. She'd been too wired to sleep earlier, but now it was catching up with her.

* * *

Cam was glad she'd decided to work only a half day. She planned to spend the afternoon baking at Sweet Surprise. Annie had many customers picking up orders for the next day, so Cam knew she'd worked ahead. But she also had two big industrial ovens—big enough to bake many pans at a time. Annie had given her the okay to use one of them so they could keep each other company.

When Cam arrived, Annie looked worried.

"What's up?"

"I haven't heard from Jake yet, and their stuff last night wasn't danger free."

"Was he going to call?"

"He was going to come over if it wasn't too late."

"Well, if it *was* too late, he might still be sleeping—if it was three in the morning or something."

"I guess that's true."

"He'll call when he's awake." Cam realized they had no confirmation that was accurate, but there was no point worrying about it until they heard differently. Besides, she had built her career on spin. It could hardly help but seep into her real life from time to time.

The two of them baked amicably for the next hour until Rob burst in.

"Did you hear about the standoff?"

A muffin tin went crashing as Cam came out of the back room. Annie had dropped the half-full tray she was transferring to her display case. Cam eyed Rob.

"Sully's house didn't have anything. Vera cooperated, so they didn't even need a warrant. She showed him where anything might be. Seemed eager."

"I bet," Cam said.

"Warrant finally came in this morning at six for the apartment—took until then to get a judge there."

"Then why didn't Jake call?" Annie said.

"They were there, just waiting until they could go in. But when the warrant came, that guy Leo, who was there when you both barged in with your phony story, was gone and it looked like he'd taken a whole bunch of stuff. They tracked him to some cabin in the mountains and he's holed up shooting."

Annie shrieked.

"No, it doesn't look like he's shooting *at* anyone. He just doesn't want them to come in."

"But eventually, they'll have to go in and get him."

"Probably, but they're trained well, and they have their vests and stuff."

Annie wandered to the back room, but a customer came in just then, so Cam had to stay and help, finding the cheese-cake with the woman's last name and sorting out that she'd paid when she ordered.

"Happy Thanksgiving!" Cam called as she left. Then she ran into the back room to see if the conversation had gotten any easier.

It hadn't. Annie had too vivid an imagination.

"Wait here," Rob said. "I'll be back in a few minutes."

Cam chased him into the front and turned him around. "Oh, no you don't! You don't come in here and stir up this mess and then disappear."

"No! I know something that should help. I'll be right back. Seriously." And he was gone.

Annie came out of the back room to find Cam cursing in her schoolmarm way.

"You'd feel better if you added some real swear words," Annie said.

"I can't believe he'd scare us like that and then disappear."

"He's right, though—they are trained. And the sergeant is cautious. So unless the guy makes a run for it, they won't go in until they're ready. Maybe they'll bring state troopers in or something."

Cam noticed her own habit at spin might be contagious, but it was better than panicking, so she didn't point that out. They got back to the baking and selling, and Rob indeed returned in just under forty minutes with a black case.

He walked straight through the bakery to the back and Cam followed him. He was setting up a police scanner. She raised an eyebrow.

"I might have borrowed this from the incident room at work without asking, but they weren't using it. Honestly, I'm not sure why. This is big news."

"What if they need it?"

"They do, but they don't seem to know it. You know the policy on scoops."

Cam walked over and swatted him. "Shouldn't you have just turned this on there?"

"Probably, but then Annie wouldn't hear and she's the one who's worried."

Cam's annoyance melted and she hugged him from behind as he fiddled with the dials, finally getting what sounded like the interplay between one of the police officers on scene and the main station.

"Annie!" Cam called.

"Just a sec!" she said, cluing Cam in that there was a customer out front.

Cam went out to help. It was more important that Annie get the scoop than her. They could fill her in in a minute. She let Annie finish helping the customer she was with, but took on the next and tilted her head so Annie knew she should go to the back.

Unfortunately, the exercise was not the stress reducer Cam and Rob had been hoping for. The dialog was sketchy and strained. The standoff seemed to be getting nowhere and the plan was not to move until some event in Blacksburg was over so they could spare a few more officers experienced in this kind of thing. It was a "wait in the woods with guns pointed" effort and only got worse for the people listening as time passed.

On the strained third hour of listening and trying to bake, Rob's phone rang. He looked confused, but answered. His first few words weren't any more enlightening, so Cam shoved a notebook at him. He wrote "Vera" in sloppy scrawl. He invited Vera to the bakery.

Cam and Annie stared at each other then looked back to Rob, waiting as he gave directions.

"She had something she was afraid to tell the police—something she wants to tell us . . . me."

"Does she know who you are?"

"Yeah. I think she figured it out. It's how she found me. The paper passed on my cell number."

"And she's coming here? With . . ."

"I think it's okay. She sounds scared, but I think she's scared of whoever got to her husband, which puts her on our side."

"Unless she's trying to pull one over on us," Cam said.

"There's three of us, right? We're okay. But maybe we should . . . let someone else know?" Rob said.

"Like who, Jake?" Annie said.

Her sarcasm was on the mean side, rather than the playful. Cam knew it was just the stress, but it was true—the person they'd normally have back them up was busy with something far more dangerous than anything they were involved in.

There was no progress over the scanner, and Annie closed up shop for the day, relieved to be done with the customers. She pulled out a bottle of wine, which Cam opened as Rob let Vera Windermere-Sullivan in the back door.

Vera waved to Cam and then scrutinized Annie.

"This is the friend I told you about who's a senator's daughter," Cam said. "Annie Schulz, this is Vera Windermere-Sullivan."

"We're sort of related," Annie said. "Your husband was the brother of my step-monster."

Vera gave a laughing cough. "Yes. I suppose that's true."

"You said there was something you were afraid to tell the police?" Rob said.

"And now I'm afraid not to, but I'm not sure how to go about it."

"They can be subtle if you think you're in danger."

Vera sat and dropped her head into her hands.

"Yesterday wasn't the first time my place was searched," she finally said. "Before Mike died . . . a day or two after Daddy's murder . . . somebody was at the house looking for something. They turned the place over. I don't know who. I wasn't home. Mike and I weren't getting along, but he blew me off and said it had to do with him. He said he cleaned it up. Do you think they found something?"

"Honestly," Rob said. "If they found what they were looking for, I sort of doubt they'd have killed Mike. Unless . . . I mean, if it was something he knew and they were keeping him quiet."

"Chances are," Cam said, "whatever the police are looking for is long gone, unless this Leo guy has it in that cabin."

"Leo?" Vera said.

Cam bit her cheek as punishment. She shouldn't have let any details slip. But maybe Vera could reassure them. "Leo was a guy who was . . . apartment sitting at Mike's other place. Do you know him?"

"Know *of* him. He's a parasite. I used to see him out sometimes, but he started calling Mike regularly a few months ago."

"Do you know what about?"

"Just looking for Mike, or that's all he'd tell me. I think he was involved in the drugs."

"Drugs?" Rob said.

They already knew that Mike had been connected to

drugs, of course, but it was better to act clueless. Maybe Vera would share something new.

"Mike had a . . . habit. It's embarrassing, really, but I guess not so uncommon for someone like him if he ran into money."

"Didn't you . . ."

"He didn't bring it home. It's why he took on the apartment. I didn't like it. I wanted to divorce him."

"But your father objected."

"That's putting it mildly. The apartment was a compromise. For both of us."

Cam wondered if she was referring to her affair.

"Why do you think your father would want you strapped to a drug-using gambling addict?"

"He suggested I didn't know everything, but wouldn't explain."

That sounded very strange to Cam, but she decided she should stay out of this. Rob had established a pretty good rapport and she would let him work it.

"So do you think Leo is dangerous?" Rob said.

"I think anyone on drugs can be dangerous, but I don't suspect he's overly competent. What do you think I should do?"

"We have a police officer friend—someone we know you can trust. He's up at that cabin tonight, but maybe we can figure out a way you can talk to him tomorrow?"

"Come to our Thanksgiving," Cam said. "I mean . . . not for dinner, but if you were to . . . maybe bring a bottle of wine, make it look like a social call . . . eat pie with us . . . something like that. We already know Jake's stopping for dessert, so that should work perfectly."

"Okay, I'll try that." Vera looked relieved.

"Can you maybe . . . spend the night with a friend or something tonight?" Rob asked.

"I'll stay with my mother. She'll like that."

Cam wasn't sure the woman liked anything, but supposed

a daughter visit probably was closer to tolerable than most things, so she smiled and nodded. They sent Vera out the door with a box of cupcakes so it looked like she'd just been treated like a VIP customer.

"What do you think?" Cam said when she was gone.

"That there's something going on," Rob said. "We've heard drugs mentioned a couple times, yet other than money disappearing and breaking into your office, Sullivan doesn't really seem to fit the profile. And then . . . I wonder . . ."

Rob sat down at his laptop and plugged in some search terms. He finally frowned and sat back.

"I can't prove it, but I think maybe this real estate fraud is a drug-laundering cover. There's money going in and out, but the properties don't seem to be moving at the same rate. I'd need to find the actual books and I don't know how I'd go about that, but maybe that was what these murders were about."

"Jake subpoenaed those records, though, right? That's how we found out Melvin was involved," Cam said.

"Yeah, and there was evidence of large political donations to Jared Koontz, but Jake won't share any more detail. I'm not sure he trusts part of what's there, and he says he can't have me running off with something that was meant to mislead us."

"Samantha suggested those donations never got there— there was a huge canceled check. Maybe that's fishy, too. I guess it depends on if the police find what they're looking for in Mike Sullivan's stuff," Cam said.

Rob smiled and said, "Maybe we really are getting closer to figuring this all out."

CHAPTER 22

Annie slept over at Cam's that night. She was too worried about Jake to be alone, and they had a big following day planned, preparing Cam's dad's place for a house full of company. Rob left a little after midnight with the promise to be back around ten the next morning with a bottle of Baileys and a vat of eggnog.

"We're going to swim in it?" Annie asked sleepily from her curled-up position on the futon.

"Yes. Thanksgiving doesn't count as a holiday if you don't swim in eggnog," Cam said, then kissed Rob good-bye.

He winked at her as he left.

"Come on, pumpkin. Let's move to the bed so I can hear if you need me in the middle of the night," Cam said, urging Annie up.

That was Cam's last coherent thought before the pounding woke her the following morning. It was almost nine and she was very glad for the uninterrupted sleep for both of them, though the banging on her front door was jarring.

She threw on a robe and made her way to it.

"Annie! I can't find Annie!"

"She's here! She was too upset to be alone is all."

Jake rushed in and ran to Annie, though his relief was nothing compared with hers, and soon Cam's apartment was deserted, save for her, as the two of them fled for a calming shower . . . or something. The details had been muddled, and Cam didn't want to stop them to clarify.

Cam made a pot of coffee and waited until the water upstairs stopped before hopping in her own shower. She preferred the water pressure all to herself.

It was a later start than they'd planned, but Cam, Rob, and Annie left for Cam's dad's around noon. Annie had left Jake sleeping at her place: working all night excused him from his day shift and some portion of dinner with his family. He promised to stop by Cam's dad's around five for the pie and witness confession moment before heading over to see his family.

Nick and Petunia were already at her dad's when they arrived, Petunia seated with a cup of tea and looking crabby about it.

"You okay? Can I get you anything?" Cam asked.

"I'm apparently in the way in there!"

Cam looked at Petunia and her protruding belly, but thought it was probably her attitude more than her girth that was hard to accommodate on a day like this.

"I made my honey buns," Annie whispered. "You want one?"

Petunia perked up. "Really?"

"Only for you. Everyone else has to wait for supper."

Cam rolled her eyes, but Petunia seemed appeased and turned her attention back to the Thanksgiving Day parade on the television. Cam willed Rob to wait a few hours before trying to suggest they switch to football. Once Nick was out here to join the effort, Petunia might go for it, but not until then.

Cam and Annie rolled into the kitchen to strategically place two pies, one cheesecake, the rolls, and the eggnog. Her dad was standing over a crockpot.

"Smell this, sunshine."

Cam went over and gave a sniff, "Ooh! Mulled wine! It smells good. Annie should give it the official thumbs-up, though. She'll know if there is something to improve it."

Annie came over and suggested just a pinch of cloves, and then indeed gave the thumbs-up. "I'll need one of those soon. Dad and Elle will be here before long."

Cam asked if Nick needed help, but he had it under control, and Cam's dad was content to play backup in the kitchen. He'd always liked helping, if not being primary chef. So Cam and Annie went out to make sure the table was set with the good china. Halfway through, Cam's dad had her add a seat.

"Didn't I tell you Vivian is coming?" he said.

"Oh, no. Lovely," Cam said, but worried a little that the table might be taken over by politics if Vivian and Senator Schulz were both present. Still, it was sort of nice to see a big meal being planned for the first time since her mom had been the primary planner. The last few years there had only been five or six of them, and this would pleasantly stretch their table.

When guests began to arrive, Petunia kicked her dad out of the kitchen to act as sous-chef herself and let Cam and her dad host the social side, serving drinks and getting people situated. Petunia could be antisocial that way, so nobody was surprised.

Supper was served a short while later and conversation was pleasant, even as political disagreement landmines were avoided. Senator Schulz and Elle were happy enough to have been invited that they were on their best behavior, and Vivian had been raised a lady, or so she had whispered to Cam and Nelson when the Schulzes arrived. So she was also keeping her opinions to herself. It seemed to be the case, too, until she wiped her mouth and spilled her confession.

"You know, Cam, I wasn't quite forthcoming. My nephew, Brian Fontana, has been working in Chad Phillips's office."

"Erm . . . we actually knew that," Rob said. "Was he spying?"

"Yes, but not politically. You see, the city got a call that Chad might be receiving a lot more in campaign donations than he was reporting. And the auditor double-checked and it looked like that was so, but there wasn't anything concrete. In particular, we couldn't tell if it was *him* or his staff. My peers on the city council agreed we should look into it."

"Without telling the police?"

"We didn't know if we had anything. He was just poking around."

Cam and Rob looked at each other and then back to Vivian. "And?" Cam said.

"They seem to have a lot more money than they've been given."

"How?" Rob asked. "Isn't that backward?"

"Well, that's the question, isn't it?"

After supper, with the arrival of both Vera Windermere-Sullivan and Jake, things began to get really interesting. Cam led them into the formal living room, which was at the front of the house and away from the family room, where most of the guests were gathered. But because Cam, Annie, and Rob wanted to be involved with the conversation, in addition to Jake and Vera, it seemed an audience had trailed them to listen in.

More shocking, though, was that when the items taken from Vera's house were discussed, Elle stepped forward.

"I think I know where that is."

Cam heard Vera gasp.

"Where what is?" Jake asked.

"The folder. Mike's folder. The one I'm sure they're looking for."

Everyone stared at her, her husband the most obviously.

"Why didn't you mention it earlier?" Annie asked.

"Your dad never would have forgiven me if I'd put you in any danger. Mike gave me something and said it was . . . a life insurance policy of sorts and he'd let me know what to do with it. That was the last time I saw him. I haven't had a chance to look at it since then, but . . . I figured since he was gone, he didn't have time to enact the plan."

"Would you mind if we went to get that?" Jake said.

"I'd rather go get it and bring it here, if you don't mind."

"Are you sure it's safe?" Cam asked.

"Of course I am. It's also very private. I'd just . . . Alden can take me."

"I'd rather escort you," Jake said.

Alden stepped forward. "I'd consider it a personal favor."

Jake sighed. "I'll wait here then."

"And we'll hold dessert," Cam said.

The silence was heavy after they left. Vera fidgeted and Cam wondered how to calm her. Finally, everyone wandered into other rooms. Annie and Cam headed to the kitchen to wash dishes, leaving Vera with Jake.

"Who would have guessed Cruella had the answers this whole time?" Annie said.

"I would have thought *you*," Cam teased.

"I'm still dying to know why they were framing me," Vivian said.

Cam jumped. She hadn't heard Vivian come in behind her, and without having seen her, her voice had sent a shock of memory through Cam to Thanksgivings years ago when Aunt Vi had been a part of their family festivities. She'd completely forgotten until then.

"Hopefully, this will all sort it out," Cam said. "It's sure nice to have you here, Aunt Vi."

Vivian laughed. "Oh, it's been so long since I was called that. Come here and let me hug you."

Cam collected her hug, and Annie dived in after her. "That means I get to call you Aunt Vi, too," she said.

Vivian laughed. "Always happy for another niece. But you know your father and I don't agree on a darned thing."

"It's okay. He and I don't agree on anything either."

Vivian laughed even harder.

"What's all this fun about?" Cam's dad had been drawn to the laughter. He wasn't used to not being the source of it.

"Just a little memory lane in here, and a niece adoption." Vivian put an arm around each girl.

Annie frowned then and stepped away, pulling her phone from her pocket. Cam thought it must have vibrated.

"They must be having trouble," she said when she looked at the screen. "Hi, Dad."

Cam watched Annie's face fall, then she ran out of the room shouting for Jake.

"That doesn't sound very good," Mr. Harris said.

Cam followed Annie as quickly as possible, needing to hear the details.

". . . same damn cabin in the woods—the one you had the standoff at yesterday. It belonged to their parents. But there's a hiding spot somewhere there. Dad drove, but he was waiting in the car and somebody grabbed her. He just saw them dragging her back into the woods."

"Damn. I had enough of that place yesterday. And it'll be hard to track anything with all the police traffic having trampled the woods already."

He got on his phone and called the station while Cam saw that Vera had turned white. She turned to Rob.

"Whatever happened with that guy Leo?" Cam asked.

"Must have chickened out. When they finally broke in, he was passed out. He must have taken pills or something. He was rushed to the hospital to have his stomach pumped, but as far as I know that's all they got from him."

Jake left then. Annie was frantic. "We can't just leave them out there on their own."

"They aren't on their own," Cam said. "The police are on their way."

"I want to go," Annie said.

"Do you have any clue where it is?"

"Sort of."

"I know." Cam, Annie, and Rob turned to look at Vera Windermere-Sullivan. She'd already retrieved her purse and had her keys in her hand. "I want to go face this bastard. He killed my father and my husband."

Cam was going to argue, but she could tell right away that both Annie and Rob were going to go, so she made excuses she was sure her family didn't believe and the four of them left in Vera's sedan. It was the most comfortable, to be sure, but was also a nice sage color that would be less obvious cruising through the wooded roads than her bright yellow Mustang.

"How do you know this place?" Rob asked as they drove. He'd taken shotgun, while Cam and Annie climbed in back.

"Mike used to take me up here when he was courting me—away from our parents and their prying eyes. We crashed on Elle once or twice, but usually it was empty."

"Not Len?"

"Naw. Lenny was the good kid—followed the rules. Not that Elle was wild like Mike, but she wasn't straight like Lenny, either."

"He's that straight? Do you know why he would hide evidence then?"

Vera took a breath. "What Mike told me is he'd done something to help Elle and that Lenny was helping him. I really thought it was all about . . . you know . . . the reconciliation plan."

"We think Len thought that, too. Did you know about that?"

"Not until they headed out to Newport News. Mike called to tell me he'd be gone and that's where he was."

"But what about the search for the file?"

"I thought that was completely separate—gambling or drug stuff. And those bigwigs . . . that murder . . . that wasn't drugs and gambling. Those are my dad's people. Not Mike's."

Cam leaned forward between the seats. "What if someone in that circle was using a real estate scam to launder drug money?"

"What?"

Vera almost ran off the road, and Rob eyed Cam seriously. He picked up the train of thought.

"It looks like maybe a company called Chrysanthemum Holdings had a lot more money moving through it than the buying and selling of real estate would indicate. We think maybe your dad found out and . . ."

"Found out? You mean he might have been killed for doing the *right* thing? That's ironic," Vera said.

"You don't think . . ." Cam started.

"No, I can see that being how it worked. He wouldn't want to deal with a drug cartel or something. He just . . . well, to me it was sort of a hazy line. He was willing to cross a lot of other ones. It's just sort of interesting that he'd get killed because of a line he wouldn't cross, rather than one he did."

Cam agreed, but didn't say so. It wouldn't make anything better. She was also a little worried that whatever she said might suggest that Vera's husband killed her father, because most of the sentences forming in her brain seemed to head in that direction. Better to filter herself and see what happened.

When they reached the cabin, it was abandoned, as was the Schulz's car. Annie began calling for her dad.

They'd beaten the police there. Cam thought they were forming a squad at the station to come out together, but at the moment, the two cars were alone.

"Where would the person who grabbed her have come from?" Cam asked.

"There are about a dozen cabins nearby, if you know the trails. They'd just need to know one of them," Vera said.

"Would that be where he took her?"

"It might be."

"Do you know anyone else up here?" Rob asked Vera.

"I don't. Mike and I haven't been here for years, and if we hiked, the other cabins were empty or else we avoided them. We were just . . . you know . . . being kids. We wanted privacy."

Annie came back then, her dad in tow.

"Have you been here before, Senator Schulz?"

"Several times. It can be hard to find privacy in town, so Elle and I have come here now and then."

"Did you see who grabbed her?"

"No. I didn't even get out of the car. I left it running and waited and then heard her scream as she was dragged off. I never caught sight of them."

Cam looked around. It was definitely roughing it—the place had only an outhouse. But she supposed she could see the privacy angle. There was a little fireplace and it was sort of romantic.

"Did you ever meet any neighbors?" Rob asked.

"Only one, and we didn't travel that way again." His chin tightened in distaste.

"And who was that?"

"Melvin Entwhistle."

"That's him! Show us which direction," Cam said. She turned to Vera. "Can you watch us go—send the police our way when they get here. You shouldn't get tangled in this."

Vera's face twisted and she nodded. Cam thought Vera looked scared to join them and relieved for a way out. She sat on a chair on the porch to wait as Cam ran to catch up with Rob, Annie, and Senator Schulz. She turned to look one last time and noticed something about Vera's demeanor besides fear. She wasn't sure she trusted Vera not to leave. On a whim, Cam picked up a long stick and dragged it along the ground as she went. She turned back to look and was glad to see a clear line in the dirt and leaves.

A fog was creeping into the mountains as they followed Senator Schulz. Cam noted the senator's shoes were probably not good for a hike—worse than her own even, which were hardly ideal. She'd worn boots, but the fashionable kind, not the hiking kind. The senator slid a couple of times before Annie sidled up next to him and gave him the little extra support he needed, at least where the trail was wide enough for two. A couple of times he paused at forks, but he seemed fairly confident which path to take, so Cam thought he knew where he was going.

"There," Rob said.

"What?" They all slowed considerably.

"I think we've cleared the area the police trampled yesterday, but there are broken branches, like maybe somebody was struggling."

"The deer will scratch their antlers," Alden said cautiously.

"No, what I saw looked more like heels being dragged. Like somebody was trying to resist."

Senator Schulz's face fell. Cam thought maybe he hadn't wanted to think about what was happening to his wife.

They'd hiked for about fifteen minutes before Senator Schulz put a finger to his lips. "There," he whispered.

Cam could see a little red through the trees, the outline of a building that was barely visible. The trail went a longer route, but a person could weave through the trees if he or she was careful.

"Should we split up?" Rob asked.

"Why?" the senator asked.

"Well, if a pair of us looks in the back, then maybe we can see a way to rescue Elle, or at least see how dangerous it is."

Senator Schulz nodded and Cam stared down at her own shoes. The boots had a heel and a narrow toe. They'd been okay on the trail, but she knew going into the deeper woods with Rob would be a bigger challenge. Still, it only made sense for Annie to stick with her dad. That was more explainable to whoever this nut was than what Cam and Rob were doing there. Cam handed Annie the stick and pointed back to show what she'd been doing. Annie understood and put it to the ground as she went with her dad.

Cam followed Rob into the tangle of bramble and shrubbery that grew under the trees. She was glad she hadn't worn a skirt, as she got caught on thorns more than once, but not far off the trail the undergrowth thinned. It was probably only a hundred feet to the cabin, but it was very slow going, and then there was a space behind the cabin with no trees that felt really exposed, so they tried to see into windows from the woods. The angle was wrong though. To see in, they would have to get closer.

As Cam tried to edge out of the trees to dart to the cabin, Rob pulled her back.

"What?" she whispered.

"I just saw him. He's pacing. It's Entwhistle, but we don't know if he's alone."

"Then we have to get closer."

"Let's try it from the side."

It meant skirting the cabin in the trees some more, but when they got there, Cam was glad they had. There was buckbrush, with its gorgeous red berries, right next to the window, and if they stayed low, she thought, it would block them from view as they approached. Unfortunately, it was a window to a small bedroom and the door was mostly closed, so they couldn't see anything.

"You hear anything?" Cam asked.

Rob shook his head, then gestured. He planned to go back behind the house again, edged up against it except where he had to skirt a spur of St. John's wort, so nobody inside could see him. Cam nodded and followed, but they stopped when they heard Senator Schulz shout.

"Melvin! Come out and talk to me like a man!"

"Drat!" Cam said as she and Rob hurried to pop their heads up into the nearest window.

They could look all the way through the cabin—other than the bedroom, it was only one room, and they could see Melvin opening the door with a shotgun in his hand.

"Where's Elle?" Cam asked.

"Over against that wall. I can see her feet. I think she's tied to a chair."

"What is it with this man and tying women to chairs?"

"You think that was him?"

"I think so. I got a look at his eyes. I couldn't tell the color in the dim light, but when I think about it now, I'm pretty sure it was him."

"Alden. You don't want to be here," they heard from the other side of the cabin.

"You're right. I'll just take my wife and we'll get out of your hair."

"I can't let you do that."

"Why not?"

"She has something of mine."

"Why would she have anything of yours?"

"She got it from that brother of hers, and I mean to destroy it."

"If she gives it to you, will you let her go?"

"I would trade for it, yes. I don't want to hurt anyone."

Cam thought he was delusional if he thought he was going to get away with this, no matter what. He'd already murdered two people. But she knew enough to know negotiating was better than not negotiating. She also knew enough to know she and Rob should just sit tight.

"I don't know where it is. I'll need to talk to Elle," Senator Schulz said.

"Maybe I should trade . . . her for your daughter."

"No! You can trade her for me—you can tie me up in there instead, but Annie stays out here."

"Then maybe I should just shoot Elle now and nobody ever finds it."

"No!" Annie yelled. "I'll do it! Trade me, Dad."

"I will do no such . . ."

"It's okay. Elle can get whatever it is and then . . ."

"But he's already killed two people," Senator Schulz said.

"I haven't killed anybody!" Melvin shouted.

Cam could hear the lowered arguing of Annie and her dad. Neither wanted to give in on this point. Cam secretly bargained to just leave Elle where she was, but in the end, she and Senator Schulz both lost to Annie's will.

Cam started to run around the cabin, but Rob caught her around the waist.

"But Annie! I mean Elle, sure . . . but Annie?"

"Annie is stronger and more athletic, and I'd put good money on her being smarter. She might even be able to talk him down, but she can certainly coordinate better with us."

"But the police will be here any minute. This situation is only going to get hotter."

"Trust her, will you?" Rob said.

Cam trusted Annie. It was the nut who was going to tie her up right now she didn't trust.

"While he's distracted, let's check the windows. Maybe there will be a chance to rescue her," Rob said.

Since it felt better to be doing something than nothing, Cam nodded and worked her way back over to the bedroom to check. She heard the voices. The exchange was being made, with Alden forced to tie Annie at gunpoint because Melvin wasn't willing to be unarmed. Thankfully, as Cam headed to the back of the cabin, she saw a shadow in the woods. She darted toward it, giving Rob a gesture to stay where he was.

When Cam reached him, she actually hugged him. It was Jake.

"What the heck is going on in there?"

Cam explained about the agreed-upon exchange, the plan to get the documents or whatever they were, and the promise to let Annie go.

"Don't go in. Let this play out."

"Cam . . ."

"No. How's this? Go with Elle. Get the stuff. Take pictures of all of it really fast, and then let Elle turn it over. Annie has a good camera in her bag in the car."

"This is *not* protocol."

"But he's promised to let Annie go if he gets the folder!"

"I suppose that's a lot more likely to work than going in firing."

Jake made his way to his fellow officers, who were waiting to round the corner, and told them the plan. They didn't seem any happier about it than Jake had at first, but they faded into the woods, so Cam thought it had worked.

She traced her way back to Rob to let him know the plan, and he told her Elle had described a hiding place up the mountain that would take at least an hour to get to and back.

"Do you think she's telling the truth?" Cam asked.

"I don't know. And I don't know why he doesn't just go with them at gunpoint, but it works better for us."

"He's probably worried about his hostages diving off into the woods. More control this way."

Rob frowned at her, "I guess. Though that's only an illusion."

"You don't suppose he has other people out here somewhere, do you?" Cam asked.

"I bet he has backup."

"We need to stick around, then, and listen, in case he's calling for reinforcements or something."

They watched as Senator Schulz and Elle walked back up the trail, knowing the police were going to join them. Jake, on the other hand, made his way down to where Cam and Rob were waiting. Cam was worried about Annie and was glad to have a police officer with them.

"None of these windows open?" he asked.

"Not on the three sides we've checked."

"I don't like this. I don't like it at all," Jake said.

"Me neither," Cam said. "Hopefully he keeps his word."

"I can't see why he would," Jake said. "Why let somebody go who knows the information? Or could press charges?"

"We don't think Elle actually knew anything. Remember what she said—it was just Mike's security. She hadn't looked. Maybe she convinced Melvin of that."

"But the charges about the kidnapping . . ."

"I guess he could be protecting somebody else," Cam said.

Rob looked at her. "Then where are *they*?"

"Keeping their hands clean," Jake answered for her. "Somebody important."

"Like somebody running for office," Rob said.

"Oh, geez. You two sure climb into some huge messes."

"This wasn't us!" Cam covered her mouth after she said it, as she knew her voice had bordered on being too loud. The three of them pressed against the cabin in silence and listened. The walking stopped, but Cam heard Annie jabbering. She thought her friend knew exactly what had made the noise.

"Shut up!" Melvin shouted.

Rob gestured to the side and Cam thought it was a good idea. It was time to hide again. She edged along the side of the house and when they heard the front door slam open, they broke into a run, Rob taking Cam's arm so her boots didn't get the better of her.

Melvin came around the house with his shotgun, and Cam saw Jake twitch. She was sure he was debating running into the cabin for Annie and locking it, but Rob held his arm. The cabin couldn't take a shotgun aimed at it, and Annie and Jake would be sitting ducks. It was better he didn't know they were there, at least until they saw Annie come sprinting out the door. Then Cam couldn't help herself.

"Annie!"

Cam saw Melvin take aim, but Jake took charge.

"Find big trees, all of you! Melvin Entwhistle, Jake Moreno of the Roanoke PD. I have a police-issued nine-millimeter handgun with significantly better aim and a lot more bullets pointed at your chest. Stop right where you are!"

Melvin quit moving.

"Drop your rifle."

"They tricked me," Melvin complained.

"Mr. Entwhistle, you took a woman against her will. This

is not a case where you can claim you were wronged. Now kick the shotgun away from you and lie facedown with your hands behind your back."

Melvin dropped the gun out to his side and got to his knees, then lay down.

Jake moved forward and handcuffed Melvin Entwhistle, reading him his rights as he did.

"He's really hot when he does that, isn't he?" Annie said.

"How'd you get out of that?" Cam asked.

"Dad and I used to do ropes as a kid—part of sailing. There's a knot that is totally tight unless you pull exactly the right spot. I just waited for my moment."

"A win for your dad!" Cam said.

"Yeah. He comes through sometimes."

Cam hugged Annie, and Rob called, "Can we come out, or should we stay in the trees?"

Unfortunately, the whiz of a bullet answered the question, and Jake had to dive for the ground. Cam thought it looked like he'd been hit.

"No!" Annie screamed.

"Stay hidden!" Jake yelled.

Cam could see he was rolling for the trees himself.

"What about me?" Melvin yelled.

"They're your people. Are they going to shoot you?" Jake asked.

A sickening *sput* answered the question. Shutting Melvin up was apparently what they wanted, well at least one of the things. On the positive side though, the gunfire had brought the police running back through the woods.

Jake rounded the house in the trees, running toward them holding his ribs.

"You're hurt!" Annie yelled.

"Yes and no. I have a vest on, so no penetration, but it stings like the dickens. You three get back away from this. Bullets came from that direction." He pointed. "So you head the other way. It might get ugly. Hundred, two hundred yards back that way, then get under or inside something. Go!"

He pushed them off, and Cam and Rob had to physically pull Annie for a while before she would move.

"Annie, if he's worried about you, he won't be able to pay full attention. We have to get out of here."

She finally agreed and they followed the line of the hill until it began sloping down again.

"There," Rob pointed out a small building and the three of them aimed for it. It was up a little hill, but looked sturdy enough to hide in, even if somebody decided to shoot at it. Unfortunately, it wasn't empty.

"Vera?"

Vera Windermere-Sullivan stopped, stone still, a deer in the headlights.

"What on earth are you doing? I thought you were going to direct the police?" Cam said.

"Nothing. Just a whim. After they got here, I came . . ."

But Cam could hear by her shaking voice she was lying. She was glad she hadn't trusted Vera or the police might not have found them. Rob moved in front of her and finished raising the bucket from the well, as that was where they were—a covered well house. In the bucket was an accordion file folder just over an inch thick.

"Give me that! It's mine!" Vera said.

"I think we'll let the police check that," Rob said, holding it out of Vera's reach as she jumped for it.

"So you killed your father?" Annie asked.

"Don't be absurd," Vera sniped. "I'm sure Mike killed my father! He had all these papers about what Daddy had done . . . Maybe they argued. Maybe it was an accident."

"Then what are you hiding?"

"Nothing. I knew if Mike gave the papers to Elle, this is where she would hide them."

Cam didn't trust what Vera was saying. It was too

halting, like she was making part of it up. "So why retrieve them yourself? Why not let the police know, instead?"

"Can't a woman be concerned with her father's reputation? He's dead. I'd like to leave him in peace."

Vera wouldn't come with them, but Annie had figured out where they were and headed them back toward the Sullivan cabin. Rob brought up the rear of the trio, looking back regularly and steering them into the cover of trees a few times just in case. Vera had run off in another direction as soon as they left and it was hard to say what or who she might be after.

"She doesn't want them to have the books or they'll take her money," Annie said when they were walking. "It's illegal money. She figures she lost her dad and husband. She doesn't think it's fair she loses the money, too."

"Even if it solves the crime?" Cam asked.

"She might just figure done is done. It was over a dirty business deal, and her dad and Mike both got caught in something they shouldn't have done, but since they are dead anyway, why forfeit the money?"

"I think there's more to it than that," Rob said. "She doesn't want something becoming public."

"Like what?"

Rob handed Cam a thin ledger. Cam opened it and could see immediately it was for accounting: money coming in, money going out. The recipients tended to be political. In fact it looked a little like the one they'd seen earlier, but the people listed were different. A few of the recipients here were known to be under investigation. And there was a political name absent from the "official version." Chad Phillips had received a great deal from Chrysanthemum Holdings.

"Election fraud?" Cam said.

"Well, and besides that—somebody hiding information from their business partner."

"Sounds like motive for murder," Cam said.

"Yeah, but whose motive?" Rob asked.

A picture was starting to form in Cam's mind that would answer that question.

T he Sullivan cabin was strangely quiet, or perhaps not strangely, considering the firefight down at the other cabin. Cam, Rob, and Annie found a police car and locked themselves in, Annie in front so somebody could work the doors if necessary. They all felt being locked behind bulletproof glass was probably a good idea while the chaos collected itself. Annie managed to use the radio to call for an ambulance, as they knew Melvin had been shot, and who knew how many more might be hurt before it was over. Nobody said anything specific out loud because Jake was still down in the fray.

"Where do you suppose Dad and Elle got to?" Annie asked. "Their car is gone."

"Maybe when they told the police the documents had been moved, the police sent them home to be out of the line of fire," Cam suggested, but she agreed it was strange.

"Or to the station, but yeah—out of the way. Jake probably let everyone know Annie got out," Rob said. Cam gave him a faux evil eye, as his idea had more merit than hers.

"Does that mean we could go home, too?" Cam asked.

"In what? We came with Vera," Annie said. "Who knows where she went after we left the well?"

"Right." Cam didn't like feeling helpless. "And Vera doesn't seem likely to be our friend after this."

Rob looked pensive, so Cam put her hand on his leg. "What?" she asked.

"It's just . . . she was so strange up there. And think about what Vivian said—that she was holding something over Melvin's head that could ruin him."

"The hidden files show support for Chad Phillips," Cam

said. "The open ones show support for Jared Koontz. We know Derrick Windermere was supporting Koontz. So Melvin must have been the one diverting money. You're right. It looks like Vera might have been forcing it because she knew about the laundering!"

"But would she kill her dad for that?" Annie asked.

"I don't know. Maybe it was an accident," Cam said. "I mean, who thinks a flowerpot is a murder weapon?"

"But Mike's death was more intentional," Annie said.

"He caught on to her. I bet she felt trapped," Cam said.

It was more than an hour later before the police officers began returning to the cars. Annie jumped out and asked the first one she saw to radio Jake, as he was probably searching the woods. The officer obliged, and even from the car, Cam could hear Jake's relief, "Oh thank heavens! I couldn't find them and I was worried."

The next feared delay was the police setting out into the woods to find Vera Windermere-Sullivan, but Jake loaded Annie, Cam, and Rob into a different police car with their evidence and headed back to town, confirming that Annie's dad and Elle had been sent back to town ages ago. Among them all, there was enough evidence that they wanted it right away, and the fewer civilians left on the mountain, the better.

Cam was shocked when, on the way back into town, Jake asked her to summarize what she thought had happened.

"This Chrysanthemum Holdings company seems to be a front for channeling drug money into elections," Cam said, passing on what they'd figured out about Vera blackmailing Melvin for a change of recipient. "Maybe she thought if Chad was a senator, her dad would let her divorce Mike and marry Chad. Maybe her dad found out and wasn't going to let her get away with it, so he ended up pelted with a flowerpot. Then when the thugs came looking for the paperwork, Vera figured out Mike had uncovered it, and she worried about whom Mike would give the evidence to. She wanted to protect her boyfriend, so Mike got pummeled, too, which is to say, killed. She thought she was safe then until Melvin realized we were snooping—he might have even told her to back off. But she took a chance in finding out what we knew and it was a fluke that Elle had the information—she knew just where it would be. She came up here and found it where Elle hid it and moved it."

"You're missing a key detail," Jake said smugly.

"What?"

"I've been talking to Lenny as we searched for you guys up on the mountain. Mike was DEA. He was undercover for this drug thing, trying to get to the big guns. He didn't know the elections piece . . . or didn't tell anyone if he did. This file, though, looks like he cracked it. Where the drug money was coming from and which politicians and scam groups were getting it."

"Holy crap! So that's how he put this all together?"

"Looks like it. Lenny was in on it, too. In fact that's why the FBI was never brought in on the kidnapping. None of the rest of us knew, but Mike had led Len to believe they were also doing something related to the search with the senator and Len had to keep cover," Jake said. "The mob thought they had a dirty cop and his thug brother working for them, but actually, they were working together on a big drug bust."

"Does Elle know?" Annie asked.

"You'd have to ask her."

Nick had successfully tricked Petunia into a day out of their condominium and Cam, her dad, and Annie had settled in to paint the stenciled design around the ceiling of the baby's bedroom. Not that Petunia would have minded the stenciling, but they all knew it would go more smoothly without her constant commentary.

"Ducks, huh?" Annie said. "So they aren't finding out if it's a boy or a girl?"

"Petunia doesn't want her baby railroaded," Cam said.

"Good girl." Annie then turned to Cam's dad. "Hey, how's Vivian doing? Did they ever figure out the angle for framing her?" Annie asked.

Cam's dad shrugged and looked around like he was about to reveal a secret.

"Melvin as much as admitted to her in the hospital that she was the easy scapegoat—she had a history with both victims."

"Is he getting in trouble?"

"A lot of trouble, but he's trying to bargain by cooperating about both Vera and Chad now. They're both being held, but Melvin could assure their conviction. There will be jail time, but not as much as kidnapping and embezzlement normally would earn."

Cam thought her dad was so cautious in what he said because Vivian was a little embarrassed to be the beneficiary of this scandal. Her party had asked her to run for the senate seat after all.

"And are you two . . ." Annie continued.

"Still seeing each other? Yes. She says I look good on her arm," he said.

Annie laughed. "That you do! You let us know when we can start calling you Mr. Senator."

Cam looked at her dad, expecting protest, but he just grinned. This might just be getting serious.

Annie elbowed her and Cam deflected. "What about *your* dad?"

"I'm thinking there is some promise here," Annie

admitted. "If he can give Elle a pass for all these crazy she-nanigans, he's got to cut me some slack."

"Yeah, who knew? Elle . . . nuts, huh?"

Annie nodded, and Cam thought she looked rather impressed. Annie always preferred a rule-breaker, given a choice.